Liz,
Thanks so
much for your
support. Hope you
enjoy the "bad boys"
of Project VIPER.
HAPPY
Reading.
Love,
Kristie
Wolf
xoxo

Too
DANGEROUS
TO Love

A MILITARY ROMANCE BY

KRISTIE WOLF

Editing by Jen Graybeal and Miranda Grant
Proofreading: Rosa Sharon at Fairy Proofmother Proofreading, LLC
Photography by Eric Battershell of O' Snap! Media
Modeling by BT Urruela
Cover and Interior Design by Laura Hidalgo of Spellbinding Design

Paperback ISBN: 979-8-9887850-1-9
Special Edition Paperback ISBN: 979-8-9887850-2-6
Ebook ISBN: 979-8-9887850-0-2

*For my mom, who inspired my love of romance novels.
This first book is for you. Thanks for sharing your Harlequins
when I was way too young to read them, and thanks for always
being my biggest cheerleader.
Love you!*

A NOTE FROM THE AUTHOR

In 2016, a friend showed me *Always Loyal*—a book featuring photographs of wounded U.S. Gulf War veterans taken by photographer Michael Stokes. As I flipped through the beautiful pages, I said to myself, "those are heroes I want to write happily ever afters for," and the VIPER series was born.

Imagine my surprise and delight when I found out that BT Urruela, a combat wounded amputee and purple heart recipient featured in *Always Loyal* was a cover model. In a heartbeat, I purchased a photo of him and I'm ridiculously pleased and proud to have him on the cover of my debut novel.

Choosing the name of my first fictional hero was just as easy as selecting my cover model. Lieutenant Christopher Daviani is named for Christopher Charles Amoroso, Port Authority Police Department, the real-life hero I was blessed to call my friend and chosen family.

On September 11, 2001, Chris responded to the attacks on the World Trade Center. During the rescue effort, he led groups of people to safety. Despite being injured, he went back in to help more people and never made it out.

Chris, I hope you are sitting on a front porch in heaven, drinking a beer like you used to do in Belmar, and bragging to your angel buddies about being a super soldier with a weaponized bionic arm.

From the bottom of my heart, I'd like to thank our nation's military, law enforcement, and first responders who run back in when others run out.

AUTHOR'S DISCLAIMER

This book contains swearing, sexually explicit language, and fight scenes.

This book also features a hero with post-traumatic-stress disorder (PTSD) who suffers from violent flashbacks and nightmares.

I've lived with a veteran who suffers from PTSD and have the utmost gratitude for our veterans and respect for their bravery, not just on the battlefield but in the struggles they face after they've come home.

To all the active military and veterans out there—thank you for your service. To the folks at the Veterans Administration—thanks for taking care of our vets.

Veterans Affairs Veterans Crisis Line: Call 988 and select 1 or text 838255.

ONE

Dr. Scarlett Kerrigan was too smart to have a panic attack about her first day on the job. She had two PhDs. One was in neuroscience, for God's sake.

But this wasn't any job. Nor was it technically her first day with Project VIPER, a top-secret Department of Defense program. For two years, she'd been working as a government contractor to develop the cybernetic technology she'd pioneered over a decade ago to meet VIPER's ground-breaking mission. Now that her life's work was ready for implementation, every aspect of her job would change.

Today, in her new workspace at VIPER's headquarters in downtown Washington, DC, and as a full-fledged Department of Defense employee, she'd begin to make history.

Or go down as the biggest failure in modern warfare.

She glanced at the box of diplomas sitting by the door to her office and prayed her God-given gifts and years of training were enough to prevent the latter from coming true. Too many people counted on her, namely the four men whose lives were in her hands.

She stared at the photos on her laptop screen of the

combat-wounded veterans she'd been hired to engineer into the nation's first generation of super soldiers. If testosterone could ooze through pixels, she'd float away in a sea of alpha hormones. And if looking at their photos intimidated her, especially the one of the rugged Navy SEAL with the dark, penetrating gaze, what would happen when she met them for the first time at the briefing in…three hours?

She pulled in a deep breath and leaned back in her chair. The leather creaked as the high back hit the windowless wall behind her.

A tap sounded at her door. Dr. Patience Fairbanks peeked in.

"Good morning, Dr. Kerrigan. Welcome to VIPER head-quarters." She stepped into the office and plucked something off the sleeve of her white lab coat. "Stupid dog hair follows me wherever I go. I should have never let my boys talk me into getting a German Shepherd puppy."

Scarlett smiled at the world-renowned orthopedic surgeon she'd met several times at the quarterly "All Hands" meetings. "I bet the dog's cute though." She'd always wanted a pet, but the subject had been non-negotiable in her stepfather's mansion.

"The big hair ball is adorable. My twins from Planet Distracted? Not so much this morning when they forgot to close the gate." She brushed her palms down her vibrant pink dress. The wrinkles smoothed along with the annoyance in her eyes. "How do you like your new office? It's quite the step up from your basement facility in the Pentagon, don't you think?"

"My office is perfect." While the walls didn't completely block the screech of the November wind, the inside of the newly renovated building featured revolutionary technology that rivaled a science fiction movie and state-of-the-art equipment as sleek as her silver metal desk. The training area occupied the underground floor. A full medical suite and the research and development laboratory encompassed the street level. Executive offices, including hers, and a briefing room large enough to hold two dozen people took up the second.

And her computer lab across the hall?

The facility that spanned half the length of the building and housed her team of bright, eager minds exceeded her wildest, geekiest dreams. But the biggest perk of all? Department of Defense funds financed this project, not her stepfather Henry Richardson or his technology empire Richardson Enterprises.

Scarlett rose from her chair. "It's great to see you again, Dr. Fairbanks."

"Please, call me Patience. Now that we're only a floor away, we'll be seeing a lot of each other, so there's no need for titles and last names." She pulled her phone out of her coat pocket. "You'll find many of us don't stand on formality around here."

"Patience it is, and please call me Scarlett." The casual manner rolled off her tongue in a refreshing buzz after coming from an environment where credentials boosted egos.

"Excellent." Patience bounced on her toes. Her straight, sleek ponytail, which matched the color of her chocolate-brown eyes, swished behind her. "Are you ready to meet the guys today?"

Guys?

Scarlett bit back a laugh. The Veterans Integration Placement and Experimental Recovery program, a.k.a. Project VIPER, was created to outfit Special Forces amputees with artificial limbs and place them in federal security jobs. Only a handful of people knew those words were the publicity icing on a complex cake with a highly classified recipe. Once her technology was networked with the embedded weaponry in the ultralight, steel-like limbs Patience had attached to their bodies, there would be nothing "mall cop" about the jobs they would do.

Not jobs. Missions.

Dangerous and deadly missions where they could just think about obliterating their enemies instead of pulling a trigger.

Uneasy, she placed her hand over the butterflies whirling in her belly like specimens in a centrifuge. She'd created this technology to save lives, not take them, but wasn't naive enough to think that defending the country came without a cost. Her work would be used to kill, but she had faith the Project VIPER team would treat their second chance to serve and shield with compassion and respect.

Once the team was networked with her technology and declared mission ready, she'd hold a dual role: further their combat capabilities and protect them from hackers. The latter required her to monitor them as they carried out missions in real time.

No pressure there.

Rounding her desk, she smoothed the tight chignon at the base of her neck. At least her hair wasn't unraveling, unlike her nerves.

Patience backed into the hallway. "Come on. I want to show you the upgrades we've made to the MedLab suite. The briefing starts in thirty minutes, so we'll have just enough time."

"Thirty minutes? That's nine a.m. The briefing doesn't start until noon." She needed those three remaining hours to wrangle her agitated nerves before she met the intense-looking VIPER operatives who were complete opposites of the professors and scientists she'd associated with most of her life. Not just North and South Pole kind of opposite. Poles on separate planets in different solar systems kind of different.

They were warriors.

Survivors.

Heroes.

She was the weird, smart girl who couldn't talk to the opposite sex unless they worked in her scientific bubble. She'd been relieved when the VIPER operatives hadn't attended any of the All Hands meetings. They'd been recovering from surgeries, mastering the enhanced strength and flexibility built into their new limbs, and training to bring them back to fighting mode.

Instead of seeking the team out, she'd studied videos of their progress and had worked day and night to ensure her technology would meet the incredible standards already set by the rest of VIPER's top-notch scientists.

Patience motioned for Scarlett to follow her. "Apparently the briefing was moved due to General Edgar's schedule. Happens all the time around here."

Scarlett rolled her eyes. "Sounds familiar." When her stepfather demanded results, he expected everyone, especially her, to rearrange their schedules to meet his orders.

She followed Patience down a brightly lit corridor, passing several silver steel doors with biometric keypads leading to specific sections of her computer lab. Prints of battleships adorned the freshly painted white walls. They stopped at a bank of elevators flanked by flags representing each branch of the military. The national anthem played in Scarlett's head as she stepped inside the elevator car.

A floor lower and a minute later, she followed Patience toward a set of double doors at the end of the hall.

"A word of advice before the briefing." Patience stepped up to a retinal scanner and dipped her head. "Don't let the guys hear you refer to their artificial limbs as prostheses."

Scarlett waited until the laser verified Patience's identity and stepped up for her own scan. "Why not?"

"They like to call their new extremities their 'steel.'"

"There is some truth to that." This morning, she'd watched classified footage of the team testing their "steel" on brick walls. Strong didn't begin to describe what VIPER's materials scientist had created.

"The guys also throw the word 'super' around a lot, like super arm. Super leg. Super limb."

"Superpower?"

Patience winked. "You're catching on quick."

The double doors opened. An antiseptic smell, like that of any other medical facility, wafted out. Patience strode into the MedLab hallway. Scarlett's eyes quickly adjusted to the dimmer lights illuminating their path down the short corridor. The clicking of her heels on the tile sounded like a pretty jingle compared to the thumping inside her chest.

They're just men.

Men who'd make jokes she didn't understand. Ask her questions she couldn't answer. God, she hadn't even met them yet, and she already felt like the awkward kid on the playground again.

Scarlett followed Patience around a corner into a longer hallway with exam rooms on one side and rest and recovery suites on the other. "Last time I was here this part of the building was still under construction. Is everything complete now?"

"Yes, including the surgical area on the other side of the floor. Did you hear that the retired trauma surgeon from the Navy we've been wooing has accepted the position we offered? Dr. Langley will be arriving next week."

"Wonderful." In the past few All Hands meetings, there had been discussions about recruiting top-level medical support in the field. "The VIPER operatives certainly look like they are physically thriving. I was pleased to hear about the progress they've made with the psychological aftermath of battle and losing a limb." For some of the men, more than one.

"It's remarkable the way they've adjusted. Their steel-like limbs aren't just their new normal. They think they're invincible, and that's only with the enhanced strength of their prostheses. Once you network their weaponry with their brains, they'll be unstoppable."

Scarlett paused in front of a room marked "Exam Four" and placed her hand on Patience's arm. She waited for two women in pale-green scrubs to pass before she spoke. "The team knows my technology won't make them immortal, right?"

"I'm constantly reminding them they aren't bulletproof, but if embracing their capabilities as superpowers helps to reinvigorate them, so be it."

"I agree." A surge of pride nearly burst Scarlett's heart. Her anxiety skittered away. This was why she'd found the courage to finally leave her stepfather's company. To make a difference in someone's life. To finally break free of the prison she'd been living in since her mother had died and to focus on what she deemed worthy. "I'm honored to be a part of their return to service."

"Glad to hear it because one of our guys needs a tweak to his steel." Patience's phone buzzed in her hand. She glanced at it and sighed. "I've got to take this. It's my ex-husband. Go on in and introduce yourself. I'll meet you in there in a minute."

Patience opened the door and nudged Scarlett over the threshold.

Harsh fluorescent light attacked Scarlett's eyes. She blinked once, twice, and froze.

Oh. My. Lord.

A shirtless man—no, *god* was more like it—perched on the edge of an examination table. Lieutenant Commander

Christopher Daviani—VIPER's first recruit and the SEAL with the smoldering gaze that burned through her laptop.

Her own gaze locked on to his shiny black prosthesis.

No, super arm.

But wasn't super the understatement of the century?

The sight of the sleek limb seamlessly attached to the flesh and bone of any person would have been sensational.

On him, it was breathtaking.

The shiny metal covered in a hexagonal-shaped pattern originated in his shoulder, where synthetic and living materials meshed like reunited lovers.

She stepped farther into the room. Awe overrode her trepidation and propelled her forward. She reached out to touch the bulky black bicep that matched the size of his real one. He bent his elbow as her finger met his steel, his movement as smooth as if the muscles that had been cleaved off along with his arm had initiated the flexion.

A squeak popped from her throat.

His full lips turned up in a smirk. "Don't worry; it's not as deadly as it looks."

She stared at the surreal man. The prototypes of the steel arm she'd seen and the photos detailing his journey from the battlefield to VIPER hadn't prepared her for the real thing. Her breath hitched under his intense scrutiny. She lowered her eyes and stopped breathing altogether as she caught sight of the Project VIPER logo tattooed in shades of black and gray on his chest.

The fanged snake inked within a triangle that represented the past, present, and future hugged another tattoo of the same hexagonal pattern inlaid in his steel arm. The artwork covered the scarring on his shoulder where science and medicine converged, making the bionic enhancement appear as natural as if he'd been born with it. While his bionic arm gave him an otherworldly aura, like a sci-fi hero from a distant planet, the solid muscle underneath his inked skin tapered to sculpted abs, making him all man.

He hopped off the exam table and leaned against it. The dark tribal tattoo on his flesh-and-blood bicep rippled with movement as he gripped the padded edge. On the other side of his body, sleek black fingers, engineered in perfect anatomical form, performed the same movement. As she stared, waiting for the table to break under the pressure of his steel, he studied her for a moment too long for her comfort. "I'm Lieutenant Commander Chris Daviani."

She slowly reached for his extended hand, stifling a gasp when flesh met metal. "Dr. Scarlett Kerrigan."

"It's a pleasure to meet you."

The hard mask he wore slipped for a fraction of a second but returned just as quickly. She dropped her gaze to his mechanical fingers intertwined with her pale skin. The warmth of his steel radiated up her sleeve and spiraled into her belly. A simple handshake with her new colleague shouldn't have sparked such a visceral reaction. Kissing her ex-fiancé James had never created such pleasure.

She peered at the white cabinets above a counter on the side of the room and dipped her head so he couldn't see the heat on her face. Maybe she'd imagined the strange response to his touch. When she looked back, he would be just a man.

Turning her head, she met his eyes and realized she'd been hopelessly mistaken.

"Something wrong?" He squeezed her fingers before he crossed his arms over the viper emblazoned underneath a light smattering of dark hair.

Responses fired in her brain, but the words bounced against her skull in an incoherent scramble. Why did Commander Daviani hold the power to momentarily steal rational thought?

Hooking his thumbs into the front pockets of his black

cargo pants, he relaxed against the exam table. "I sure hope nothing is wrong, Dr. Kerrigan, because we're counting on you to get us back in action."

And there it was, proof he was just a man, like every other one in her life, who needed her brain to reach their goal. Granted, his motivations weren't greedy like others who wanted to profit from her genius. He sought survival, honor, and the ability to serve his country. Yet, she was his means to an end.

She squared her shoulders and clasped her hands in front of her. "You will be back in action. Very soon."

He rubbed his short, dark beard, which matched the color of his cropped hair. Silvery-gray flecks rimmed his deep-sapphire eyes. "Tell me, how do you plan on doing that?"

"I know you've been fully briefed on my role here at VIPER."

"I was, but I want to hear it from you since my life is in your hands."

She pulled in a full breath and latched on to the topic she not only understood but dominated. "Tomorrow, a neuro-transmitter will be implanted into your cerebellum that will network with your brain stem and cerebrum."

Tipping up her chin, she met his gaze. He held out his steel and studied it like he was following along with what she explained. "My software will communicate between the transmitter and the central processor engineered into your arm. Once I network the two, we'll begin testing your weaponry. While we're testing, my team and I will be reeval-uating the cybersecurity protocols to ensure the network that activates your weaponry is protected from hackers."

"And you're sure your code is secure?"

Her defenses rose at the challenge in his voice and the sharpness in his gaze. "It's virtually unhackable."

"Virtually?" His eyebrows rose to his hairline.

Her hackles rose too. "When it comes to cyberspace, no system is one-hundred-percent secure, but mine is nearly impenetrable."

"Bold statement."

Sweat pooled in her cleavage. She tugged the lapels of her suit jacket. This conversation was too intense. *He* was too intense. "Yes, it is a bold statement, but it's the truth."

He raised his hand to his face and examined it more closely. "I'm told your technology will let me shoot deadly lasers from my arm with just my thoughts. No need for bullets like regular guys."

Scarlett noted skepticism laced with excitement in his voice.

"Correct." She rubbed her hands together, displeased to find her palms sweaty despite having confidence in her work. "My technology also enables you to feel sensations with your prosthesis—" She shook her head. "I mean steel."

He extended his black index finger and lightly touched the back of her hand. "Like the softness of a person's skin."

"Yes." She bit the inside of her cheek as his metal digit glided over her knuckles. "You'll be able to sense if someone's flesh is cold or—"

"Hot?"

Energy buzzed through the room, making it seem smaller than it had been moments ago. In her twenty-seven years, no man had ever looked beyond her brain except Commander Daviani. He seemed to be looking everywhere.

It's the technology he's enthralled with. Not me. Never me.

She reminded herself of that fact as she paced to the other side of the small room and back again. When she opened her mouth, jittery words tumbled out. "Yes, you'll be able to feel hot and cold, among other sensations. You'll also be able to envision the exact point you want a laser to hit.

My technology will shoot that laser from one of the two-hundred and eighty-six points in your arm and calculate the proper trajectory so it finds your target with ninety-nine point nine percent accuracy. You'll be so leading-edge every comic book hero will be jealous of your powerful, special body."

He gripped her arm. "Do you always ramble and pace when you're nervous?"

She stopped moving and peeked up. Amusement replaced the fascination in his eyes she'd seen moments ago. Indignation simmered in her veins. During the four intense interviews she'd survived to get this job, not once had she succumbed to her nervous babbling habit or paced the room. She'd even kept it together when Admiral Edgar, whose imposing stature, cocky swagger, and gray mustache made him look like the leader of an old west outlaw gang, had vetted her. Why did she allow Commander Daviani to turn her into a nonsensical mess? "I'm not nervous, and I'm not rambling."

She couldn't argue the pacing part.

Leaning closer, he inhaled as if collecting the patience to deal with her quirks.

"Yes, you are. On both counts." He released her and straightened from his perch on the examination table.

She stiffened and stretched to her full height. At five feet eight, she usually met most men eye to eye or damn near it, but not so much with Commander Daviani.

"I hope it's first-day jitters, Dr. Kerrigan. When the shit starts to get real and cyber enemies come gunning for us, my team and I need to know you know what you're doing when it comes to the tech."

Scarlett sucked in a breath. The technology community hailed her as royalty. Scientific circles called her a female Einstein. She might not be comfortable with the silly titles or comparisons, but nobody questioned her work, especially a cocky SEAL who seemed to take pleasure in making her uneasy.

She stepped toward him. "I can assure you, Commander, I know what I'm doing."

"Good." His gaze locked on hers and held tight. "We're counting on your big brain to get us back in the field where we belong. And to bring us home alive."

She girded herself against the gravity of his words. "I take my responsibilities very seriously. I promise you'll be safe with me."

Every muscle in her body tensed while she waited for him to decide if he could trust her. She believed her bravado-packed words with all her heart, but he was a man, not a computer simulation or a machine. When it came to his future, she couldn't make absolute assurances, yet she wouldn't rescind her promise. She would keep him safe, not only to protect her reputation but to protect his life.

He held his arms out to the sides. The VIPER logo on his chest stretched along with his steel. A slow smile spread across his chiseled face as his sharp gaze stayed locked with hers. "Then I look forward to working with you, ma'am."

TWO

Chris slipped into the briefing room and searched for the rambling doctor he'd met in MedLab. He spotted her golden hair that smelled like honeysuckle amid the group of Pentagon suits gathered near the head of the conference table. Before he could catch her eye, Patience strode toward him, a frown flattening her ever-present smile.

"Sorry I got delayed earlier. I was stuck listening to my ex-idiot's lame excuse about why he was going to miss another one of the twins' baseball games. Did you and Dr. Kerrigan have a nice chat?"

Nice? He forced himself not to look at the beautiful genius he found more than nice in too many ways. Instead, he flexed his steel fingers into a fist and focused on Patience.

"Need me to teach your ex a lesson?" He'd never use his enhanced strength unless in battle, but he'd be happy to have a conversation with the guy about how to treat a lady.

Patience's frown vanished as she batted her eyelashes. "You say the sweetest things, but I wouldn't want you to hurt yourself. His head is made of stuff denser than your steel."

She touched his arm. "How's the flexion now after I tweaked it?"

"Great. I'm ready for more than training." God, he itched for more. Months of one excruciating surgery after another, followed by a rehab regimen even NATO would condemn as torture, had left him hungry for action. He needed a real mission with a purpose, or he'd explode, likely in his sleep, which would be a very bad scenario.

"I know. I know." She rolled her eyes. "And I'll tell you what I tell my little hellions. Be patient. Scarlett's technology is the last phase in your return to action. Give her time."

Scarlett.

He rolled the vibrant name that seemed at odds with the awkward beauty around in his mind. Blocking out the chatter, he stepped forward to study her a bit more closely than necessary. With her conservative navy pantsuit, she should have blended in with the department's upper echelon. Instead, she reminded him of a delicate flower among a mess of ugly weeds.

The subtle curves he'd itched to wrap his hands around but hadn't dared touch called to him from across the long silver conference table. He raked his steel hand through his hair, his fingers tracing a path to the tattoo on the back of his opposite shoulder. "I don't know. She looks too fragile."

"You mean too fragile to turn you into a fighting machine?"

"Yeah." He shook his head, still in awe of what he had become and what he would further progress into once the beautiful genius finished her work. When VIPER found him at the military medical center in Bethesda, Maryland, he'd had a broken collarbone, a collapsed lung, and a missing arm. His career and life, as he'd known it, had been over. But VIPER had offered him a job and a higher-than-high-tech prosthesis.

It was top secret.

Weaponized.

Dangerous, like him.

Too dangerous for a nervous woman to be responsible for.

Behind him, his teammates argued about whose steel had performed the best during this morning's five a.m. training session. Instead of joining the good-natured, yet obnoxious debate, he watched Patience interrupt the powwow near the podium and lead Dr. Kerrigan toward them. The genius's wide, deep-green eyes ringed in amber and her slim fingers clasped in front of her spoke volumes.

Her melodic voice floated through his mind.

I promise you'll be safe with me.

It was a bold statement he'd pushed her into making, and hell if he hadn't enjoyed hearing her voice rise with strength and catch when he'd touched her. He believed she meant every word of her promise. But believing and delivering were two different things. She needed to be as good as she claimed. He'd skirted death once. He doubted if the Grim Reaper would be so accommodating next time.

Holy testosterone in a test tube.

Scarlett's gaze fixed on the VIPER operatives standing under the gigantic American flag pinned above the entrance to the long conference room. She'd thought the military brass now taking their seats around the massive conference table appeared impressive, but raw adrenaline simmered from the VIPER team in pulsing waves.

She forced her focus away from Commander Daviani and zeroed in on the tallest of the group stepping toward her.

"*Buenos dias,* Dr. Kerrigan. It's a pleasure to finally meet you. I'm Captain Nicolas Romero."

Green Beret. Orphan from Toledo raised in foster care with a degree in computer science from West Point. Or the tall, dark, and Hispanic one who likely captured hearts with just his sultry smile and sensual accent. Not to be confused with the tall, dark, and brooding Commander Daviani leaning against the wall behind him, who didn't seem to think she could do the job she'd been hired for.

Shaking Romero's hand, she pulled up his file in her brain.

The horrific photos taken shortly after his transport had been ambushed flashed before her eyes. Blood and burns had covered his face. Torn, pulpy flesh had hung from his right shoulder and his hip socket where his arm and leg had been blasted off. She couldn't stop imagining their counterparts decaying in the sand like the remnants of a gutted hyena.

She shut down the images of the broken soldier and focused on the heartthrob in front of her. "*Mucho gusto*, Captain Romero." She hadn't spoken Spanish in a while, but the greeting rolled off her tongue effortlessly. "And please, call me Scarlett."

"Only if you'll call me Nic." He flashed a grin. White teeth sparkled against his olive complexion.

She vowed to use her knowledge to ensure he kept smiling and would never again endure what she'd seen in those photos.

The third VIPER operative, this one almost as tall and lankier than Nic but equally solid, nudged him aside. "I'm Major Lincoln Taylor, F-22 pilot and top of my class. You can call me Linc."

Nic chuckled. "He forgot to mention how big his ego is."

"Shut your pretty face." The Air Force Academy grad, with a major in aerospace engineering and hours upon hours of flight time, speared an icy glare at his teammate. His glacier-blue eyes and the harsh angles of his face matched the untamed Alaskan land he'd grown up in. Although he'd lost both legs when his jet had crashed in the Middle East, his gait, which she'd marveled at in the videos, appeared steady and even.

Patience pushed herself between the men and tsked like a mother. "Behave yourselves on Scarlett's first day."

Before Scarlett could return Linc's greeting, the fourth VIPER operative strode up.

"I'm First Lieutenant Kane Darren, Force Recon, United States Marine Corps." He tipped an imaginary hat. "Pleased to meet you, ma'am."

"Please call me Scarlett. Ma'am reminds me of a few boarding school mistresses I'd like to forget." She should have told Commander Daviani the same thing earlier when he'd addressed her as such, but she'd been too busy defending her expertise.

"Scarlett it is." Dimples winked in both of Kane's round cheeks. "And a fine pretty name."

She couldn't help but grin at his country twang or how he moved as gracefully on his steel leg as Linc did on two. His file said he'd been fast and agile before losing his limb thanks to years of running high school track and hunting in the hills of the Appalachian Mountains. Now the country boy would be unstoppable. "How are things in West Virginia?"

"Things are fine, thank you, and bless you for asking."

Bless him. How anyone could be so happy after being the victim of an improvised explosive device was one of those things only God could explain.

Linc narrowed his eyes. "Don't go scaring our genius away with your redneck, so-called charm. I need her smarts to get me in the air."

Story of my life.

Linc sounded like every other male she knew, from the

middle school basketball player she'd tutored so he wouldn't get kicked off the team to Commander Daviani not even an hour ago.

Their means to an end.

Kane hooked his thumbs into the waistband of his cargo pants. "Watch the redneck comments, Fly Boy, or the next time I go home, I won't bring back Uncle Pat's apple pie moonshine. And we don't give a crap about your flight time."

Home and moonshine.

The empty place in her heart twanged like Kane's accent. She hadn't known the love of family since her mom had died sixteen years ago. She barely remembered the sound of her mother's voice but hadn't forgotten how it had felt to be held in her loving arms.

Linc stepped up to Kane and poked his chest. "First, bringing moonshine into this was a low blow. I've admitted your Uncle Pat's is almost as good as my cousin's in Alaska. Second, who do you think is going to fly your sorry, ugly asses to the fighting? The goddamn stork who brought your sorry, ugly asses into the world?"

Kane rubbed his knuckles into the top of Linc's spiky blond hair. "You pilots are all the same. Egotistical pricks. Cease the assholery, will ya?"

Assholery? Was that a word? It so, it wasn't one anybody in her professional circles used.

Nic turned to her and winked. "Don't listen to these *idiotas*. Knowing how to treat a lady isn't in their blood."

"And it's in yours?" Kane raised a sandy-colored eyebrow. "If you're so blessed with charm, then why did the barista at the coffee shop this morning turn you down?" He looked at Scarlett. "Cheesy pickup lines are still cheesy even when you throw in a few pretty Spanish words, don't you think?"

Think?

Yeah, she thought a lot, but not about topics like dating.

The familiar butterflies jitterbugged in her stomach. These men, with their action-flick hero faces, hard bodies, and what appeared to be good-natured ribbing, registered way out of her element. Like off the periodic table. "I, uh, don't really know."

He winked one of those cornflower-blue eyes. "I thought geniuses knew everything."

Not this genius. Having a skyscraper IQ opened a lot of doors but also locked her behind many.

Kane tapped her on the shoulder. "That's okay. We'll let you slide, being it's your first day and all."

Laughter, genuine and honest, bounced between the men. Well, except Linc, but the hard line of his lips tilted up a smidge. She laughed along, the sound nervous to her ears, but the butterflies in her belly eased their dance by a few beats. These guys were funny in a crude way she'd never experienced. She didn't have any siblings, but it didn't take a genius to realize their insults and playful punches were a macho way of conveying how much they cared and respected their brothers-in-arms.

VIPER's director Will Thompson entered the room. She nodded a greeting and stepped aside to let him pass. Her shoulders collided with a hard body behind her as fingers grazed her hip.

"Careful, Dr. Kerrigan." Commander Daviani's deep voice rumbled in her ear. "This can be a dangerous place for someone like you."

Like me?

Her breath caught, and she coughed, unable to argue the point. This room, this building, held too much masculinity. Too much normalcy with talk of dating and family. Too much of everything she'd never experienced. But she'd made the choice to leave the familiarity of Richardson Enterprises and venture into scary territory. Revealing apprehension wasn't an option. At least not any more than she'd already displayed during her meeting with Daviani's bare torso.

She squared her shoulders as she turned to face him. "I can handle myself, Commander."

"Call me Chris."

She nodded. "Please call me Scarlett."

"Noted, *ma'am*."

Director Thompson cleared his throat from his spot at the head of the table. "Ladies and gentlemen, please take your seats." He motioned for Scarlett to take the chair closest to him.

She glared at Commander Daviani—Chris—before she turned away. He'd heard her tell Kane she didn't like to be called ma'am, yet he'd said it in a teasing manner with an undertone she couldn't pinpoint.

Director Thompson pressed a button on the computer console built into the head of the table. The DOD logo on the screen that took up the entire wall at the end of the room switched to the Project VIPER snake and triangle. She listened as Thompson briefed Admiral Edgar and the other Pentagon brass about VIPER's progress and thanked each team member for their service and for volunteering to be part of the project.

Color swamped her cheeks as he expounded on how her technology would be the catalyst to change the face of modern warfare. She was used to being the center of attention among her scientific peers, but this was different. This attention came from a former military intelligence leader whose expertise didn't come from research and study but from down-in-the-trenches experience. His black suit against his coffee-colored skin housed a trim physique honed from years of service. The dark gleam in his eyes hinted at things he couldn't speak about as the leader of an "if I tell you, I'll have to kill you" kind of program. If the scars on his bald head were any indication, he'd barely survived some of his experiences.

She perused the VIPER operatives in the front row who entrusted her with their bodies. Their lives depended on her success. Commander Daviani met her gaze as if he'd been waiting for her to search him out. With unabashed curiosity, he stared at her with those stunning sapphire eyes. She'd be damned if she let him see how much his interest unnerved her.

THREE

Scarlett didn't look away from Chris's scrutiny. His respect for her upped a click. But only one. He wouldn't believe the hype about what she could do for VIPER until she delivered.

Kane rolled his chair toward him. "Hey, did you get a gander at our new genius?"

"Yeah. I met her in MedLab. Couldn't they have hired someone a little less—"

"Less what? Sexy?" He softly whistled through his teeth. "Relax, dude. It's not like she's going into battle with us."

"I know, but she'll be monitoring us from headquarters while we're in the field. She's an integral part of the team. The pressure might be too much to handle for someone who's never been responsible for the lives of others. How stressful could it have been working for her stepdaddy at Richardson Enterprises?"

Director Thompson cleared his throat and glared at them.

"Busted," Kane sang under his breath as he scooted his chair away.

Chris tuned out the rest of Thompson's dog and pony show for the higher-ups and studied Scarlett's slim fingers clasped on the table. Her white knuckles revealed her nerves. And were her hands shaking? He leaned a hair closer. Fuck, they were. He eased back into the soft leather of his seat and crossed his arms over his chest.

Inaccurate intel had led to the disaster that had stolen his arm and left his men dead. The officer responsible for the fuckup had been new to the team. During the final briefing before they'd moved out, her eyes had held the same apprehension as Scarlett's did right now.

When the room cleared, Chris pulled Thompson aside. "Are you sure Dr. Kerrigan can handle this?"

"Trust me, Daviani." The director wiped sweat off his head with a handkerchief. "She may seem a bit odd, but she's the best of the best. Play nice and don't scare her off. VIPER needs her. She may not know it yet, but we all need her."

Hours later, Chris tossed his tablet onto the nightstand and draped his flesh-and-bone arm over his eyes. No matter how many times he read about Scarlett, the facts didn't change. Thompson hadn't been kidding. She was the best of the best, at least on paper. Kane was right too. Sexy didn't even begin to cover it.

He gently grasped the little knob on the bedside lamp between his steel fingers and turned. "Got it."

While the weaponry Scarlett would network between his brain and his arm would only be active during training and battle, his enhanced strength was always functional. He needed to think about every motion, every touch so he didn't exert too much force or pressure and break something.

Or someone.

He turned his head to the fist-sized hole in his wooden headboard. Eventually, he'd get around to fixing it. Right now, it reminded him that his post-traumatic, stress-induced nightmares sometimes became physical. The mandated therapy sessions he attended twice a week helped, but the demons in his traumatized brain were by no means laid to rest.

As he closed his eyes, the words his ex-wife Natalie said before she'd left lacerated him.

"I'm sorry, but I can't handle you."

He clenched the sheets with his steel hand. The soft cotton tore under his grip. "Shit."

Scarlett's gentle voice whispered through his mind.

"I promise you'll be safe with me."

"Where the hell did that come from?" As he questioned why the nervous genius's voice flitted through his mind on repeat, the burning in his chest lessened. Despite not fully trusting in her capabilities, something about her calmed his troubled thoughts. But trust and yearning for a peaceful night's rest had nothing to do with why he pictured her in the cold, empty spot next to him.

Never going to happen.

Even if she wasn't his colleague, he couldn't let another woman into his bed—or his life. Forget about his heart. His turbulent past and hazardous future made him too dangerous.

FOUR

The IT technician's voice boomed through the shooting range. "Heads up! LTH weaponry coming online."

Kane pounded on the protective glass separating the observation room from the four shooting bays. "Not LTH. V-Strikes."

Chris snickered from the bay next to him. The LTH acronym for the laser-taser hybrid weaponry they were testing today wasn't cool enough, so they'd renamed it. *V* for VIPER. Strike because the strikes from the protons that would soon stream from their limbs were potent enough to inflict a multitude of dangerous and deadly things.

If we ever get back into the field.

Scarlett had been at headquarters for weeks now, and they were finally getting around to testing their capabilities.

A prickle originated in the corner of his eye. He winced as an electromagnetic current traveled down his neck and streamed into his shoulder. The activation of the V-Strike weaponry only jolted him for a few seconds, but it burned like he'd been scorched from the inside.

"Fuck, that hurts." Nic shouted from the bay next to him.

Chris cursed his agreement as he glanced into the observation room. Scarlett stood by the safety glass.

A mischievous smile quirked her lips as her laugh sounded over the intercom. "I warned you. I know the sting of activation is uncomfortable, but it's necessary to let you know your weapons are live. Your bodies will get used to it in time."

She's enjoying the hell out of this.

Why wouldn't she enjoy his discomfort? He'd been a dick to her these past few weeks. He wasn't proud of his tactics to coax her into talking to him beyond a few words or a head nod. But when he called her "ma'am" or goaded her into defending her technology, he enjoyed the sexy-as-hell way she put him in his place. He wanted more of her spark. Burned to pull it out even though he had no business with her beyond what she could do for his career.

Not just for his career.

For his life.

Without VIPER, he had nothing.

Kane cursed. "You call that a sting? That hurt more than the time I tore out of Mr. Hayfield's pasture with the cops on my tail and jumped an electric fence. Didn't spill a bit of the whiskey I'd been drinking with his daughter though." He peered down at his crotch. "Are you sure I'll be able to have kids someday with all this juice running through me?"

Chris watched Scarlett, entranced as the flush in her cheeks deepened to a brazen shade of pink.

She tensed and averted her eyes from Kane's groin. "The team who invented the V-Strikes is made up of scientists smarter than I am. I promise your virility won't be compromised."

Linc glanced between his legs. "My boy didn't survive a

plane crash and double leg amputation to be fried by some subagency's technology."

Nic eyed his own family jewels. "Nobody's smarter than Doc. If she says our manhood is safe, it is."

Scarlett's shoulders dropped away as she steepled her hands in front of her chest and nodded. "Thank you, Nic."

He bowed low. "You are very welcome."

Chris grimaced at another sting, this one inside his chest. Dammit, he shouldn't be jealous of how Scarlett's shoulders relaxed when Nic joked with her. Or how she laughed when Kane showed her videos of the Pygmy goats on his family's farm. Even Linc, with his sullen attitude, made her smile every so often. The gap between him and the beautiful doctor was his fault though. Well, partly. She hadn't gone out of her way to be his friend either.

Yeah, friends.

That's not how he dreamed about her at night.

"Get your heads out of your asses and quit the chitchat about your junk so we can get started." He faced the end of the forty-foot shooting bay, eyeing the hanging black-and-white paper targets in the shape of the human body.

He looked through the thick safety glass separating the shooters. To his right, Nic hummed some of the hip-hop music he liked to listen to. To his left, Kane's leg vibrated like a child's wind-up toy. In the final bay, Linc stood motionless, all coiled energy ready to strike. Chris's own idiosyncrasy was silently reciting the pertinent facts needed to complete the mission or counting down the time to execute. But instead of hearing his own voice in his head, he heard Scarlett's directions from this morning's training brief.

"You control your weaponry."

"You visualize where you want the laser to hit your target."

"You think about what level of damage you aim to inflict."

"You command your body to fire."

"If you can think, you are in control. If you're in a situation where you lose the ability to think, headquarters will control your weaponry remotely."

He prayed he would never be in a position to test that last capability as he reached for the infrared eyewear on the ledge next to him and slipped it on. Without it, he wouldn't be able to see the path of the V-Strikes engineered to be undetectable to the human eye.

Once he learned to master his new power, he could temporarily incapacitate a person or stop a heart, depending on the intensity and the anatomy he targeted. V-Strikes would leave no trace as they left his body, no trace on the clothes they fired through, and no trace on his victims unless he wanted to leave evidence of his assault. They could also cut a hole in glass with the precision of a laser, penetrate a bulletproof vest, or blast through brick with the force of an explosion.

The technician gave the command to fire. Chris focused on the center of the bull's-eye and envisioned a tiny hole in the center. The excitement steadied him as he prepared to engage.

Fire!

The electromagnetic current rippled in spiraling twists around his arm. A thin red laser surged from the front of his bicep and streaked toward the target.

Bull's-eye!

He raised his arm to shoulder height, awe and exhilaration rushing from every pore of his body and visualized a strike to the kneecap.

Fire!

A V-Strike flashed from his fingertip in a downward arc.

Bull's-eye!

Next to him, Kane let out a whoop as a V-Strike shot from his knee and hit between the target's eyes. Linc fired simultaneous strikes from his thighs while Nic hummed a tune and fired rapidly from each of his steel appendages. Chris continued visualizing different target areas and intensities as he moved his arm to test if he really could strike from any position. Satisfied he could, he turned from the target, visualized it as a brick wall, and focused on decimating it.

Fire!

He spun in time to see the target disintegrate into smoldering ash.

Fucking bull's-eye!

His body buzzed as he tore off his goggles and turned to the observation room. Scarlett stared at him with a mixture of joy and confidence and a good dose of "I told you so" on her face.

He mouthed, "Nice job," and turned away. He'd doubted her science fiction technology and had made no secret about his misgivings. Now, the things he could do with his new arm were out of this goddamn world.

Maybe she was smart enough to keep him and the team safe.

An electromagnetic jolt seized his arm. A second later it fizzled, signaling he was no longer activated. No longer dangerous, at least with a laser. But there were no maybes about whether he'd be a danger to Scarlett if he ever acted on his nightly fantasies. She may be VIPER's genius, but she wasn't his to touch and never would be.

Pride surged through Scarlett. After years of researching, experimenting, and dreaming, her vision was a reality. This was only the beginning, not just for combat-related advances but for so many other applications she could create to save lives.

Kane raced into the observation room and pulled her into a hug. "That was more exciting than breaking a skittish colt. You're amazing, Doc."

She stiffened in surprise as Nic yanked her away for his own hug.

Linc held out his fist. "Way to go, Doc."

She touched her knuckles to his with ease as if accepting celebratory hugs and fist bumps was something she did every day at the office. A stiff nod from her stepfather, not even a handshake, was all the paltry praise she'd been accustomed to. The VIPER way was much more gratifying, even if it only came from three out of the four.

A weird feeling settled in her gut. While she didn't expect cartwheels from Chris, more than a passing acknowledgment of her accomplishment would have been nice. She wasn't used to worrying about impressing her colleagues. They typically went out of their way to impress her. Why did she need Chris's admiration? Was it because she was undeniably attracted to him? One shouldn't have anything to do with the other. He didn't see her as a woman but as his ticket out of training and into the field. His "nice job" should have been adequate.

I should have never let Beth talk me into watching a romantic comedy last night.

Life wasn't a flirty movie with a happily ever after. VIPER certainly wasn't anybody's happy anything. As cool as the technology was, the guys had landed here because they'd lost a limb or two and had nearly died. Her path to VIPER hadn't been covered with roses either.

She should have been happy with the funds and resources Richardson Enterprises provided. Should have been able to trust her stepfather with the technology she'd pioneered. But Henry had only considered her a dollar sign, not a child to be loved, let alone a woman with feelings. If fate held a happy conclusion for this story, sappy music wouldn't accompany it. VIPER's happy ending would be when the team came home alive.

Director Thompson stepped into the observation room. "Listen up. We've confirmed a live site for the beta test of our communications and biofeedback systems."

"About time." Chris rubbed the scruff on his chin with the back of his steel hand. "Where and when?"

"At the Naval Academy—your alma mater. The test will take place next Thursday. Governor Bradley is hosting a fundraising gala where he's expected to announce his presidential candidacy. VIPER will be present under the guise of providing additional security, but our primary objective is to test our comms in a field setting."

Scarlett nodded. "Makes sense."

Bradley, a veteran himself, was an outspoken supporter of wounded vets. She heard he'd visited each of the team members, not once but several times, after their returns stateside. The Naval Academy grad was also a classmate of Admiral Edgar and had served with him in the Navy. Even though Bradley didn't have a hand in VIPER's inception, rumor had it he held enough security clearances to know about the project and enough clout to suggest recruits. For his support, the men in this room owed him their careers. The solemn nod Chris sent her way said he knew it too.

"Will our weaponry be active?" Linc pointed at a target and mouthed, "Fire."

"Didn't you hear me?" Thompson eyed the team one by one. "I said, 'Under the guise of providing security.' If a guest drinks too much, you can use your muscle to escort them out."

"You mean we're *bouncers*?" Nic cursed under his breath.

Man, they're like the snakes inked on each of their chests. God help any enemy within striking distance.

Thompson held up his hand. "There's brass at the top who need more convincing that VIPER is worth the investment. Many of them will be present and scrutinizing the way we operate. Even the slightest slipup could convince them we aren't fit for missions, so stop whining and focus on the job you were recruited for. We need the dollars to keep flowing from the Pentagon. Without them, we're defunct."

The weight of keeping Project VIPER alive settled like a concrete wall on Scarlett's shoulders.

Thompson looked up at Kane and Linc, who both towered several inches over him. "You two are needed in MedLab." He pointed to Nic. "Human resources needs to see you."

Chris straightened from where he leaned against the safety glass as everyone filed out. "Sounds like if all goes well, we'll be back in action soon. Isn't that right, ma'am?"

She refrained from hurling one of the colorful adjectives she'd learned from the guys. "Why can't you call me Scarlett like everyone else?"

"The others call you Doc."

"They don't do it to make me angry."

"And you think I call you ma'am to piss you off?"

"I know you do. Why?"

His lips turned up at the corners. The appreciative look she'd hoped for earlier lit his gaze. "Because you're a lot more fun when you let out the woman inside."

His words triggered the unnerving sensations only he could ignite. "What are you talking about?"

He took a step closer, his body inches from hers. The walls of the glass-enclosed room seemed to shrink from the heat of his proximity. "I meant it when I said nice job. These guys are about ready to explode more spectacularly than the target I obliterated if they don't get back in the game. Thanks for your efforts in getting us there."

Her lips parted into a small O. Praise was the last thing she'd expected to hear.

Oh, she thought he was a jerk, but he was also a selfless hero, a protective, caring leader, and a whip-smart engineer who understood most of the technology jargon she threw his way. Who was this man who managed to infuriate and please her within the space of a few minutes?

When she found her voice, her steady words were in complete opposition to the quivering in her belly. "Thanks for the compliment, and you're welcome, but you didn't answer my question."

"About the woman inside?" His gaze bore a hole into her as if his eyes were equipped with technology engineered to see into her soul. "I know, Scarlett. I know."

FIVE

A brisk wind blew Scarlett's ponytail into her face. She burrowed her chin into the collar of her black peacoat. A smile warmed her cheeks when she spotted her best friend Beth maneuvering through the evening rush-hour crowd. They met with a hug in the middle of the sidewalk, and Scarlett warmed up even more. "I've missed you."

Beth stepped back. Her dark mass of loose curls shone like a halo under the streetlights. "I've missed you too, girl." Her amber-colored eyes lit with excitement as she tugged Scarlett inside Gallery Place. "Come on. We don't have much time to find the perfect dress for your big fancy gala tomorrow. I can't believe you didn't tell me about it until this morning."

"Sorry. I know your project has been keeping you at the office late and I've been busy too." And preoccupied with analyzing the conversation she'd had with Chris at the shooting range a few days ago.

What had he meant when he'd said, "You're more fun when you let out the woman inside," and followed it up with the equally vague, "I know?" She was about to ask Beth's opinion on the matter when a gaggle of teenagers stopped short in front of them to take selfies with their phones.

Beth giggled. "Remember when we were young and silly?"

"Barely." Scarlett groaned as she unbuttoned her coat.

"Let's be like that again and take selfies while you try on dozens of gorgeous dresses."

"Dozens? How about just one or two. You know I hate shopping. And parties."

Since falling under her stepfather's guardianship at the age of twelve, she'd been expected to attend the lavish gatherings he threw for his clients. She'd hated every minute of struggling to make small talk with women who called her odd behind their wineglasses. Even worse were the conversations Henry drew her into for the sole purpose of showing off her knowledge like she was his trained monkey. "Do you really think I need something new? I could wear the black gown I wore to Henry's birthday party."

"Boring, like the coat you're wearing." Beth stopped and pointed to a slinky sequined gown in the window of a boutique. "Now something along those lines would be perfect."

"No, you would look great in that. Not me." Beth's petite curves made her look fantastic in anything, while Scarlett resembled a lanky teenage boy. "Besides, I work for the Department of Defense. Not exactly a field where I need to worry about fashion."

Beth smoothed the front of her faux fur jacket. "I work for a government agency too. You don't see me dressing like I'm going to a funeral."

Scarlett fingered the hem of her coat. Her wardrobe wasn't dull. It was sensible, like writing code.

"Come on." Beth guided her to the escalator. "Someday

you'll thank me for talking you into buying a sexy little number."

"I really don't see why I would ever do that."

"You know, for someone so smart, you aren't real bright sometimes."

Scarlett sighed. It wasn't the first time she'd heard those words. She was proud of her hyperintelligence but could admit she lacked insight into some of the nuances of life other people could easily see.

"Powerful clothes broadcast a statement. And speaking of powerful—" Beth fanned herself with her hands. "The hot vets will be there. Maybe you'll find yourself in the arms of a real American hero."

"Please stop referring to my colleagues like they're man candy." She should never have described the team's physical attributes over a bottle of wine the other night. "They're so much more than 'hot vets.'"

"I agree. They're handsome, heroic, and totally fancy-party-date material." She looped her arm through Scarlett's. "Think of the gala like the prom you never went to."

Or the homecoming dance. Or pizza and a movie with a boy.

How was she supposed to date without being educated on it? Henry had shipped her off to boarding school to "nurture her genius" within days of her mother's death. The academies she'd attended had rarely offered social events. When they had, she'd been the outcast among the other students, who had been years older. Besides, Henry had never approved of activities outside of academics.

Beth whistled as her gaze fixed on a shop window at the top of the escalator. "Wait until the hot vets get a load of you in that sexy number."

Scarlett shook her head. "No way."

SIX

Scarlett peered at the dress hanging on the back of her office door. She should have never let Beth talk her into buying the too-tight, too-red, too-revealing gown with the slit up the thigh. "Even geniuses make mistakes," she muttered.

She picked up her phone and sneered at Beth's most recent text message.

> Beth: Have fun tonight and flirt with a hot vet while you're at it!

"Enough with the 'hot vets.'" She dropped her phone on the desk and pressed her fingers to her temples. Flirting was not a subject she'd been schooled in. God knew she had no practical experience in how to attract a man. She hadn't even needed to bat an eyelash to gain her ex-fiancé's attention. James had known her since they'd been teenagers.

Maybe she could take an online course about how to catch a man's eye.

Who was she kidding? She'd be the first woman to fail "Flirting for Dummies." Laughing at herself, she rose from her chair and headed down the hall in search of coffee to calm her nerves. As she turned a corner, a wall of muscle and steel halted her progress.

"Whoa." Chris gripped her shoulder.

She flattened her hands against the unforgiving planes of his chest. His unique earthy scent, infused with a hint of sweat, drifted into her nose.

"Are you okay?" He released her and stepped back.

She dropped her hands from his chest and rubbed her shoulder. It still felt warm. "Yes, sorry. I wasn't paying attention to where I was going because I was thinking about the beta test, and the governor and—"

What you'll think of me in my gown.

Patience strode out of the kitchen. "Chris, there you are. I wanted to thank you again for watching the boys last night." She turned to Scarlett as she massaged her temples. "This guy saved my life when the meeting with my custody lawyer ran late."

Scarlett studied the circles under the tired mother's eyes, which had been growing darker by the day.

Chris touched Patience's shoulder. "You're a great mom. Your ex won't get them."

"I know." She pulled in a deep breath and smiled. "The boys won ribbons at the science fair this morning with the potato clocks you helped them make."

"Excellent. I had a lot of fun hanging out with the rug rats." He cocked his head to Scarlett. "I bet you won the kindergarten science fair with a potato clock."

Patience laughed as she backed down the hallway. "Don't be ridiculous. She was probably in preschool."

Heat rose to Scarlett's cheeks as she skirted around Chris and entered the kitchen. She knew Patience wasn't teasing her about being above average. She wasn't so sure about Chris.

At the counter, he slid next to her and reached for the "Science is Hot" mug she kept among the other cups by the sink.

Their shoulders touched.

Electric sparks zipped down her arm.

He leaned into her as he reached for the coffeepot and poured. "You look like you could use this."

Her response lodged in her throat. Why did he get so close for no good reason? And why wasn't she backing away?

Slowly, he pressed the mug into her hands. "Who gave you this cup?"

His intoxicating scent mingled with the coffee and swirled deliciously between them. Warmth rushed through her fingers and into her cheeks. "My friend Beth."

"Good to know."

What did that mean? The question flew from her brain as his gaze traveled from her reddened face down to the *V* of her blouse and back up. His lips twitched into a smirk, bringing the dimple in his left cheek to life.

"I'll see you at the gala tonight, ma'am."

Coffee in hand, she stared at his backside encased in those black cargo pants he wore so damn well. Dammit. He was a government asset. It was her job to serve and protect him.

Stop ogling his ass and remember that.

SEVEN

The silky hem of Scarlett's red gown tickled her ankles. Her thin, matching heels jingled on the shiny wooden floor like a pretty song. As she walked toward Patience, the sureness in her step soared to red-carpet worthy.

When she'd arrived at the venue at the Naval Academy, security had whisked her up to the mezzanine level, where she'd been drawn into conversations about her work with VIPER. Despite her nerves, she'd spoken intelligently.

Effortlessly.

Nailed it.

Patience sidled up to her. Her black sequined gown shimmered under the lights hanging from the barreled ceiling.

"My, my, Scarlett. I do believe you have yourself a suitor. The guy with the great hair hasn't stopped eyeing you, and who can blame him? You look stunning."

"Thank you." She touched the loose curls brushing her shoulders and glanced around the balcony. A man by the railing with wavy blond hair and a neatly trimmed goatee smiled at her. His tall, lean frame gave him an authoritative air. The laughter on his handsome face and the chuckles from his friends, however, said there was nothing pretentious about the attractive stranger.

"What's the matter? You look like you made a scientific breakthrough and don't know what to do with the information."

"It's been…" Her newfound confidence waned as she fiddled with the communications device in her hand. "It's been a long time."

"Since?"

"Since I've talked to a man I don't work with, never mind one who appears interested. Can I ask you something? As a friend?"

"I did your hair and makeup for a fancy party. We're besties now. Ask away."

Delight coursed through Scarlett. Beth was her only girl-friend. Now it seemed she had two. "What if he talks to me and I clam-up? Or worse, I ramble like a simpleton. I don't have much experience talking to men in social situations."

"Oh, honey, just be yourself. Any man would be a fool not to fall in love with you."

Two fools who only loved the organ in her skull came to mind. The rest of her could be donated to science as far as Henry and James were concerned.

Patience nudged her with a sequined hip. "Go talk to him."

Scarlett's communication unit beeped with a request from Thompson to meet him by the stage.

Saved by the boss man.

"Duty calls." She bid a hasty goodbye to Patience. Maneuvering through the crowd, she made her way to the edge of the mezzanine, where it narrowed into an interior balcony spanning the length of the cavernous room. She stopped to admire the rich dark wood of the matching balcony stretching across the other side of the grand hall and inhaled the tasty scent of filet mignon.

The band struck up "The Marines Battle Hymn" as she hurried toward the stairs at the far end. Before she descended, she paused to study the fairy tale scene below. Sixty tables draped in shimmering gold cloth covered the polished wood floor. China plates, crystal goblets, and gold-dusted red roses glittered as six hundred supporters dressed in tuxedos, military uniforms, and colorful evening gowns enjoyed a fine meal.

She glanced at the communications unit in her palm being tested tonight. When the team went on missions, the devices, which resembled black smartphones, would provide real-time location data, a touch video screen, and bio feed-back so sensitive it could report a change in blood pressure or heart rate.

Chris's and Nic's were entirely embedded in their steel arms. The central processing units of the devices were housed in Kane's and Linc's steel legs, but the screens were strapped to their wrists. The audio, which streamed to their ears without earpieces, was temporarily down while headquarters ran a diagnostic test, but the video was functional.

Later, when the crowd cleared, Scarlett would use her device to activate the team just long enough to make sure their weaponry came online without a hitch. For now, she used it to pinpoint their locations.

Nic leaned against the wall in the southeast corner. She zoomed out to see what had put the smirk on his classic features. Two twentysomething women eyed him up like a decadent dessert. Who could blame them? He made tall, dark, and pretty look sinful in his dress uniform.

Kane stood to the left of the stage. His intense gaze contrasted with his boyish features as he tipped an imaginary hat to a passing couple. She'd seen him brandish his country boy gesture many times these past few weeks and always found it charming. So did the woman, based on the way she looked over her shoulder and smiled at him.

She found Linc near the entrance staring at the Wright B-1 hanging from the arched ceiling. Even through the screen, the desperation to fly again shone in his icy Alaskan gaze. She didn't doubt he'd hop in the replica of Orville and Wilbur's aircraft and soar among the clouds if given the opportunity.

She spotted Director Thompson to the right of the stage, talking to Governor Bradley. Chris should be there too. Where was he? Her lungs constricted. Was something wrong? She initiated a search on her comms unit. Seconds later, a green dot on the screen confirmed he was *near* his assigned position.

As she found him in the crowd, he looked up, his gaze zeroing in on her like a heat-seeking missile.

The breath she'd recovered was stolen again.

Holy naval hotness.

She licked her lips and stared at the blue service coat stretched across his broad shoulders. Her gaze lowered to the lean *V* of his torso and fixed on the gold stripes at his cuffs. Desire purred in her veins. She'd seen his hard, scarred body under the uniform he wore, felt the way his hands, both flesh and metal, warmed her skin. She had a feeling when he was with a woman, there was nothing gentle about this officer.

Was the heat in his eyes real or a trick of the lighting? She needed to look away before she got burned, but his gaze held her tight.

He knows what he does to me.

His lips spread into a knowing grin as if to say, *damn sure I know.*

* • ⌖ • *

Chris prayed the biofeedback functionality in his comms unit was offline, along with the audio. Scarlett didn't need to know the sight of her on the balcony in the shimmering red gown had caused his heart to stop beating momentarily.

From her perch above, she held his stare, carrying herself with a confident grace he found sexy as hell.

She shifted her stance, her eyes still on him, and the slit in her gown parted to expose creamy skin halfway up her thigh. The clouds outside the tall arched windows also shifted and let in the moonlight. The illumination bathed her in a surreal glow, reminding him of an old painting he'd once seen of a young beauty standing on a widow's walk, searching an angry sea. Scarlett reminded him of that girl.

Watching.

Waiting for her lover to return.

Sweat formed on his brow. His stomach twisted in a knot as he realized he didn't want Scarlett to merely be his lover. He wanted her to be the girl waiting for him to come home.

Scarlett tore her gaze from Chris and headed down the stairs. Her comms unit had flashed a biofeedback warning. Chris's vitals had spiked for a moment. Had it been a glitch? She made a mental note to ask at the debrief later as she wound through the maze of tables toward them.

Governor Bradley spotted her and extended his hand in welcome. "Ah, there's the woman I've been hearing about."

She accepted his handshake and met his warm gaze. "It's a pleasure to meet you, sir."

"The pleasure's all mine. Director Thompson and Commander Daviani have been raving about your outstanding work."

Scarlett stole a glance at Chris. He'd been raving about *her*?

The governor took a step closer and lowered his head to her ear. "You know, Dr. Kerrigan, I've been privy to *everything* about VIPER. I'm a wounded veteran myself, and I'm honored we could provide the site for your beta test." Something caught his attention and he waved. "Henry, glad you could make it."

Scarlett froze as her stepfather emerged from a crowd of politicians.

No, no, no.

She'd feared he might attend because he supported Bradley's run for the presidency. Before she'd left her office for the gala, she'd checked the guest list—again—and his name hadn't been on it.

Henry beamed a wide smile at Bradley. "Governor, glad to see you've met my brilliant daughter."

She turned her cheek for Henry's kiss as he reached her side. "You didn't mention you were attending tonight."

"Well, I should be at the technology summit I spoke at in Europe yesterday, but when my buddy Will said you'd be here, I adjusted my schedule."

She managed to nod as she stared at Henry and Director Thompson shaking hands. *They know each other?*

Henry hadn't mentioned that tidbit when she'd told him she was taking a job with a DOD project headed by a retired Army officer named Will Thompson. Or had he? She tried to recall the conversation, but Henry's "you're an ungrateful brat and I made you what you are today" speech upstaged any other details.

Governor Bradley patted Henry on the back. "Good to see you. Hey, I was sorry to hear Richardson Enterprises didn't win the DOD contract for the submarine upgrades. Better luck next time."

Henry sucked in his whiskey paunch and rubbed a hand over his thinning gray hair. "If the government wants the job done right, they should award the contract to the best instead of the cheapest."

Bradley mirrored Henry's gestures, except he didn't need to suck anything in, and his hand smoothed out a full head of white waves. "Awarding government contracts would be easy if cost was the only factor considered."

"What *should* be considered when awarding contracts is—"

Scarlett cleared her throat, eager to shut down Henry's impending lecture. She touched Chris's bicep. "Commander Daviani, this is my stepfather, Henry Richardson."

Henry offered his hand. "Thank you for your service."

Chris gripped it with his steel.

Henry gawked at the technological marvel. "You're lucky to have my daughter on your team. It's kind of like having the CEO and founder of the top technology company in the world on your side, know what I'm saying?"

"Forgive me, sir, but I do not. Maybe you can explain."

Scarlett refrained from gawking at Chris's comeback.

Henry tugged on his jacket lapels. "I'd be happy to explain why Scarlett and I make a great team. When her mother died unexpectedly when she was twelve, I couldn't leave the little thing all alone, so I did what any noble man would do. I made her my kin. Sent her to the best schools. I guided her education myself. So, you see, Commander Daviani, Scarlett's an extension of me. A two-for-one deal."

A muscle ticced in Chris's jaw. "With all due respect, sir, she's not a package deal. She's one of a kind."

Henry's jaw dropped. So did Scarlett's. Aside from her mom, she'd never witnessed anybody call her stepfather out on his arrogance. Her respect for Chris escalated to reverence.

Bradley slapped Chris on the back. "And this man is one of a kind too. I'm proud to have his support tonight."

A flush crept into Chris's cheeks. "I'm proud to be here, sir, and thankful for the support and compassion you've shown me and my team."

The surprising emotional display sent Scarlett's heart into spasms.

Bradley pointed into the crowd. "Ah, there's my nephew."

The attractive man with great hair and goatee who had smiled at her on the balcony headed toward them. Eyes the same warm blue as his uncle's met hers. She covered her belly with her palm. Henry's unexpected appearance and Chris's quick rise to her defense had her insides twisting like a double helix.

Chris placed his steel hand on the small of her back. "Are you okay?"

"Yes, I'm fine." If fine meant having the attention of two handsome men and not knowing what to do with it.

Bradley's nephew smiled at her. "Uncle Bob, aren't you going to introduce me to the smartest, not to mention the prettiest woman in the room?"

The governor clapped the younger version of himself on the shoulder. "Dr. Kerrigan, this is my great-nephew, Ryan. You two have a lot in common. He's a cybersecurity professor at American University and a big fan of yours. Now if you'll excuse me, it's almost showtime." He winked at his nephew. "Don't ask for an autograph and embarrass yourself. You have a family reputation to uphold."

"Don't worry. I'll take good care of her."

EIGHT

Chris seethed as Ryan Bradley kissed the back of Scarlett's hand. The irrational urge to crush the professor's fingers swamped his steel. Punching Henry Richardson's arrogant face felt entirely justified though. "Excuse me. I've got to check in with my teammate."

The throng of waiters parted for him as he made his way to the other side of the stage.

"You okay?" Kane glanced around the room. "Got a biofeedback alert about your elevated heart rate."

"Must be a glitch." Like the glitch in his brain making him jealous when he thought of Scarlett with another man. Hell, back at headquarters the other day, he'd even asked who'd given her the "Science is Hot" mug because he needed to know she wasn't sipping after-sex coffee with anyone.

"Hope your glitch won't compromise the beta test."

"It won't." *The only thing compromised is me.*

"Who is Doc talking to?"

Chris glanced over his shoulder. Scarlett laughed at something Ryan Bradley whispered into her ear.

And now I want to break your other hand, buddy. "Governor's nephew."

"Dude, why are you so pissy? Lighten up. This is our big night." Kane tapped his steel leg. "Soon we'll be using these bad boys to save the freaking world. Chicks dig superheroes, you know."

Except Scarlett.

She seemed to like the brainy type.

Kane whistled low. "Don't you think our genius looks hot?"

Smoking hot. Sexiest. Woman. Ever. "She looks nice."

"Nice? Don't you know how to compliment a woman? No wonder you're always cranky. When was the last time you got laid?"

Natalie's face popped into his head. Christ, had it been that long? His relationship with his ex-wife had started to unravel long before he'd lost his arm, so yeah, it had been over two years since he'd been with a woman. After VIPER had patched him up, he'd turned down plenty of opportunities to cash in on his wounded hero status. He didn't want sympathy, and he couldn't bring a woman home to his bed.

Especially not Scarlett.

She didn't deserve a man with a dangerous body, mind, and job. She deserved someone who came home to her each night. Someone who couldn't hurt her. Someone like the governor's damn nephew.

The voice of the communications leader back at headquarters echoed in his ear. "Governor live in sixty seconds."

Chris confirmed his position. A few more hours and VIPER would be cleared for active missions. It was what he'd been trained for and much less painful than watching Scarlett talk to another man.

The emcee's voice boomed from the stage. "Ladies and

gentlemen, please welcome Maryland Governor Robert Bradley."

Chris shoved Scarlett out of his mind. Feelings had no place in a mission.

He raised his hands to applaud as the governor approached the podium. A painful prickle splintered near his right eye.

What the hell?

The activation test wasn't supposed to happen until after the room cleared, but the unmistakable current snaked around his arm.

No. No.

His comms beeped with a biofeedback alert as he whispered, "I've been activated."

The communications leader cursed. "Daviani. You've been compromised. Exit. Now."

He spun from the stage and replayed Scarlett's instructions in his mind.

"You control your weaponry."

He stepped toward the exit and visualized strangling the electromagnetic current with his steel.

Stand down! Cease fire!

The V-Strike didn't follow his commands. He dove to the floor to try and throw the deadly laser off target as it pulsed from the back of his bicep.

Governor Bradley grunted.

Chris sprang up.

An eerie hush swathed the room as the governor clutched the podium with one hand. He grasped his left arm with the other. Long seconds later, his legs buckled. A collective gasp broke the silence as he collapsed.

"Governor down. I repeat, governor down," someone shouted.

Cold fear ensnared the viper on Chris's chest.

I shot the governor.

He swiveled his head as time took on the slow-motion pace of an overly dramatic scene in an action movie. Guests sat stunned in their seats, their mouths moving, their voices a fuzzy background noise. Chris stood frozen as Bradley's security detail rushed past him toward their fallen leader.

They have no idea it was me.

He shoved past the news-hungry reporters and hurried to a side exit. The sting of deactivation hadn't seized his shoulder yet. Whoever had hacked VIPER's network could still remotely control him. He was an active weapon in a room full of six hundred people.

Bolting through the exit, he yanked the inch-long screw-driver device he always carried out of his pocket. The door banged against the stone wall. His curse carried over the sound as he popped open the manual override compartment housed in his thumb.

Scarlett appeared beside him and grabbed the device. "Give me that."

"Get back inside. I'm still active."

She inserted the tip and twisted. "Not anymore."

"Daviani." Thompson's voice cracked in her ear sharper than the cold wind. "Take the limousine back to headquarters. Everyone else, hold your positions."

"Roger that. I'm taking Scarlett with me." He grabbed her elbow and tugged her toward the sleek black vehicle twenty feet away.

"Roger that," Thompson said. "Area is secure. Bradley is alive. Muting comms until we regroup."

Scarlett's heavy breaths puffed out in white clouds as she typed into her unit. "Thank God the governor is all right. My team is reporting—"

Chris tightened his grip on her elbow. "Not a word until

we get in the car." He scanned the area as he yanked open the door and pressed her inside.

She hiked up her dress and scrambled into the limo. He slid in behind her. Panic-laced adrenaline coursed through him as they sped away from the curb. With the ferocity of a wild animal, he clawed at the neurotransmitter in the back of his neck that made him one of the most dangerous humans on the planet. "Dammit, Scarlett. I could have fried you back there."

"No, I don't think you would have." Her fingers flew over her comms unit. A graph came up on the screen. "Look."

"I don't know what that represents, but *you* need to know this. *Never* come near me again when I'm not in control."

"But you were in control. This data confirms the V-Strike's intended target was the governor's heart. When you hit the ground, you must have thrown off the trajectory. That's an issue we need to fix because the V-Strike should have hit its target regardless of your position, but your swift reaction saved the governor's life."

"I got lucky." Panic spiraled into boiling rage. Whoever had hijacked his body and had made him an uncontrollable danger would pay. "You said the network was unhackable."

"I said virtually." Her brow furrowed as she typed into her comms unit. "No network is one-hundred-percent secure, especially if someone on the inside compromises it."

The limo bumped over a pothole. She jolted off her seat as her comms unit dropped to the floor. In a tangle of limbs, she reached for her device. He yanked her back. The slit in her dress tore a few stitches nearly up to her hip. He clamped his hand on her thigh to steady her. "Are you saying someone betrayed us?"

"It's possible." She shook her head. "I don't have enough facts yet to draw an accurate conclusion, but—"

She bit her lip and dropped her gaze. Underneath his

hand, her slim leg shook. He gripped her chin with his steel and forced her gaze up. The dread in her eyes shone like jewels from the glow of the white lights lining the carpeted floor.

"I know what you're thinking because I've drawn the same conclusion." The sounds of traffic mingled with his words that cut his heart like a knife. "There's a traitor among VIPER."

A shaky sigh jittered from her lips. "I don't want to say it because it's unthinkable, but it's the only plausible explanation."

He smoothed his thumb over her jaw. "Tell me more."

She leaned into his hand as if drawing his strength to steady herself. Her creamy soft skin under his palm and the scant space between his fingers and whatever she wore underneath her dress didn't steady him one bit though. Closing her eyes, she breathed in deeply. When she pulled back, confidence sparked in her wide emerald gaze. His respect for her kicked up a notch. He'd been worried about her nerves stealing her focus when shit got real. They'd seemed to for a moment, but apparently, his touch awakened some strength-giving source deep-seated within her soul.

It also revved his warrior side and thirst for action.

"Okay, let's talk this out." She gripped both of his hands and squeezed. "Your weapons systems can only be activated via multiple-factor authentication—a code and two biometric signatures. For tonight's testing purposes, I'm the only person who could have activated you via my comms device."

"Is it possible for anyone else to know tonight's activation code?"

"It shouldn't be, but hackers evolve faster than the technology created to stop them."

"How about your biometric signatures? How could a hacker have gotten those?"

"It's possible they could have gotten them from hacking into our network, but our security protocols on that are locked up tight. My best guess is someone found a way to get them while I was at the gala."

He brushed his thumb along the tip of her index finger. "I understand how someone could lift your fingerprint from an object, but what about your retinal signature? There weren't any scanners on the premises."

"I've heard rumors about new technology." She glanced out the window and studied the DC skyline. "The person who procured my credentials and the hacker aren't necessarily the same person. The hacker could be anywhere in the world, but if there's a traitor feeding him information he could be close and could strike again."

"Fuck." He yanked his hand from hers and slammed his steel against the leather seat. Tonight's fiasco would surely delay the team being cleared for missions. If another breach occurred, the project would lose its funding.

Her jaw trembled. "Do you think my theory is true?"

"Yes." He leaned in and inhaled her honeysuckle sent. "And not knowing who the enemy is pisses me off."

"My network being violated pisses me off. I'm excellent at my job and nobody compromises my work or my reputation. I *will* find the person responsible. I promise you."

Desire slammed into him harder than a bullet. The picture she presented in her smoking-hot gown and those red lips promising results rivaled any spy movie heroines he'd seen on the big screen. His rumbling desire quickened to flowing lava. He'd had glimpses of a backbone underneath her softness. He needed to know *every* part of the woman who held his life and his existence in her hands.

Now.

. . .

***

Chris slipped his steel into her hair and lowered his head to hers. Anticipation stole her breath. Even her sexually uneducated brain couldn't mistake his intention.

She braced both palms flat on his chest and felt the coiled snake inside, armed and ready to strike. Nerves only a neuroscientist knew existed danced in the flames.

Holding her breath, she tensed in delicious anticipation as his mouth brushed hers. He tensed too, as if waiting for an order to proceed. The feather-light contact, and the lack of something harder, deeper, pulled a soft moan from her throat and parted her lips. He took advantage of the breach and slipped inside. As their tongues met, sparks sizzled on their skin and short-circuited her brain.

She should push him away. Instead, she dug her fingertips into his chest and held on for dear life.

Another sound she didn't recognize sprang from within. Tension coiled deep and hot within her middle. He tightened his grip on her hair and angled her head. Deeper, harder, he kissed her, exploring every inch of her mouth like a warrior on a mission. And like his willing prey, she surrendered, letting him control the kind of kiss she'd dreamed about but never thought a woman like her would experience.

Breathing his name, she begged without knowing what she pleaded for.

To stop?

Kiss her for hours?

Forever?

She glided her hands along the hard planes of his chest to his equally hard bicep and harder steel and squeezed. "Chris, I don't understand."

Nothing made sense. Not what happened at the gala or

this kiss or the rioting hunger she knew without any research or evidence only he could satiate.

"Me neither but fuck it." He banded his arm around her waist and lifted her onto his lap. His long, rigid length rocked against her ass. A breathy moan left her lips. Again, he took advantage of her surprise with a force as strong as his steel and awakened all her dormant desires, pulling them to the surface.

The limo hit a bump and propelled her into the air. He manacled his arms around her waist as she slammed down onto his erection.

"Fuck, Scarlett."

The silvery-gray flecks in his eyes flickered like sunbursts. His fingers slid up her leg and glided under the frayed slit in her dress. Ropes of fire coiled between her legs as he tickled her buttery-soft skin at the edge of her panties. She dug her nails into his biceps, somehow knowing the tremors under her hands didn't stem from pain but painful desire.

Breathing heavily because that's all the function her body would allow, she closed her eyes against the thrilling, confusing madness.

The whir of the partition separating them from the driver jerked her back to reality.

"Excuse me, Commander." The driver held a phone through the space. "You have a call."

Something dark flashed in Chris's eyes as he set her beside him.

Stretching, he reached for the phone. "Daviani."

She scooted across the limo seat and brushed her fingers over her swollen lips. His kiss had just blown up her world like a chemistry lab fire, but he didn't appear affected by the inferno. His clipped words, rigid posture, and tense jaw as he spoke to the person on the other end were the mark of a decisive leader, not a man who said, "Fuck it," and kissed her with abandon.

"Roger that." He flung the phone on the seat. The hard planes of his jaw sharpened as he waited for the partition to close. "Thompson said the Pentagon is calling for VIPER to be put on hiatus until further review."

"No. They can't—"

"Yes, they can. Listen to me." His voice held a chilling, determined edge. "I need your big brain to find the bastard who betrayed us before all the surgeries, all the torturous rehab, and all the promises the Pentagon made me were for nothing. I need you angry and determined and so on top of your game, you rule the fucking universe. Understand?"

"My brain, right." The rush of emotions drained with the reminder of her purpose. He might think she was pretty. No doubt he desired her sexually. She'd felt the irrefutable proof. But the part of her he coveted was and always would be her mind. She didn't need data to draw that conclusion. Life had already taught her the lesson.

She channeled her disappointment into the anger and determination he'd requested and vowed not to use one more brain cell to examine the illogical, highly inappropriate kiss they'd shared. She drew back her shoulders. The neckline of her gown strained against her breasts. He needed her to save VIPER and, from the desperation in his demands, to save his life.

"Cyberspace is my battlefield. I'll find your enemy. When it's time for steel and V-Strikes, I'll let you know."

He dropped his gaze to her cleavage. A heartbeat later, he looked back up, his features a dangerous blend of raw beauty and simmering frustration. "Steel and V-Strikes? Is that all I am to you?"

The professional mask she'd jammed over her post-kiss letdown slipped. Exquisite heat rose to her cheeks. Jumbled emotions her brain couldn't categorize or quantify confused her, but one question begged to be asked.

Is a big brain all I am to you?

She opened her mouth. The phone rang like a command to shut down the loaded question.

Chris reached for it. "Daviani." His turbulent gaze held hers as he listened. "Roger that." His rigid body didn't even flinch as the limo hit another bump. "Thompson wants to see you in his office as soon as you return to headquarters."

NINE

"I'm…I'm fired?"

Director Thompson pulled a tissue from the box on his desk and wiped at the sweat on his brow. "I received a call from the Pentagon a few minutes ago. They are demanding your termination immediately."

Scarlett sank into a chair, not trusting her legs to hold her upright. She bunched the material of her dress in her fists.

"I'm really fired?" Maybe she'd heard him wrong the first time. Stress could make people misconstrue words.

He flipped open a manila folder on his desk and shuffled papers. "Yes, fired."

No, no, no. Anger and disbelief buzzed through her ears in a paralyzing racket. She'd made a promise to the team to return them to action and to Chris to save the program. "But, sir, I think someone from the inside is leaking information. It's the only plausible reason for what happened tonight."

Thompson rose from his chair and braced his hands on the desk. "The Pentagon was clear. You are to be removed from the premises with no further involvement with VIPER."

She rose too, her legs steady despite the panic racing through her red-clad body. "But I haven't even been to my lab yet or talked to my analysts. Or been debriefed. How can I be fired without telling my side of the story?"

"The program is now being seen as too much of a liability." He narrowed his gaze. "VIPER is in danger of being disbanded because you failed to keep it safe."

Her heart sank to her high heels at the cold truth. She understood his disappointment, but why his lack of faith? He'd begged her to work for VIPER. Had said they were going to change the world. Help people. She'd thought his convictions in her abilities were as sturdy as the steel in Chris's arm. She'd been wrong. He was right about one thing though. She did fail, but someone had helped get her there.

Why wasn't he giving her the chance to find out who?

"Please, sir. Let me stay on a provisional basis until I find the traitor. Then I'll gladly step down."

His eyes didn't meet hers. "You failed, Scarlett. Governor Bradley almost died because of the disaster you caused. You know about his involvement with VIPER and how much this program you've put in danger of being canceled means to him. His people said he personally called for your termination. I wish you nothing but the best in the future."

Chris arrived at the briefing room as the team filed in.

Kane slapped him on the back. "Way to liven up a dull party. But did you really have to show off by striking down the governor? Couldn't you have danced with a lampshade on your head like a normal party crasher?"

Chris smiled. Leave it to Kane to lighten up the heavy

shroud cloaking the brightly lit room crowded with the communications team and Scarlett's analysts.

Nic appeared next to him. "Hey, *hermano*. How's the arm?"

Tension eased out of Chris's shoulders. When Nic had first joined VIPER, he'd referred to his teammates as *amigos*. Chris couldn't recall exactly when *amigos* had graduated to *hermanos*, but it hadn't taken long. The four of them were more than friends. They were brothers, no matter the language.

"You're crazy if you think you can beat any part of me, but I'll let it slide because of your rough night. How's Doc doing? I bet she's never had to deal with a shitshow like this before."

"She's good." The sexy, confident woman he'd kissed in the limo was more than good, but where was she? A quick glance around the room confirmed she hadn't snuck in while he'd been joking with Kane and Nic.

Linc drummed both of his steel legs with his fingers, fidgeting like a kid stuck in the house on a rainy day. "Someone attacked us, and all we can do is sit around and wait for the techies to figure out who. If I had my F-22, I'd take down—"

Nic elbowed him in the ribs. "Who? The Taliban? ISIS? The hot dog vendor on the corner? We don't know who the goddamn enemy is, but our genius will figure it out."

"I know she will, but it will take time. I don't have time. If we lose our funding, the only flying I'll be doing is from my seat in coach."

Kane rolled his eyes. "Calm down, Fly Boy. Doc promised we'd be mission ready soon. She won't let us down. In the meantime, stop worrying about your flight status and start acting like you're a part of this team. Once Doc delivers us an enemy, we'll need to be ready to retaliate."

Chris nodded. "Let Scarlett do her job so we can do ours."

And stop thinking about our kiss so I can do mine without my dick getting in the way.

He'd thought tasting the beautiful scientist would unravel the caution tape she hid behind.

It had.

Damn, it had. More than he'd anticipated and more than enough to have made him momentarily lose his focus. If Thompson hadn't called, Scarlett would have been under him before they'd hit the city limits.

The mission hadn't been a total failure though. When he'd demanded she find the motherfucker who'd hacked them, she'd steeled up with the type of razor-sharp determination he needed from the woman who held his life in her hands. Her wall had slipped for a second though when he'd asked if steel and V-Strikes were all he was to her. His focus had nearly crumbled when she'd pulled her shoulders back and those gorgeous breasts had almost popped out. And he couldn't forget how the slit in her gown had offered easy access to the place he dreamed about devouring with his mouth.

And his cock.

Did he really want to forget? He had no choice. They existed in opposite worlds, hers safe and logical, his dark and dangerous. The two colliding on anything more than a professional level would be disastrous.

Director Thompson marched up to the podium. "Take your seats."

Nic held his hand up to the side of his mouth as they sat at the table. "He doesn't look so good."

No, he didn't. His rumpled tuxedo and sweaty bald scalp made him look twenty years older than sixty-three. The man had been Special Forces in the Army followed by a career as a field agent with the CIA before a near-fatal head wound had forced him to retire from the agency. Why was he acting like this was his first crisis?

Chris glanced over at Linc and Kane to see if they noticed their leader's uncharacteristic behavior. They were huddled together, talking.

Thompson glared in their direction. "Shut up, you two."

"Sorry, sir." Kane straightened in his seat. "I didn't think we were starting because Doc isn't here yet."

Thompson stiffened.

The hair on the back of Chris's neck stood up. "Where is she?"

"Dr. Kerrigan has resigned her position effective immediately."

A chorus of "What?" accompanied by several expletives echoed from the others in the room.

Chris's heart thumped against his ribs. She's gone? This didn't make sense. The woman he'd kissed not even an hour ago wasn't a quitter. He may have thought she couldn't handle this job when they'd met, but now? He believed she would follow through with the vow she'd made to save VIPER. Then again, he'd never expected his own mother or his wife to abandon him. Death had even taken his father away. Everybody he'd cared about had ditched him eventually and left him with scars he couldn't heal. Why should he put his faith in someone he barely knew?

Because she's not like them.

Somewhere in the space of striking down the governor and kissing her senseless, he'd begun to trust her. He believed in her suspicions about a traitor. Believed she was committed to VIPER. Believed in her.

She wouldn't leave unless…

He jumped to his feet. "Why did she resign?"

A reassuring sense of camaraderie flooded him when the rest of the team stood too.

Thompson's dark skin flushed with red-hot anger. "Sit your asses down."

Chris ignored the order and pressed further. "It's our bodies and brains she enhanced. We deserve to know why she left."

"And your bodies and brains were compromised because she didn't do her job." Thompson slapped his palms onto the table. He cleared his throat as his fingers slid across the wood into fists. "In light of tonight's events, Dr. Kerrigan's departure is for the best. Effective immediately, nobody in this room will have any contact with her. Are we clear?"

Chris nodded along with the rest of the team and sat down. It was clear they weren't going to get any more information about Scarlett's alleged resignation. As for the part about not having contact with her? That wasn't clear at all.

TEN

Scarlett dropped her head on the steering wheel. She should be at her desk devising a plan to find the hacker instead of sitting in her car outside of her townhome, but she couldn't bring herself to walk up the stairs and close the door behind her. That felt like admitting defeat before the war began. Before she defied Thompson's "no involvement" directive, she needed her best friend, a glass of wine, and a good cry. Tomorrow she would track down the bad guys without the resources of the United States government.

Good luck doing that without breaking any laws.

A car door slammed. She jerked her head up and tensed when a familiar figure emerged from a sleek black sedan parked next to her. A confrontation with her ex-fiancé wasn't in her plan. The sooner she got rid of him, the sooner she could have a pity party with Beth, clear her head, and search for clues about the breach.

She slid out of her two-door compact and took her time standing, hoping she didn't look as rattled as she felt. Enough light from the lamppost showed James hadn't changed at all.

His green eyes, which she'd once thought shined like wet moss in the sunlight, now reminded her of sludge at the bottom of a smelly pond. She wrinkled her nose as the stench of his cologne assaulted her nostrils. It was the antithesis of Chris's forest-after-a-rain-shower scent.

James held both his arms out wide, inviting her in for a hug. "Scarlett, you look stunning."

Instead of stepping into his embrace, she clasped her hands in front of her.

He dropped his hands to his sides. "Your dress is the same color as the rose you wore in your hair on New Year's Eve when we were... How old were we?"

"Eighteen. I was eighteen. You were twenty-four." Henry's party had not been where she'd wanted to ring in the New Year. She'd wanted to hole up in her room with her laptop and a bag of chips, but Henry had always got his way when it came to her schedule.

"We shared our first kiss when the clock struck midnight. Do you remember?"

How could she forget? When she'd gone down the stairs, she'd been pleased to see the son of Henry's friend had grown into an attractive man while he'd been in Europe completing his education. His magazine-cover-worthy smile, slicked-back hair, and wire glasses perched on a perfect nose had given him a sexy professor kind of air she'd found alluring. When he held out his hand and pulled her onto the dance floor and into his arms, she hadn't felt like an awkward teenager. For the first time, she'd felt like a normal girl with a handsome guy at her side.

"What do you want, James?"

"Why so short, darling?" He adjusted his paisley power tie. "Aren't you glad to see me?"

"You know I'm not. Tell me what you want and leave. It's been a long night."

"I know. I saw the news. Guess your little project didn't go well. What's it called again? Vixen? No, that's not it. Vamp?"

She stiffened as a hand pressed into the small of her back and a familiar scent surrounded her.

"VIPER." Chris sized up James. "It's called Project VIPER."

She stole a glance at the solid mass of testosterone flanking her. Chris's faded jeans and black leather jacket made him look even more dangerous than he did at head-quarters. If his eyes could shoot V-Strikes, there'd be a body on the ground at her feet.

James nodded his head toward Chris's steel hand. "Is this one of your veterans?"

She cringed at the way he said "veterans," as if Chris was a pet. "This is Commander Daviani."

James brushed his suit jacket. "Tell me, Commander, did she get you a job as a mall cop?"

Chris stepped onto the sidewalk in front of the smaller man. "What did you say?"

James had the good sense to back up. She wasn't surprised to see he hadn't changed—full of bravado but no substance.

Scarlett placed her hand on Chris's arm. While watching him rip James to shreds would be gratifying, this wasn't his fight. "Commander Daviani is kind of a mall cop. As in the National Mall, you know, the one in our capital, near where the president lives. He's responsible for guarding our nation, its leaders, and the places we hold sacred. So unless you're willing to answer to him, I suggest you keep your nasty comments to yourself."

Scarlett's tirade pulsed in her ears. She'd never spoken to James with such malice before, not even the night she'd walked out of his condo and never looked back. By the way his mouth hung open, he was as surprised at her words as she was.

He regained his composure. "Let's not be snippy. I was hoping you'd invite me in for a drink so we can talk about us."

The thought of her and James being an "us" again made the mini crab cakes she'd eaten at the gala threaten to come back up. "There never was an us. There was only you and the sacrifices you expected me to make for the company."

"What I wanted was for us to be together. Richardson Enterprises would have been ours someday. We could have been the most successful couple in the world."

"That little fantasy is what you wanted. You never cared to even try and understand why I needed to move on with my career."

"Come on, Scarlett. Can't we keep the past where it belongs and move forward?"

Asswipe.

Shithead.

Dickwad.

The team would be proud if they could hear the litany of insults she'd picked up from their conversations. "The past belongs front and center, so I can learn from my mistakes."

"And you leaving the company was a grave error. You've played the Good Samaritan and saved the wounded." He glanced at Chris like he was a vagrant off the street. "It's time to come back to work. You're obviously not in a safe environment. Henry said he'll double your salary."

"Did he say he'll double *your* salary if you get me to agree?"

He reached for her hand. "Be reasonable. There's no need to make this difficult."

Chris's steel fingers snapped around James's wrist. He glared at him as he released his hold. "It's time for you to leave. You enjoy the rest of your night, John. Or was it Jerry? Sorry, I can't seem to remember."

She held her breath as her past and present engaged in a silent battle to win her loyalty.

Her ex-weasel backed down first. "We're not done here. I can tell you're tired and upset. We can talk about this tomorrow night at Henry's when you're in a better mood. He's expecting you for dinner at seven."

Chris's attention stayed fixed on James until he drove away. As the sedan rounded the corner, he lowered his face to hers. "Who was that?"

Her heart rate sped up at the tension in his voice and the heat of his breath on her cheek. He always held a quiet intensity, like he kept the animal inside on a tight leash. Tonight, something darker and more intense roared underneath the surface, scaring and thrilling her at the same time.

"That was someone I'd like to forget."

"I'm going to need more details."

The tense set of his jaw matched the expression on his face right before he'd kissed her. If she ignored his question, maybe he'd resort to extreme tactics to get an answer.

Would another kiss be so bad?

Yes. Very bad.

"James is an old family friend and VP of Engineering for Richardson Enterprises."

Chris's gaze sharpened. "And what about the 'us' bullshit?"

She hated admitting she once thought herself in love with the pretentious bastard. "He's my ex-fiancé."

Chris tilted his head. The movement was slight, but she caught his surprise.

Her shoulders slumped. She wanted to get out of this dress and call Beth, not waste time talking about her failed engagement. Her relationship with James solidified what she'd come to realize over the years. Her mind made her extraordinary. Everything else about her was forgettable.

Fallen leaves skidded along the sidewalk. She turned and climbed the steps to her front door, shivering as the wind kicked up a notch. "I have a lot of work to do if I'm going to find the party responsible for tonight's breach. Why are you here anyway?"

He gently placed a steel finger to her lips. Her body stiffened as she watched his dark gaze fix on her front door. "Is anyone supposed to be in your house?"

She shook her head.

"Listen to me carefully. Get in your car and lock the doors. Don't move until I come out."

She hesitated for a moment.

Steel fingers grasped her chin. "You stay there. Understand?"

He released her as he reached into his jacket and pulled out a gun. She shuddered when she heard the nearly silent but unmistakably deadly *click-click* of a bullet loading the chamber.

"Go," he growled.

She raced down the stairs in a flurry of red. She was almost to her car when a woman's scream tore through the wind.

ELEVEN

Chris turned the doorknob. Locked. He didn't hesitate as he rammed his steel into the door. With a grunt, he shoved it open. He raised his weapon and quickly scanned the area. A flash of black at the far side of the room darted through a doorway. He ran over the threshold and knocked over a plant sitting inside the entry. The pot cracked against the wall as he raced after the footsteps into the kitchen and out the open screen door. He halted at the top of the steps and scanned the small fenced-in backyard.

Empty.

Still wielding his gun, he ran the short distance to the swinging gate and barreled into a common courtyard.

"Shit." He lost them.

Crouching down, he studied the damp grass. Footprints. Two men in boots based on the size and shape. He turned to the gate. A heavy severed lock hung from a metal ring. His instincts screamed to give chase, but investigating the feminine shriek he'd heard from inside the house took priority.

He hurried across the yard and up the three concrete

steps. All seemed to be in order in the spacious kitchen except for the open back door. He bent down to examine the lock. Tiny scratches indicated it had recently been picked.

"Scarlett?"

Chris spun on his heel and leveled his gun at the female voice coming from a short hallway off the kitchen. A petite brunette staggered out with her hand pressed to the back of her head. She gasped as she raised her gaze.

He lowered his gun. "It's okay. I'm a friend of—"

Heels clacked on the hardwood living room floor, followed by a gasp. "Beth."

He whirled toward the screech and aimed. "Dammit, Scarlett." His words rushed out along with his breath as he lowered his weapon. "I told you to stay in the car."

She wrapped Beth in a hug. "What happened?"

"Somebody broke in. Stay here."

He jogged down the hallway Beth emerged from and nudged open an ajar door with his foot. The walk-in pantry with floor-to-ceiling shelves appeared orderly enough to be featured in one of those home shows. He turned and headed back to the equally neat kitchen. A crimson smear on the wall caught his eye.

Blood.

He hurried to Scarlett and guided her and the sniffling brunette into the living room. Everything appeared untouched except for the plant he'd knocked over and the cherry credenza against the wall opposite the couch. The doors hung open and a cardboard file box with the lid halfway off teetered on the cabinet's ledge. Papers spilled out from the opened drawers. A few file folders dotted the floor.

He motioned the women to the couch and stood over Beth. "You're bleeding."

She touched the back of her head. Tears gathered in her

red-rimmed eyes as she pulled her hand away from her wound and saw the blood.

As he closed the front door, he assessed Scarlett. Her face hadn't gained much color, but at least she wasn't crying too.

That's my tough genius. Keep it together.

He ran back into the kitchen and filled a dish towel hanging on the stove with ice. Thank God he'd ignored Thompson's order to stay away from her. He'd come here for answers. He'd get them once Beth was settled. Asking why someone would break into her home and why she'd been engaged to the asshole named James would have to wait until he ensured the rest of the house was secure.

The makeshift ice pack chilled his steel hand as he stalked back into the living room and handed it to Beth. He accepted her thanks as he surveyed the scene. The rich red, gold, and moss-green pillows scattered about the sofa and the colorful vases on the fireplace mantel were as perfect as furniture staged in a showroom. Although the only sign of foul play was the messy credenza and nothing of value seemed to be missing, his heart raced. Someone had broken in to steal something specific and Beth had gotten in the way.

With efficient moves, he checked the coat closet and stairwell, careful to avoid the speckled dirt from the fern he'd knocked over. "I'm going upstairs. Stay here until I get back."

Scarlett opened her mouth to say something but closed it as if she thought better.

"I mean it." He pointed to the couch. "Stay."

He jogged up the stairs to the upper level and nudged the open door at the top with his foot. The small room, likely meant for guests, held only a neatly made bed with a simple patchwork quilt, a nightstand, and a small dresser. A quick check of the closet confirmed it was empty, as was the adjacent bathroom.

When he opened the final door at the end of the hall, the smell of honeysuckle drifted into his nostrils.

Scarlett.

Inhaling, he scanned the slate-gray walls of her bedroom, his gaze landing on the silky, indigo-colored comforter. Everything appeared in order except for the delicious and dirty turn his thoughts were taking. Spinning from her bed and visions of the beauty in red naked underneath him, he checked the master bathroom. The countertops gleamed. In the spacious walk-in closet, her clothes hung straight and neatly in a color-coded system. Tidy and meticulous, like he'd expected.

He headed back down and found Scarlett's gaze. "Everything seems to be in order upstairs." Everything except his thoughts about what he'd like to do to her in the big bed. That fantasy train was barreling headlong down a dangerous path.

He cocked his head to the stairs leading to the lower level.

Scarlett nodded. "I know—stay until you get back."

Chris flipped the light switch at the top of the stairs and hurried down. At the bottom, he paused. "Wow."

A flat-screen television hung above a wooden L-shaped desk that took up half the wall space in the large room. Four computer monitors, two open laptops, and a printer sat at different levels on the various shelves built into the massive unit. Open spiral notebooks and file folders littered the desk, along with a couple of overturned picture frames. Wheeled whiteboards covered in formulas he couldn't begin to understand flanked either side of the desk like prized artwork. The only wall in the room not resembling NASA's Mission Control Center housed a closet with white double doors hanging wide open.

He stepped between the support columns evenly spaced

in the center of the room and assessed the damage. A dozen or so upended file boxes spilled from the closet. Papers and folders lay scattered across the beige carpet. Every one of the drawers in the desk hung open. Paper clips, notepads, pens, and other office supplies mingled with the plundered paperwork. A collage of framed diplomas hung crooked on the white wall as if someone moved them in a hurry, likely to check for a hidden safe.

After a quick sweep of the bathroom and the storage space, and a marvel at the number of Scarlett's degrees, he headed up.

At the top of the stairs, he found both women on the couch where he'd left them. "Your friend needs to get to the hospital."

Beth lowered the ice pack to her lap. "I'm fine."

"You hit your head hard enough to make it bleed. You need to get checked out."

"I'm not going to the hospital. Not again."

"Again? Something like this has happened before?"

Scarlett rubbed Beth's back. "She was involved in an attack on the street a few years ago."

The thought of someone hurting the pretty brunette with eyes the shade of honey had him clenching his steel fingers into a fist. Instead of punching something, he pulled his phone out of his pocket. "I'm really sorry, but you do need to get checked out."

Scarlett shifted in front of Beth like a shield. "Do not call 9-1-1."

"Agreed. No cops." Her protectiveness added to his desire to peel back her layers and discover what else hid inside the intriguing genius. "I'm texting Kane. He's had the most medical training out of all of us. He's at a bar a few blocks away."

"I'm not letting my best friend be checked out by

someone who's been drinking." Scarlett stood. Her heel caught in the hem of her dress and launched her forward. He grabbed her under each elbow and saved her from the same fate as the toppled fern. Glaring at him, she shrugged off his help.

He brushed his steel over his head to the back of his shoulder and rubbed the tight muscle. "Kane isn't at the bar to drink. I asked him to stick close in case I needed backup. Linc and Nic aren't too far either. We'll handle this."

She narrowed her eyes. "You never told me why you came here tonight. And why is everyone lurking around my house?"

"Something didn't sound right when Thompson said you'd resigned."

"Resigned?" Her eyebrows shot to her hairline. "I promised I wouldn't let you or the team down and I meant it. I didn't willingly leave. Thompson fired me."

The knot in Chris's gut unraveled. He hadn't wanted to believe that she'd abandoned VIPER—abandoned *him*—but after a lifetime of being left behind, he needed action to back up words. Fuck, had she delivered.

"We'll talk about your involuntary departure later." He turned to Beth. "Are you okay with Kane checking you out?"

"I'm sure I'll be fine with him. He's part of VIPER, right?"

Chris nodded. He didn't doubt Kane would be fine with her too. "I know this must be tough considering your past trauma, but can you tell me what happened here tonight?"

Beth wiped her eyes. "We had a breakthrough at work today and I was too keyed up to go home. I decided to come over and wait for Scarlett so we could celebrate after her big night. I also wanted to see her in the dress I picked out." Her eyes brightened. "She looks fantastic in it, don't you think?"

"Yes, she looks nice."

Nice?

Kane would slap him upside the head for the lame-ass compliment again, but he didn't dare voice how he really felt about Scarlett's appearance. He had enough trouble ignoring what it did to his body and his focus. "Tell me what happened next."

Beth placed the ice pack on the coffee table. "I let myself in with my key. I figured I'd pour myself a glass of wine and watch a movie until she came home. While I was in the pantry getting a bottle of wine, I heard a noise behind me. I turned around, and there was a man with a gun. I remember screaming and jumping back. I guess I hit my head on the wall and passed out. When I woke up, I was sitting on the floor."

"Did you get a look at the guy?"

"Not a good one. All I saw was a big goon in black clothes and a mask with a gun. He was huge." She gestured with her arms to show he was both tall and wide.

"When did you get here?"

"About thirty minutes ago."

Kane appeared in the doorway. "Hey, what's up?"

He motioned to Beth. "Someone broke in, and Scarlett's friend got caught in the middle. I need you to do a concussion assessment while I chat with Scarlett downstairs."

Kane took off his black cowboy hat as he perused his charge with appreciation. "Of course."

Scarlett stepped in front of him. "This is my best friend, Beth. You'll take good care of her, won't you?"

He held up his hand in a three-finger Boy Scout salute. "I'll treat her like my own sister."

"You'd better."

Chris placed his hand on Scarlett's back and led her to the stairs. Considering the drama of the last six hours, he had to give her credit for how well she was holding up. He hoped she could hold it together when she saw the mess the intruders had made of her office. "I have to warn you, it's not pretty down there. Someone broke in to search for something. Do you have any idea what?"

"Come on. I'll show you."

She pushed past him and hurried down the stairs. He paused at the bottom as she marched through the maze of papers and files scattered about the carpet, past the ridiculous number of computers, and into the open bathroom door. Seconds later, she walked back out, holding a small pink cardboard box. As she leaned against her desk, a triumphant smile stretched across her face.

He tilted his head. "Is that what I think it is?"

"Yup."

She dug inside the container, pulled out a black hard drive, and waved it in the air. "This is what they were looking for."

Laughter bubbled in his throat. He wrapped his arms around his belly as the swift and strong reaction gained force and doubled him over. When was the last time he'd laughed this hard? "Most people would hide their valuables in a safe instead of their, um, you know, feminine products."

"Safes can be cracked, but from the way you cringed when you said feminine products it's clear you wouldn't have thought to look in a box of tampons either."

"You're pretty proud of yourself for outwitting the bad guys, aren't you?"

She cradled the box like a Grammy. "Yes, I am."

"And what if the intruder was a woman?"

She shrugged. "She probably has her own tampons."

Chuckling, he stared at the self-assured, sarcastic beauty. Where had she come from? He'd seen glimpses of her before, but never to this extent. Now was a good time for her to emerge from hiding. She'd need all the confidence she could muster to get through the battle ahead.

He took the hard drive from her hand. A jolt of electricity surged up his arm when their fingers brushed. "What's on here that's so important?"

Excitement sparkled in her eyes. Whatever she was hiding in her tampons was valuable, and she was damn proud of it.

"It depends on who's in control. For some, it could mean freedom." She crossed her arms over her breasts and rubbed her biceps. "For others, death."

"Explain."

"I'm cleaning as I talk." She stepped to her desk and picked up a shattered picture frame. "Ouch." Her fingers flew to her mouth as the pieces fell to the floor.

He jumped to her side. "Did you cut yourself?"

"Yes." She spoke as she wrapped her lips around her index finger.

Desire rolled through his groin as she sucked the blood from her cut. He looked at the photo to stop his gaze from wandering to other places on her body he wanted to treat with oral attention. A young blonde woman with a sharp resemblance to Scarlett hugged a smaller version of herself. "Is this you and your mom?"

She nodded as she sucked.

Gently, he pulled her finger from her mouth to examine the wound. A prickle of blood oozed out of a small slice at the tip. He grabbed a tissue from an overturned box on her desk, her sweet-smelling hair tickling his nose.

"Your mom's very beautiful." He wrapped the tissue around the tiny cut. "You look like her. What's her name?"

Wetness pooled in Scarlett's eyes and clung to her dark lashes. "Jacquelyn. Her name was Jacquelyn. She died of an asthma attack when I was twelve. Couldn't find her inhaler." A fat tear rolled down Scarlett's cheek, followed by another.

He ignored the warning bells in his head and pulled her into his arms. She stiffened, but he didn't abandon his attempt at comfort. Instead, he wrapped his hand around the back of her neck and massaged through the silky blanket of her hair until she relaxed into his embrace.

"I'm sorry." She sniffed into his neck and apologized again.

"Nothing to be sorry for. I get it." He opened his mouth to tell her about his grief, about how he understood loss, but closed it before the words could escape. Emotions were already running high. Being this close to her was dangerous enough without bringing up his own sob story.

What was even more dangerous? Her body against his felt so right, like she was the key to feeling whole again. It wasn't fair he couldn't pursue the woman who could be the missing piece to the messed-up puzzle he'd become.

He silently cursed.

When had life ever been fair to Christopher Daviani?

A small hiccup jumped from her mouth. She wiped her eyes with one hand and held up the hard drive with the other. "This is my life's work. Most of the cybernetic research I've done since I was a teenager is contained in here."

He continued to hold her in his arms despite the lecture he'd just given himself. "You said *most* of your work is on the drive. Where's the rest of it?"

"I have a copy in a bank vault, along with my written notes. The rest is in my brain, but I can't continue my work without the information stored on here." She clutched the drive. "Other than that, my research isn't anywhere else. Not even in a shared environment like the cloud. I can't afford to take any chances. If someone wants it bad enough they will find a way to get to it."

"So you're a cybersecurity expert who doesn't think information contained in cyberspace is safe?"

"I am, which makes me an authority on how vulnerable cyberspace is. This is my passion. Cybersecurity is a necessity. And when people offer you millions of dollars to buy your passion, you learn how to protect it."

Holy shit! First, the smokin' hot red dress and now her surprisingly arousing cyber talk about passion and millions of dollars. He stepped back before she felt *his* passion growing against her belly. "Millions?"

"Yes, from corporations and foreign governments mostly. At the risk of sounding overly dramatic, if my work fell into the wrong hands, the outcome could be catastrophic."

Pieces of the puzzle swirled around in his head like thought bubbles in a cartoon.

VIPER hacked.

Governor shot.

House ransacked.

Valuable research.

He wasn't sure how it all fit together, but one thing was certain. Scarlett was the common denominator. "Pack a bag. We're getting out of town."

"I'm not going anywhere." She bent to pick up papers. "I have a physical and virtual mess to clean up."

He cupped her elbow and tugged her up to face him. "Armed intruders broke into your home. I don't believe it's a coincidence it happened on the same night your system was hacked and I—a member of your team—struck the governor. I'm not sure how it's all connected, but I'm sure you're in danger. What's inside your brain is the ultimate prize, and God only knows what they'll do to get their hands on your research and on you."

TWELVE

Chris waited by the curb while Kane helped Beth climb into his pickup truck. She glared at them as they met by the hood.

"She doesn't look too happy." Chris eyed the sullen brunette. "How did you convince her to get checked out at the ER?"

"It was easy. I promised her ice cream afterward. Apparently, she's a sucker for mint chocolate chip." He tipped his cowboy hat. "And for a country gentleman."

Chris snorted. "When you get to the hospital, the story is simple. Home accident. I don't want this on anyone's radar, not even the police. At least not until we have answers."

"Agreed. How's Doc holding up?"

"She's as happy about being a target as Beth is about going to the hospital." He detailed the night's events and what he needed help with to transfer Scarlett to a safe location where she could work on uncovering who the hell had messed with VIPER.

"I'm on it." Kane whistled through his teeth. "Too many

things going wrong in one night. Something big is brewing. Don't worry; we got your back. Take care of Scarlett."

"And you take care of Beth, and I don't mean hitting on her."

"You take all the fun out of playing the hero. Did you know she's a scientist with one of the federal health agencies? Can't remember which one, but I do know she's working on a classified project. Kinda sexy, don't you think? Or did you not notice she's hot 'cause you only have eyes for scientists in red?"

Scarlett stalked into her walk-in closet and slammed the door with enough force to rattle the full-length mirror hanging on the back. Chris's explanation about why he thought she was in danger echoed in her ears.

"What's inside your brain is the ultimate prize…"

"Prize? I'm not anybody's prize."

But I am.

For more than half her life, she'd been treated like the blue-ribbon cow at the county fair.

As she tore clothes from hangers and drawers and tossed them into a suitcase, her mother and Henry's frequent argument replayed in her mind.

"But Jacquelyn, the child is brilliant. You're doing her a disservice by not enrolling her in an advanced program. Her mind needs nurturing. With the proper guidance, she'll have her doctorate by the time she's eighteen. Imagine what she could do for my company."

Scarlett smiled as she thought of her mom's response.

"I'm not sending my daughter a thousand miles to live at some stuffy academy. She's already different from the other children. She'll lose an important part of herself if I take her away

from kids her own age. She's doing very well attending public school in the morning and college for math and science in the afternoon. Besides, I'd miss her too much."

The arguments had always been the same, and Scarlett still felt guilty for being the reason her mother and Henry disagreed. In the end, Henry had always acquiesced to his wife's wishes no matter how many times they'd battled about Scarlett's so-called gift. When her mother died, Henry finally won. Days after the funeral, he shipped her halfway across the country to an elite boarding school for the gifted. Tonight, someone else who desired the ideas in her brain had forced her away from home.

A knock sounded on the closet door. "Almost ready?"

"Almost." She picked up a T-shirt and shook it out harder than necessary. Where was this safe location he was whisking her away to? Was it on the grid? She needed a fast wireless connection to find the hacker. And what about the traitor at headquarters?

"No further involvement with VIPER," she said, mimicking Thompson's angry voice.

What was right, and what was wrong? She chewed on her thumbnail and stared at her suitcase. She'd made a promise to find the traitor and would do whatever it took to achieve her goal. As for the consequences of her actions, she'd deal with them after she found the bad guys.

Standing on tiptoe, she reached for the black metal box on the top shelf and pulled it down. She quickly spiraled through the combination lock and opened the case. The black, sleek pistol felt cool in her hand as she tucked it into her laptop bag.

Once she'd packed enough warm clothes for a week as Chris had instructed, she reached around her back for the zipper of her dress and pulled. It didn't budge. She tried again and cursed when the slider wouldn't descend even a centimeter.

With a huff, she twisted the door handle and peeked out. Chris sat on the edge of her king-size bed, his gaze on his phone. Every nerve ending shimmied at the thought of a man in her private space. Sure, James had been in this room, but he was a weasel. Chris's presence narrowed the room to him, her bed, and thoughts of how the contrast of his steel hand and her silk comforter would feel against her skin.

She squeezed her thighs together against the telltale ache that had barely sparked for James. If she sat down next to Chris, would he take her in his arms like he had in her office and fan the spark into a flame hot enough to burn or was he only being an honorable guy?

She opened the door farther. His earthy scent wafted in. She hoped it would linger until she was able to come back home.

He looked up. "Why aren't you changed yet?"

She lifted her hair off her neck as she glanced over her shoulder. "I think my zipper is caught in the material of the dress."

He rose and motioned for her to turn around. The air in the room receded as she slowly spun. Steel fingers brushed the indent of her slim waist, lingering for a moment as if he wasn't sure if he was committed to touching her. She held back a sigh when he retreated a step but couldn't suppress the shiver when he changed his mind.

The tiny hairs on her arms sprang to attention as his cool metal brushed her back a fraction above the zipper just beneath her shoulder blades. She felt a tug and heard him mumble, "Got it." Tooth by tooth, he exposed her bare skin.

Slow.

Steady.

His breathing sped up in correlation to the zipper's

descent. She felt his hand tremble as it skimmed the small of her back. Smelled the leather of his jacket as he leaned closer. Confidence erupted within her. His primal reaction had nothing to do with her genius mind.

"Guess battle isn't the only thing your super arm is good for." The sultriness in her voice surprised her.

With a soft, sexy chuckle, he turned her in his arms to face him. "Dr. Kerrigan, are you teasing me?"

His sizzling sapphire gaze burned her. Although she didn't have much experience recognizing desire in a man, her conclusion about him being turned on didn't waver.

"Why is it okay for you to tease me nearly every day, but I can't give it back? What's the matter, Commander? Can't you take it?"

"Yes, ma'am, I can take it." His gritty words crunched like gravel. "And then some."

She held her breath, frozen in the most intimate moment of her life. What was the sensual woman she'd momentarily become supposed to do next? She swayed toward his heat and silently asked for guidance. Anticipation created vibrations so intense she thought she might splinter into pieces if his lips touched hers. Instead, he retreated from the foolish course she'd lamely attempted to lead them down.

"You need to get dressed." He pointed his steel finger to the closet. "We have a mission, and your mind is the key to achieving our goal. Got it?"

She certainly did get it.

Loud and clear.

THIRTEEN

Scarlett rolled her suitcase out of her bedroom to where Chris waited at the top of the stairs.

"Ready?" He took her bag.

As she followed him down, the evening's events whirled in her mind until hysteria fizzed in her chest. "Sure. Why wouldn't I be ready to leave my home for a fun-filled vacation, complete with danger and espionage? Did I have to pay extra for the goons with guns, or was it the deal of the week?"

He nudged the front door open with his foot and stepped aside to let her by. "When did you become such a smart-ass?"

The November wind struck her face. She barely felt the cold slap, but his question lodged a hysterical laugh in her throat and made her cough. "Smart" had been used to describe her more times than she could count. As for the "ass" part? Never. She liked the two together. It matched her mood, which teetered toward unhinged.

It also made being the smart girl sound less lonely.

Chris hurried past her down the front steps and opened the passenger door to his black SUV. He placed his hand on the small of her back and guided her in. "I broke the lock on your front door. Linc is on his way to fix it. He'll do a thorough sweep of the place and install a security system."

"Thanks."

"The guy's got other talents besides being one hell of a pilot, but don't tell him I said so. We don't want him to become any cockier than he already is." He winked as he shut her in.

She turned up the heat as he stowed her laptop bag in the back. As he slid into the driver's seat, she turned to him. "When do you think I'll be able to come home?"

"Depends on how quickly you can identify the enemy."

"That could take days. Weeks."

"Well then, that's how long we'll be gone."

Red flags waved in her vision. The thought of being alone with Chris concerned her almost as much as hackers and traitors. And what about the moment of stupidity in her bedroom when she'd thought he was going to…to what?

Kiss her again?

Rip her gown off and throw her on the bed?

Those thoughts had been mortifying.

Face it. I'm not the gown-ripping, throw-on-the-bed type.

She covered her legs with her jacket and smothered her senseless fantasies. She needed to focus on what she knew. Science and math. Her haven. Conducting experiments and writing code held an elegant logic she understood. Chris and his f-bombs, and God, the way he'd kissed her with his talented mouth, had awakened urges and desires she'd never experienced before.

He'd called her beautiful, like her mother. Was it possible he found her attractive, or had his compliment been polite conversation? Had she been so enamored with the thought of him desiring her body instead of her mind that she'd convinced herself the attraction was mutual? Maybe the hard arousal she'd felt against her backside in the limo had been the product of adrenaline and had nothing to do with wanting her.

But even if he did desire her, she wanted more than just screwing around while she searched for the traitor. She wanted somebody to love all of her.

Mind.

Body.

Heart and soul.

Did such a man exist? If he did, would she know what to do when she found him? That was a problem even her exceptional brain couldn't solve.

Chris handed her a burner phone. "Kane will give one to Beth so you can check in with her. You left your phone upstairs like I told you to, correct?"

Nodding, she silently cursed at the list of things she'd lost tonight. First, her job and reputation, now her phone and house for the foreseeable future, and most frightening of all, her sense of security. She trusted Chris and the team to protect her while she plunged into a cyber hunt but panic still threatened to suck her under.

"Linc's here. Let's go." He backed out of the parking spot as a black pickup truck pulled next to them, the exchange like a well-orchestrated dance.

"Sounds like you devised a plan before you got to my house."

He checked the rearview mirror and guided the SUV down her quiet street. "The only plan was making sure you were all right. We *knew* you didn't desert us."

Warmth and his earthy scent mixed with the rich smell of leather encompassed her like an impenetrable forest. They believed in her commitment to Project VIPER. Believed in *her*. She swallowed the emotion clogging her throat. "I swear on the hard drive in my bag, I won't stop until I solve this."

He chuckled, the rich sound diffusing the gravity of the moment. "Those are some serious fighting words."

She winked. "What else would you expect from a smart-ass?"

As she relayed the humiliating "you're fired" conversation with Thompson, the city of Alexandria passed in a blur. Her voice cracked a few times when she got to the part when Thompson had told her she'd failed, but she held it together long enough to get out the entire story, including his warning to stay out of the investigation.

Chris stopped at a traffic light and angled his body to face her. "We figured you were coerced into resigning and not outright fired, but now it makes sense why Thompson forbade us to have any contact with you."

Forbade? Chris was ignoring direct orders.

Not good, not good.

Her gaze jumped from window to window as if the military police would pull up and start shooting at any moment. "You can lose your job if Thompson finds out we're together. Take me home. I'll call the police and they can investigate the break-in, or maybe Thompson can help. He's angry now, but he won't want to see me hurt."

Chris flashed those intense eyes at her again before he hit the gas. "I don't trust the police to protect you. I respect our men in blue. Hell, my dad, rest his soul, was a cop, but they don't have the training or the superpower I have." He held up his arm for emphasis. "Besides, we don't know who we can trust."

"Why can't we trust Thompson? He's committed to VIPER. It's ridiculous to think he'd want to see it fail."

"Is it ridiculous?"

A war waged inside of her between what the facts pointed to and what she wanted to believe. "But he's on our team."

"Then why on earth would he say you resigned instead of telling us the truth?"

"Maybe he was trying to save my reputation."

"Or maybe he lied to protect his own." Frustration edged his voice as he leaned closer. "Until we uncover the reason for his bullshit story about your resignation he can't be trusted."

Scarlett stared past Chris through the window at the headlights on the other side of the road. "No, no. This is all too much. Why would Thompson fight to bring me on board but not fight for me to stay?"

"Look, I never said he's our guy." His tone softened. "I'm merely using him as an example to make you realize everyone is a suspect."

She hesitated as she thought about how easily she got along with all her colleagues. "I can't imagine anyone at headquarters wanting to hurt me."

"I know you don't want to think someone is targeting you, but tonight's events point in that direction."

Silence filled the SUV as the reality of the situation permeated her brain. Even though the idea of having to investigate every coworker for treason sickened her, he was right.

He took the next exit. When he stopped the car at another traffic light, he trapped her with his gaze. "People are after you. Once you pinpoint who, I'm going to make them pay. Want to know why?"

She didn't say anything. The feral expression on his face and the intensity of his tone stole her breath.

"Because nobody fucks with a member of my team."

"Thank you." Her insides turned gooey despite his hard-as-steel words. Chris and the guys were the team she was responsible for. She never imagined they would consider her part of their team. "But I don't like that you're going rogue on my account."

A big smile crossed his face before he headed onto the highway. "You mentioned Thompson told you to stay out of the investigation." He smiled into the night. "Looks like you're going rogue too."

A hot rush of excitement zinged through her veins. The scientist part of her should be terrified about the danger and consequences ahead, but the sheltered schoolgirl overdue for an adventure said, "Hell yeah." Biting her lip, she placed her hand on his warm, hard thigh. "Well, Commander, I guess that makes us partners in crime."

"Yes, ma'am. I believe it does."

FOURTEEN

Chris turned the SUV into a fast-food burger joint ten miles from Scarlett's house. He eased between a broad pine tree and a dumpster at the end of the lot.

Partners in crime.

He liked the way it sounded, although partners in bed would be much more satisfying. Scarlett looked like she could use a good round of sex. The way she'd bit her lower lip when he'd said they were "going rogue" had punched him with a vision of all the things he wanted to do to her mouth. If he leaned over a few inches and…

A rap on the window derailed his fantasy. He snapped his head to the side and gave Kane the finger.

Scarlett rubbed her eyes with the heel of her hands. "Huh? Where did he come from? I didn't even hear him pull up."

"Jealous about our stealthy superpowers *your* technology isn't responsible for?" Chris winked as he opened the door and got out.

"Now who's a smart-ass?" she called after him.

The comeback made him laugh all the way to the passenger side. Her eyebrows rose when he opened the door and offered his hand. "What? Surprised I'm a gentleman too?"

"Floored." She accepted his chivalrous offer and stepped out.

He inhaled her honeysuckle scent as he shifted his hand to the small of her back and guided her to Kane and the classic baby-blue Buick he leaned against.

Kane nudged his cowboy hat back with his knuckles as he straightened. "Nic is with Beth at the hospital, listening to her complain about waiting for a CT scan while I drop off this beauty."

Chris exchanged keys with him. "Thanks, man. Were you followed?"

"No. You?"

Chris surveyed the empty parking lot for signs of a tail and shook his head. Alarm flashed in Scarlett's eyes. He gently took her chin in his steel. "Nic took care of the traffic cameras in your area. The pretty boy's a decent hacker. You're safe."

She nodded, but the tension didn't ease from her shoulders. Even though he was surprised by the way she'd kept it together tonight, he'd gotten glimpses of the panic she was struggling to control. He scrambled for a better way to reassure her she wasn't in danger. He came up blank. She was in trouble.

Lots of it.

Kane pointed to the classic car. "Not a scratch. Grams will never make us corned beef and cabbage again if you so much as put a ding in the bumper."

"Don't get your panties in a bunch. Tell Grandma Ava I'll take good care of her baby."

Kane helped transfer the bags to the Buick. "Guess I'll

relieve Nic before Beth convinces him she's well enough to go home, or before he convinces her to have a sleepover."

"Nobody is sleeping with her, understand?"

Kane snickered. "No promises. Stay safe."

Adrenaline, with a sizable dash of jealousy, rushed through Chris as he watched Kane roll away in his SUV. Unlike his buddies, he couldn't ask the woman he'd be spending the rest of the night with to join him in bed. He had to get his raging libido under control before he got back in the car. His superpowers didn't include getting his dick to stand down when the woman he dreamed about every night would be sitting inches from him for the next three hours.

"Let's get some food." He grabbed her hand and led her toward the burger joint. "We have a long drive ahead of us."

"Where are we going?"

"To a cabin in western Maryland. We'll be safe there for a few days."

"Does it have a fast wireless connection?"

"Most women I know would be asking if it has running water and heat."

"Most women you know aren't searching for a cyber-criminal."

He chuckled as he held open the door to the restaurant. The different sides of Scarlett he'd witnessed tonight, the cursing and teasing, the promises to save his job, threatened to snap his control. Hell, in her bedroom, he'd almost pulled her into his arms close enough to feel his hard cock. Simply thinking about how hot she would look stretched out on her bed, naked and all his, screamed reckless.

Who'd known the awkward, reserved scientist would be trouble?

A few minutes later and a couple of number fives in hand, they headed back to the Buick.

Chris set the bags on the hood. "I know it's chilly, but

Kane will have my head if we spill even a drop of ketchup in this car. Mind having a picnic? The trees will block the wind, and we're far enough off the road not to be seen."

"I thought you said we weren't followed."

"We weren't, but it never hurts to be careful."

Nodding, she watched him set out the food picnic style as she slipped on her ski jacket. "Tell me more about this cabin."

"I called my friend Billy while you were packing and asked him to stock it with food and firewood—you know, the other essentials we'll need to survive."

"Sounds like a nice, quiet, distraction-free place. Exactly what I need."

"Right, distraction-free." He chewed his late-night dinner as he faced the biggest distraction of his life. Maybe talking about technology, threats, and traitors would cool his jets. "Tell me more about why someone would be willing to commit a crime to get your research."

"First, tell me why we're on the run in Kane's grand-mother's car."

He stroked the hood like a kitten. "Nobody will be searching for us in an old Buick. She's pretty spectacular, isn't she?"

Scarlett shivered as the wind kicked up. "As cars go, yes, I suppose she is."

He stepped closer to her to block the chill. "Don't let Kane hear you say that. He helped his grandfather restore this beauty. Before he left for his last deployment, he promised Grandpa Darren they'd put the finishing touches on it together when he came home, but the old man died before he returned."

"Oh, I didn't know. Poor Kane. How heartbreaking."

"When Kane came home minus a leg, his grandmother moved out here from West Virginia to care for him. Left the farm with her brother's family and drove this tank out here by herself. Once Kane was well enough to leave the hospital, he moved in with her."

Scarlett giggled. "Kane lives with his grandmother? How hysterical and sweet at the same time."

"Yup. She cooks dinner for the team once a week. You should come sometime."

He could picture her sitting around Grandma Darren's kitchen table with him and the guys, eating Irish cooking, drinking beer, and letting herself relax like she was one of the family.

His family.

She dropped her gaze. "I don't think that's appropriate. We're coworkers. Well, sort of, since I'm not with VIPER anymore, but you said I'm still part of your team."

"Kane's my teammate, and we eat meals together all the time. What makes you so different?"

"So many things."

"Like what?"

"Everything." She took a few steps toward the trees and halted. The wind blew an empty cup across the blacktop as she turned and strode back. "The way I was raised. The way I was educated. The way I don't know how to talk to people. The way you—"

"You talk to people all the time."

And she had no problem talking to the governor's nephew.

She spun to the trees with a huff, as if his ignorance about who she could and couldn't talk to annoyed her. He let the pacing continue until she leaned against the car with what appeared to be defeat on her shoulders. Something clicked in him. "Scarlett."

His tone got her attention. Even in the shadows of the crappy parking lot light, he could see the uncertainty in her eyes. "Tell me what you were going to say when I cut you off."

She stuffed her hands in her pockets and leaned against the car next to him. "Shouldn't we go?"

Even if the hacker, the traitor, and the intruders parachuted into the parking lot with guns drawn, he wasn't leaving without the answer. "Not until you tell me what's on your mind."

"Okay," she whispered to her shoes. "I was going to say the way you make me nervous makes me different. Most women would know what to do with that reaction, but I don't."

Their hips brushed. Electricity slung south to his cock. Part of his brain told him to retreat. The other part would die to see how far he could push her. "In your bedroom, did I make you nervous when I pulled down your zipper and exposed your little secret?"

"S-secret?"

He braced both hands on the hood of the car as he nudged her honeysuckle hair away with his nose. "Who would have thought the buttoned-up genius wasn't wearing a bra under her dress?"

He pulled his head back in time to see her swallow. Fuck, how he wanted to sink his teeth into her petal-soft skin and taste what he starved for. "I felt you tremble underneath my fingertips, but your reaction didn't feel like nerves." He waited for her to push him away, but she didn't, so he pressed his luck. "Tonight, I met a funny, sexy woman. She's in there somewhere, isn't she?"

She closed her eyes, her chest heaving. When she opened them, they held a sadness he hadn't noticed until just now. "Yes, she's in there, but she's been buried in the dark for so long she doesn't know how to come into the light."

He nudged her chin. "I'd love to meet her. All of her."

FIFTEEN

A sharp ring saved Scarlett from responding to the heavy words hanging in the wind.

Chris grabbed the phone from his pocket and jerked it to his ear. After a few moments, he passed it to Scarlett. "It's Beth."

She took the device from his hand, careful not to graze his fingertips. He'd already ignited enough heat in her body. She spun away and crunched through dried leaves toward the dumpster. "Are you okay?"

"Only a slight concussion. Aside from feeling like I have a hangover and being forced to go to a hospital again, I'm all right."

Scarlett stopped under a bare oak and leaned against it. The cool bark offered a welcome balm to her heated body. "I'm so sorry this happened to you."

"Stop apologizing. I should be the one saying I'm sorry. If I hadn't passed out I could have gotten a gander at the goon and given you a better description."

"Or you could have gotten shot. No more apologies. Go home and rest."

"I will, but first, Kane, in that sexy cowboy hat of his, is taking me to the diner for ice cream."

Scarlett chuckled. "You weren't kidding when you said you'd get a date with one of my hot vets one way or another."

"Speaking about hot vets, Chris is sexy as sin. And let's talk about that black bionic-looking hand? Imagine the things he can do with it, if you know what I mean."

Oh, she could imagine. "Just because you plan on taking advantage of your hero doesn't mean I am."

"Well, you should."

No way, not going to happen.

Thinking about Chris in anything but a professional manner bordered on unethical. "Even though I was fired, we're continuing to, uh, work together."

Beth sighed. "Ain't that the shame of the century? But seriously, be careful. I don't know what happened tonight. Kane said he's told me everything he can, and it's not much, but he promised me that Chris will keep you safe. Please let him do his job and listen to what he says."

"Promise." Scarlett ended the call and walked back to her —what? Bodyguard? Protector? She handed him the phone. The remains of their impromptu picnic were gone.

How pathetic am I? The most romantic date I've ever had is fast food on the hood of a car.

He opened the passenger door. "Let's go."

Once inside, he steered onto the dark road and headed toward the entrance to the highway. "Is Beth okay?"

Scarlett inhaled the car's light vanilla scent. Longing pierced her heart. Grandma Darren's kitchen probably smelled like vanilla, along with sugar, spice, and everything Scarlett had lost when her mom died and she'd fallen under Henry's rule.

"Yes, Beth is fine. Kane is taking her to get something to eat."

"I hope he behaves himself." Chris sped up the ramp to the interstate. "Lately, he's been playing the wounded hero sympathy card with the ladies quite successfully."

She tried to suppress a yawn, but it mingled with a laugh. "Don't worry about Beth. She's a love 'em and leave 'em kind of girl these days. It's Kane we should be worried about."

"You said she was attacked. What happened?"

"Two years ago, Beth and her fiancé Danny were walking back to her apartment from dinner. It was late. And dark. They took a shortcut down an alley when a man jumped them and shot Danny right in front of her."

"Holy shit. What happened to them?"

"Beth suffered a broken arm and a concussion." She swallowed. "Danny died."

Chris reached over and covered her knee with his steel. "I'm so sorry. Did the police catch the guy?"

"No, but something he said during the attack points to him being the same man Beth had met on an online dating site when she and Danny had briefly broken up. When she canceled because she and Danny had gotten back together, the guy went from a lunch date that never happened to a stalker in a matter of weeks."

"What kind of stalking?"

"Creepy text messages indicating he'd known her whereabouts. Sexually explicit emails detailing what he'd planned to do when they met in person."

"Is he still harassing her?"

"No, thank God. Shortly after the attack she moved from our hometown to a place around the corner from me and hasn't heard from him since." Scarlett fisted her hands in her lap. "I tried my best to find him. So. Damn. Hard. My failure kills me. It kills me, even more, to know he's still out there and could resurface at any time."

Chris squeezed her knee. "If he does, you'll get him. I'm sure of it."

His faith in her, along with his touch, warmed the cold space in her heart. "Danny was more than Beth's fiancé to me. He was my friend. I lived next door to him until my mom married Henry and we moved to the DC area." A smile teased her lips. "He and Beth were the only kids who treated me like I was normal."

"You *are* normal."

"No, I'm not. I'm exceptional except for when it counts. I should have found Danny's killer, but I failed my friends. And I failed you tonight."

"You're not responsible for what happened." He checked the rearview mirror again.

She sighed and glanced at the silver moon peeking through the clouds. "Logically, I know I'm not, but I feel like I am. I promised you things would go well, and they didn't. And I'm definitely responsible for Beth getting hurt at my house."

"Bad timing. Stop beating yourself up and start telling me more about what's on your hard drive."

She leaned over and touched his shoulder. "I've taken the technology that lets you control your super arm a step further."

"How much further?"

"So much further, your mind will have the ability to control not only your body but your environment."

"Are you saying I could make things move simply by thinking about it?"

"Yes. You wouldn't even need a magic wand, only my technology in your brain and in the object. Imagine someone with a spinal cord injury who's lost all motor function, even speech. They could think about opening the back door to let the dog out. Or change the thermostat without pressing any buttons. Or even drive a car."

"Providing independence and freedom."

"Precisely. And if someone who couldn't speak needed to find an object, say a misplaced inhaler, she could think a command to find it, and the object would flash and beep. I'm working on making the object fly into her hands, but such applications are a few years down the road."

Chris glanced at her. "Did you choose this line of research to prevent others from dying in similar scenarios like your mom?"

She offered a weak smile and nodded, surprised, and touched he remembered the conversation about her mother. "Now imagine an IED in a battle zone. Or a bomb in a crowded airport. No timer. No trigger. No detonating device. Just the thoughts of a psycho and boom."

"Damn, Scarlett. That's intense. Who else knows about this?"

"I haven't published my findings yet, and I've tried to keep it under wraps as much as possible, but the scientific community is small. I've collaborated with trusted sources."

"And your research is why your ex-asshole and your egomaniac of a stepfather want you back at work so badly."

"Yes. They'd love for me to develop the environment control software under Richardson Enterprises. I left because the DOD wanted my work to improve and save lives, not make them a fortune or bask in the glory of being the first to market with a groundbreaking product."

He touched his steel fist on his chest. "And I thank you for trusting the DOD with your work instead of giving it to Richardson. What's his deal?"

"Henry grew up without a dad and with a verbally abusive mother with an addiction to drugs and alcohol. Since he never experienced the stability of a loving home, he tries to control everyone and everything. At least that's my take on why he acts the way he does."

"Did he try to control your mom?"

She smiled, despite the aching hole in her heart. "One time, about a year or so after they'd gotten married, I overheard him demanding she change her dress because he thought it wasn't classy enough to impress his client they were meeting for dinner."

"What did she say?"

"She told him to go to hell and said something about being a fool for not seeing through his charming façade."

"Did he try and control you?"

She smiled at the shift in his tone from curious to concerned. "He tried to control my education, but Mom pushed back. When she died, he finally got his way."

"Your mom sounds like she was a tough woman. You're a lot like her."

"That means a lot to me. Thank you."

"It's the truth. And what's James's excuse for being an asshat?"

She snickered, adding "asshat" to the growing list of colorful insults she'd learned. "About ten years ago, James's father, who was a good friend of Henry's, lost the family fortune to gambling debts. When his mom found out they were broke, she ran off with someone years younger. Shortly after, he disappeared. They never found a body to confirm the rumor he was offed by his loan shark. According to what my mom told me. Henry was disappointed in his old friend but took James under his wing because he felt sorry for him. I think James emulates Henry, instead of his father, who let him down."

"I think James needs to find a new role model. Do you think he had something to do with the break-in at your house? His appearance while it was being invaded, as if he was there to create a distraction in case you came home early, and occurring on the same night your program was hacked, is a big coincidence. And what about dear old dad?"

He lifted his steel off the steering wheel to air quote his last three words. His black fingers caught the light of the passing cars.

She stared at the beauty of his strength as fat snowflakes landed on the windshield. "It wouldn't make sense for Henry or James to have someone break into my house and steal my research. Like you said, I'm the other half. They could easily lure me somewhere and torture the information out of my brain."

"That's not funny."

No. It was terrifying. "While Henry hasn't gotten over me leaving the company, I'm the only family he has. I think he and James saw an opportunity to convince me to come back, figuring my confidence would be shaken after what happened at the gala."

"Aside from profit, why is it so important you work for him?"

"Henry takes full credit for the scientist I am today. It's like he believes he hasn't gotten the proper return on his investment yet. And it's a matter of pride. Nobody says no to the great Henry Richardson."

Scarlett rested her head on the seat and watched the minivan in the lane next to them. She wished she *did* want to work for the family business. If her mother hadn't misplaced her inhaler, if Henry had cared for all of her, not just her mind, she could have spent the second half of her childhood knowing the love of a family like the one she imagined inside the minivan.

"Get some sleep." Chris patted her hand with his steel. "We'll talk more in the morning."

Sighing her agreement, she pressed her body deeper into

the soft leather. She was safe, at least for now, with the strongest man she'd ever met.

"Chris." His name slipped from her lips in the dreamy seconds before slumber. "Thanks for treating me like part of the team. In case you're wondering, you aren't only steel and V-Strikes to me."

Moments after she gave in to exhaustion, the car jerked to the left. Her eyes flew open. Blurry taillights dotted her vision as they veered into the adjacent lane.

Chris cursed over the blare of honking horns and swerved the Buick into its proper place.

Her heart slammed against her ribs as she whipped her head toward him.

"Sorry." His voice cracked. "There was something in the road."

"What?"

"I don't know." He stared straight ahead. "Go back to sleep."

Chris hadn't been lying about something in the road. His jaw. It had dropped to the wet asphalt the moment she'd declared he was more to her than steel and V-Strikes.

Had those words come out of her mouth, or had his mind been playing tricks? He'd taken his gaze off the road to search her face for some indication of sincerity for only a second. Long enough not to notice the debris obstructing the lane.

He squeezed the steering wheel again and cursed under his breath. If his steel fingers left dents in the powder-blue cover, Kane would have a hissy fit. He couldn't let Scarlett get any further into his head. It was dangerous enough she already occupied a space. Once they identified the traitor and found the hacker, his emotions would settle. For now, he had to keep his mind clear, his dick in his pants, and his eye on his end goal—protect Scarlett so she could find the enemy and save VIPER from losing its funding.

He checked the clock on the dashboard. Three more hours to their destination. He flipped on the radio and lowered the volume, hoping the music would silence Scarlett's words singing in his brain.

SIXTEEN

Chris stared down a set of yellow eyes illuminated by the orange glow of the breaking dawn. "Move it, buddy."

The buck in the middle of the road leading to the cabin cocked his head as if to say, "Dude, do you know what time it is?" The crunching tires over the snow-dusted gravel sent him scurrying into the trees.

With great care, Chris drove over the deep potholes lying in wait to swallow the tires of the Buick. An overgrown branch scraped along the side. He cringed as the harsh sound wailed like music in a horror movie right before the psycho jumps out of the trees with a chainsaw. He glanced over at Scarlett to see if the eerie noise had woken her. She'd been snoring softly for the past hour and still slept soundly.

No psycho. No damsel in distress. No need for steel and V-Strikes, but she'd need his protection soon. Her mind and research were valuable assets someone wanted to possess.

Chris knew she didn't mean to flaunt her brilliance but to have figured out how to control things with one's thoughts? It was no wonder he held her in awe. Thanks to

Scarlett, his existence hovered a few feet over the line between reality and science fiction. Without VIPER, he'd be as good as dead. Lost, with no purpose and no future. Or he *would* be dead, like every team member on his last mission.

The words of his shrink echoed in his brain.

"It's not your fault the others didn't survive."

"It's not your fault your wife left."

Yet it was.

He hadn't shared his uneasy feelings about the young officer with his team.

He'd hurt Natalie.

No amount of psychotherapy would change the truth.

He peeked at the woman he dreamed about. The blood in his soul would stain her perfection.

As he continued down the bumpy road toward the cabin, his phone rang. "Shit," he whispered as he quickly answered and switched it to vibrate.

"Yeah?" His scratchy voice hurt his own ears.

"Good morning, happy camper. Make it to the cabin yet?"

He winced at Billy's morning-person volume as he glanced at Scarlett's silent form. "We're almost there."

"Good. I'm about to head to the clinic but wanted to make sure you arrived okay. I turned on the heat and lit a fire in the bedroom. There's plenty of food. Oh, and Marie was shopping the other day and bought new sheets, a comforter, and a rug. She said the place needed some personality."

"Thanks, man." He knew he could count on Billy to help him out, no questions asked. "And tell Marie thanks too. Let me know how much I owe you."

"No need. I've already worked out a payment plan. The next time you're out here, I'm going to drop all three kids off at your cabin for some quality Uncle Chris time and take my wife on a date. Until then, you and your friend will be nice and cozy."

Yeah, nice and cozy.

"Marie also wants to know when you're finally going to call Natalie and sign the papers to make the place officially yours. She's hoping you'll let her do more decorating."

The cabin legally belonged to his ex-wife. Natalie wanted nothing to do with the tiny place she'd inherited when her father had died shortly before Chris left for his last mission. He had fallen in love with it. The lush forest and quiet solitude felt more like home than any other place he'd lived, save for the small apartment he'd shared with his dad in New York City. During their quick divorce settlement, he'd asked Natalie if he could buy the cabin from her. She'd surprised him, offering it as a parting gift of sorts.

"Tell Marie it's on my to-do list."

"Good. She's been driving me nuts with color swatches for your living room."

Chris laughed through a pang of jealousy. He'd learned early on in his short-lived marriage that Natalie liked the romance of a military husband but couldn't handle the reality.

Regret suffocated him and probably always would. He'd thought her experiences growing up as an Army brat and the foundation of their love would get them through the uncertainty and instability of the SEAL lifestyle. The night before he left for his fateful mission, they had what he'd thought had been a sincere conversation about going to counseling. He wasn't the giving-up kind. Natalie was. Marie, on the other hand, supported Billy with steadfast strength, from tearful deployments to joyous homecomings and everything in between.

He said a quick goodbye to Billy. Seconds later, the phone hummed in his lap.

"Yeah?" he croaked, tired of talking.

"It's me. I'm at Beth's. You can tell Scarlett she's fine."

"Christ, Kane. Please tell me you didn't sleep with Scarlett's best friend."

"Of course not. She seemed like she needed company. We talked, that's all. Then she went to bed. Alone. I'm sticking around in case she wakes up and needs anything. What's up on your end?"

Chris gave him a quick recap.

"Holy shit. Thompson lied? And are you saying someday soon Grams can tell her car to drive her to bingo?"

"Who knows? Maybe. Our genius is smarter than we ever dreamed."

"Let's make sure we keep her safe. By the way, my buddy got us a bunch of tickets to the Army-Navy game. Think Scarlett will want to come?"

"I don't think she's the football type."

"We'll just have to convince her that she is. It can be a team bonding event."

"Let's save the project before we plan extracurriculars."

"Roger that."

Chris hung up as he stopped the Buick in front of the cabin. The place hadn't changed since he'd visited three months ago for Marie's thirtieth birthday party. The roof of the wooden porch sagged, and the dark-green door needed painting. Other than those flaws, the little structure appeared sturdy, with thick log walls and a solid stone chimney. He cut the engine and added "trimming the ivy clinging to the porch rails" to his list of chores.

Or maybe not.

He liked the wild aura it gave the property, like it existed eons away from civilization. The perfect place to hide out, especially since it wasn't in his name yet.

Procrastination does have its uses.

He promised himself to suck it up and contact Natalie about signing those papers.

Soon.

Even as he thought the words, he knew he'd keep putting it off. The last time he'd seen her had been in his lawyer's office a few days before VIPER had given him a new arm. Although she had no reason now to recoil from his broken body, he couldn't risk seeing pity and revulsion on her face again. Not with the memory of it always haunting him.

He stepped out of the car and yawned at the bronze-colored sky. Leaving Scarlett in the warm seat, he carried their bags in. As Billy had promised, groceries lined the counter. In the small bedroom, a fire burned in the pot-belly stove. He threw back the comforter and headed outside to get Scarlett.

His phone vibrated in his pocket as he jogged down the stairs. Halting at the bottom, he pulled it out and jammed it against his ear. "What's up?"

Nic whistled through his teeth. "Someone's been staking out Doc's place."

Cold confirmation satisfied Chris's suspicion. Scarlett was in danger and more than he'd originally thought. He jogged down the steps. "Did you get the plate number?"

"Yeah. I ran it."

"Glad to hear your computer science degree is being put to work." Chris crossed the grass clearing to the car.

"Bite me. The plate belongs to a dummy corporation called JS Holdings. I'll keep digging."

"Keep a close eye on Thompson. He lied to us. Scarlett didn't resign; she was fired."

"Why would he lie?"

Chris stopped by a tree and studied the twigs on the ground like they were tea leaves. "Don't know, but we can't trust him until we get to the bottom of this."

"It's probably some political bullshit. Like our pay grade's not high enough to be told the whole story or some other red-tape crap."

"I hope so." As he ended the call, he prayed Nic's assumption was correct. A traitor on the team was bad enough, but their leader? He searched his memories for signs of irregularities in Thompson's behavior. Sure, he'd seemed to get jumpier as the beta test had approached, but a sweatier-than-usual bald head didn't justify accusations of treason.

Digging his steel fingers into a tree branch, Chris concentrated on the bite of the rough bark he shouldn't be able to feel at all. He squeezed his fingers harder, envisioning his power flowing up his arm until the branch snapped in his lethal hand. With a grunt, he crushed the broken pieces in his grip.

God help whoever fucked with him and his team.

He gathered Scarlett in his arms and carried her into the cabin. Once she was snug under the covers, he pulled out his pistol and checked the chamber. A soft snore flowed from her as he placed the gun on the nightstand.

"Looks like you might need my steel and V-Strikes after all," he whispered into the darkness.

He removed his boots and stretched out next to her, rolling onto his side to stare at the beautiful woman sleeping next to him. Despite the danger he posed while he slept, he needed a moment, just a blissful speck in time, to simply be with her away from the madness. A calmness settled over him as he let himself relax into the comfort only the woman beside him could bring.

He let his eyes close.

Only for a minute.

SEVENTEEN

"**G**et away."

Scarlett bolted straight up in bed at the frantic voice. Her eyes ping-ponged around the unfamiliar room. Where was she?

A loud crash followed a string of curses.

Chris?

She jumped out of the bed and ran to the closed door on the left side of the room where the uproar had come from. "Chris."

"In here."

"Are you all right?"

"Fantastic."

She backed up. "Uh, okay. It sounded like the goons from last night were holding you at gunpoint."

"No goons. Just taking a shower. I'll be out in a minute."

She sat down on the bed she didn't remember falling asleep in.

What a way to wake up.

Strange place.

Loud scream.

Violent crash.

Her gaze landed on the nightstand. The black gun catching the sunlight on its barrel was a harsh reminder of why she'd woken up in a secluded hideout.

So much for a quiet cabin in the woods. She closed her eyes to try and calm her racing heart. A second later, she whipped her gaze toward the bathroom door. Chris stood on the threshold, the sight of him sending her heart pounding harder than when she'd thought he was in trouble.

The sunlight from behind bathed him in a white glow, like a supernatural deity materializing from another realm. A black towel slung low around his hips rested centimeters under the delectable indents where his carved abs tapered south. She opened her mouth to say his name. The air trapped in her lungs wouldn't let the word escape.

Say something. Anything.

She couldn't. Didn't even try, afraid if she did, his image would vanish into the sunbeam, lost to her forever.

The divine man in the doorway made no move to pull his towel tighter around his waist. He only stood there with his lips spread in a cocky grin.

He knows what he does to me. The bastard knows, and he's enjoying every minute of it.

He rubbed his chin with his slick, black fingers. "Sorry about all the noise. Sleep well?"

She couldn't answer, too entranced by his hand. What would it feel like if he touched her because he wanted—no, desired to feel her flesh against his steel? Cool? Hot? Strong? Gentle? All those things at once?

"Uh, I guess I slept okay. You?"

His gaze landed on the pillow next to her. "Best sleep I've had in a year."

She studied the indent in the soft cotton. Had they shared the bed last night? A pleasurable ache sparked in her belly and spread low into her core at the thought of doing more than merely sleeping. "What was all the commotion in the bathroom about?"

"A critter decided to join me in the shower."

"What kind of critter?"

"Small. Furry. Some kind of spider. Scared the shit out of me. Don't worry; I killed it with a shampoo bottle and a shaving mirror."

"Sounds like a lot of ammunition for a spider."

He winked as he sauntered to the corner of the small room where their bags lay. "Just doing my duty to protect you."

As he bent over to retrieve his duffel, his towel rode up, revealing the tightest ass cheeks she'd ever seen. Granted, she didn't have much data to draw an accurate conclusion about her observation, but based on the information at hand, she was confident his ass was perfection.

He stood up. The wide expanse of his chiseled back and the tattoo on his left shoulder came into glorious view. Over the dips and valleys of his muscles, the World Trade Center was etched on top of the American flag. A police shield, "9/11/01," and "Never Forget" was inscribed underneath. She'd wondered about the tattoo on the couple of occasions she'd observed Patience examining him in MedLab after a training exercise. The viper ink she understood. All the guys on the team sported the same one. Chris had mentioned his father was a cop. Had he died in the 9/11 attacks?

She was about to ask him when he spun around. "Hot coffee is on the stove. Eggs and bacon are warming in the oven. Give me five minutes and we can eat breakfast—well, lunch together. It's almost noon, and we have a lot to discuss."

He flashed her another wicked smile as he strode into the bathroom and closed the door.

She fell back onto the sheets, grabbed the pillow next to her, and covered her face. His earthy forest scent confirmed they'd shared the bed last night. "Best sleep in a year" was how he'd described his slumber. Funny thing was, it had been the best rest she could remember in a long time too.

She hugged the pillow to her chest and sat up to assess her surroundings. Aside from the nightstand with the gun on it and a pot-belly stove glowing with embers, the bed was the only other piece of furniture. Nothing hung on the walls. No curtains adorned the windows. Either nobody lived here, or Chris sorely needed a decorator. The only personal touches were the throw rugs on the floor and the matching plaid comforter. She ran her fingers over the thick, soft material. The navy-blue and forest-green shades suited him.

Rising from the bed, she padded to the window that faced a large clearing on the side of the cabin. A dilapidated shed stood on the edge of the forest. Bare oaks and maples mingled with thick pines as far as she could see.

We're all alone. In the woods. With one bed. And he's laughing at me with his teasing smile.

Talking with him last night about traitors, technology, her mom, and even the danger had been easy. Discussing how he made her nervous, however, had ranked harder than the last exam she'd taken in school. And when he touched her? She couldn't think of any experience to rival the feel of his flesh and steel on her skin.

She speared her fingers into her knotty hair. *No more inappropriate thoughts.* Today she would act like she did on any given day at headquarters, like a professional.

Because every day at the office starts with a view of Chris's naked ass.

The bathroom door creaked. She looked over her shoulder, vowing to stop wasting time dreaming about his spectacular backside.

"Are you sure you slept okay?" The silver-gray flecks that matched his long-sleeved T-shirt sparked in his gaze. "Your face is flushed."

She leaned against the window. Distance was a necessity until she could erase the memory of him shining like a god in a towel. "I'm fine."

"A shower will perk you up. I'll make us some toast and meet you in the kitchen."

She watched him leave, her vow to stop thinking about his ass posing the biggest challenge of her career.

After a quick critter-free shower, she pulled on her lacy bra and panties. Her cheeks flamed as she recalled Chris's comment last night about her lack of undergarments. What inappropriate words would come out of his lips if he knew she wore silk and lace under her suits every day?

Maybe the girl she'd been before Henry had sent her away lived inside her somewhere. Despite being different, her preteen years had been about as normal as any other kid, she guessed. She used to giggle about boys with Beth and ride her bike to the park with Danny. She'd even been invited to the sixth-grade Winter Party by Tommy Marlon. She'd never got to wear the shimmering blue dress she'd picked out with her mom and never got a goodnight kiss when Tommy walked her home. Instead, she'd wept at her mother's funeral.

Mom was right.

She had lost a vital part of herself when Henry had sent her away. Was it time she tried to find it? She picked up her brush and pulled it through her wet hair. It snagged on a knot. The prick in her scalp matched the pain in her past. Was her penchant for wearing satin and lace underneath her sensible clothes a substitute for the pretty dress she never wore?

The intoxicating smell of bacon drove her to forget about her musings and finish dressing. After pulling on jeans and a light-blue V-neck fleece, she quickly dried her hair. She opened the door to the main room and smoothed the natural waves she straightened every day. Her hand froze on top of her head as Chris's denim-clad ass greeted her.

A hot man who cooks. Now there's some serious porn.

He turned from the stove, a pot of coffee in his steel and nodded to the small wooden table set with two plates heaped with bacon and eggs, coffee cups, utensils, and a container of butter. With his free hand, he held out her chair.

Stop being a gentleman.

She crossed the small living room and stepped into the even smaller kitchen. His thoughtfulness and the repeated views of his ass made it hard to stop wishing he'd use his hand to sweep everything off the table, lay her flat, and eat *her* for breakfast.

She shivered, despite the warmth from the fire in the hearth, as he slid up behind her.

"Sit."

Powerless to ignore his command, she dropped into the chair. His gritty tone cued her memory to play the words he'd moaned when he'd kissed her.

"Fuck, Scarlett."

How had he made such a foul word sound like a caress?

Was he a dirty-talking, bossy alpha in bed? James had never said anything when they'd had sex other than, "Hurry up and come. I have work to do." But she'd never found the glorious release Beth claimed to experience regularly, and James had never cared to discover why she hadn't.

Chris would care though, and he'd know how to get her there. She believed that as sure as she believed in the big bang theory.

What a bang it would be to explore her convictions.

She squashed her errant dream and pointed to the

counter lined with boxes and cans of food. "Did a fairy come and stock the place for us?"

"I told you last night I called Billy. An old military buddy." He placed toast on the table and sat down. "He's a retired Navy doctor. Runs an urgent care clinic not too far from here."

Steam wafted from the coffee to warm her face. She wrapped her hands tighter around the mug. "Is this his cabin?"

He paused for a moment. "No. It's mine."

"Oh. It's nice." She wanted to suggest that curtains on the floor-to-ceiling windows flanking the fireplace and a few throw pillows on the brown couch would liven things up, but she wasn't here to impart her interior design wisdom. "Any news from the team?"

He reached across his chest and rubbed his shoulder.

Icy goose bumps pierced her skin despite the fire at her back. He had a habit of rubbing his 9/11 ink when he was uneasy. "Has something else happened?"

"Not yet. Nic said someone staked out your place last night. Whoever broke in hasn't given up."

She dropped her toast. "Did Nic see who it was?"

"He got a license plate number. It's registered to a dummy corporation. He'll keep digging until he gets a name."

"Christ." She squeezed her fingers into fists on top of the table. "How many times can I be violated in one night?"

"Linc and Nic already fixed your door and installed a new security system. If anyone goes near your place, the team will be alerted."

Warmth spread through her body. Is this what it felt like to have real friends? Besides Beth, she didn't have anybody who would go out of their way for her. "Please tell the team thanks. For everything."

He took both of her hands and turned them over. With a gentleness that surprised her, he peeled her fingers back from their tight balls and massaged her palms in slow circles.

"I'm okay, Chris. I'm not going to break into hysterics." Although the parts of her James had ignored for so long broke into a frenzied dance with each firm stroke against her skin.

His gaze dropped to her V-neck. "I know."

She glanced out the large windows. The lack of curtains left her feeling as exposed as she did under Chris's heated gaze. Both scenarios unnerved her in different ways. "Are you sure nobody but the team knows we're here?"

He released her hands. "We're as safe as we can be for now. If whoever is looking for you thought you left town, they wouldn't have wasted time casing your street last night."

She picked up her fork and toyed with her scrambled eggs. What he said made sense. "Any good news to balance the bad?"

"Yes. The governor is fine. His camp is spinning his collapse as a severe undiagnosed allergy to crab meat. Since crabs are like the state food of Maryland, the public feels bad for him. His presidential announcement is getting more exposure, all positive since the incident."

"That's great news. The allergy angle is brilliant. I'm glad we didn't hinder his campaign."

"Me too. I have a lot of respect for that man." He rose and picked up the coffeepot from the stove. "More?"

"Please."

She stared at his muscled arm as he poured. The *N* for Navy on the sleeve of his T-shirt had a star at the top right about the size of a nickel, the perfect size for a—

She slapped her palms on the table. "Retinal scanner."

Coffee sloshed out of her full cup onto the back of her hand. She cursed as the steaming liquid seared her skin.

He slammed the pot down on the stove. "Shit, did you get burned?" He grasped her elbows and lifted her from the chair. With strong hands, he guided her to the sink and fiddled with the faucet.

She jerked as the water hit her scorched skin.

"Give it a minute." He held her in place with his solid body.

"You don't understand." She twisted her torso to face him. "I figured out how the hacker got my retinal signature."

"Great. Tell me. But you're doing it right here until I say you can move."

Her back stiffened. "Are you always this controlling?"

"Yes, ma'am."

Scarlett's lips twisted into a smirk. "I'm so excited I won't even call you an ass for the ma'am comment."

"I know I'm an ass, and I'm okay with it. Now tell me what you've figured out."

"There's been rumors about a group of scientists in China who developed a retinal scanner the size of a dime. There've been no confirmed reports of a prototype, but speculation has caused significant buzz within the biometric community. If someone was in possession of one last night, and I looked straight at it for a few seconds, it could scan my retina."

"Wouldn't you notice someone holding a device up to your eye and saying, 'Please, Dr. Kerrigan, focus on the pretty red light?'"

"You're funny. Think about it. If it was your mission to secure someone's retinal scan in a large group setting, and you had a device like I described, what would you do?"

"I'd conceal it on my body, engage you in conversation and—"

"Steal my biometric print." She turned back to the sink and tried to pull her hand away from his grip. His steel arm snaked around her waist and pulled her against him. "Stop moving. The longer the water cools the burn, the better."

She huffed as she leaned back into his chest. "If someone embedded the device in, say, an American flag pin, it's feasible my retina could have been scanned without me being the wiser."

"Nice job, Sherlock Holmes." He smiled into her hair. The more she talked about her revelation, the more her body relaxed against his. "What do we do now?"

"I'll send out inquiries to colleagues working in the biometric space. Ask if they've heard anything about a proto-type. And I'll scan the security footage from the gala to narrow down suspects based on who I talked with last night."

"Good plan. I'll make a list of every person who knows about VIPER's capabilities, ask the guys to do the same, then cross-reference. Everyone is a suspect, with Thompson, your stepfather, and your ex-asshole at the top of the list."

He reached around her, twisted the faucet handle, and turned off the water. Patting her pink skin, he spoke into her ear. "Feel better?"

She rubbed her fingers over the burn and sighed. "Yeah."

Satisfaction dripped from her lips long and slow, like how he'd fantasized about making love to her.

She nodded to the bedroom. "I'll grab my laptop and get started."

He took a big step back to give her plenty of room to pass and enough space for his body to cool. His thoughts about what he'd like to do to her between the sheets they'd slept in last night didn't cool down at all.

Selfish bastard.

He'd had no right to risk hurting her in the throes of a nightmare because he'd craved the peace she brought him. A few minutes was all he'd meant to spend at her side until he'd calmed down. Usually when his head hit the pillow, it took about an hour for him to fall asleep. He'd thought there would be plenty of time to absorb her serenity, to appreciate the contrast of her lashes against her fair skin, and stare at the relaxed set of her pretty lips before he went on the couch. He'd miscalculated, gently easing into a dreamless sanctuary he'd never wanted to wake up from.

He shouldn't want her. It was wrong.

Unethical.

Dangerous.

But given the opportunity, he wouldn't change a thing about where he'd woken up this morning. He couldn't do it again though. The dent in his headboard, and Christ, the way he'd hurt Natalie were harsh reminders that he'd gotten lucky last night. He wouldn't risk Scarlett's safety again to assuage his demons.

A few minutes later, after they cleaned up breakfast and Scarlett ensured their network connections were untraceable, he studied her over his laptop. "Tell me this, Einstein. How are you going to get the video from the gala? You're not employed by the United States government anymore and don't have access."

Determination and pride shone in her eyes. "This is my battlefield, remember? You think the bad guys are the only ones who know how to hack?"

The bold words flowed from her pretty mouth with the promise of sweet retribution and the suggestion of a rebellious side he'd yet to meet. Even though he couldn't claim the badass woman he sensed inside, he couldn't wait to be introduced.

EIGHTEEN

Heavy boots stomped on the cabin's porch. Scarlett yanked her gaze from her laptop to the door, cold air hitting her skin as it flew open. Chris stood on the threshold, a pile of wood in his arms.

"You smell like the forest." She inhaled the scent of pine needles and fresh air as he strode past her to the fireplace.

"I stopped to chop some wood while I checked the grounds."

She shifted in her chair at the kitchen table, her thighs involuntarily clenching as she pictured man and machine wielding an ax in the twilight. She wondered if he'd taken his shirt off.

Damn. I should have joined him for some fresh air.

He dropped the logs on the hearth and headed toward her. "Any luck with the license plate Nic sent you?"

"No. Whoever set up the dummy company it's registered to—this JS Holdings that Nic uncovered—knows what they are doing."

"How about the security footage you procured?" He studied the laptop screen over her shoulder. "Find anything?"

His warm breath teased her neck as she rolled her shoulders back to alleviate some of the stiffness from hunching over her laptop for hours. "No. Almost every man at the fundraising gala wore some sort of pin on his jacket large enough to hold a prototype. American flag. State of Maryland. And the women in evening gowns? There are dozens of places to hide a miniaturized device. Buttons, bows, flowers, jewels. And don't even get me started on the military people. They have enough bling on their uniforms to hide ten devices."

He thrust his shoulders back. His T-shirt strained against the wide expanse of his torso. "Mine could hide dozens with all of my ranks and awards."

She swatted his steel arm. "And your ego is so big, you could hide a full-size scanner in your inflated chest."

He threw his head back and laughed. A smile lit his face. This wasn't the sarcastic smirk he wore when he made fun of her, or his playful grin when he joked with the guys. It also wasn't the knowing stare he'd burned her with from the bathroom doorway this morning. This was pure joy, and it was beautiful.

Her anxiety level dialed down to edgy. Hackers and traitors on the loose, men with guns stalking her, and Chris's hulking presence were a recipe for frayed nerves with a side of fear. Dessert was a heaping spoonful of sexual attraction she had no clue how to act on. Leaning into his hard chest and enjoying the way her body had pressed against his when he'd held her by the sink had been the most decadent position she'd ever been in.

He opened the refrigerator, grabbed a bottle of water, and twisted off the cap. "I'm sorry to get you off track. You really have no idea how funny you are though."

She stared for a moment as he drank, wishing it were her lips against his instead of the bottle.

Stop being the nerd with a crush on the quarterback and talk to him.

"Being told I'm funny isn't something I hear very often, at least not since I joined VIPER."

"You've been hanging out with some really boring people because I think you're hysterical." He sat across from her at the table. His long legs brushed hers underneath. "Have you heard from your biometric sources?"

"Yes. They confirmed there are prototypes like the one I described for sale on the black market. I've asked them to do more digging to see if there's any chatter of an acquisition by an American entity. Any word on what's going on at headquarters?"

"I just talked to Linc. Thompson has directed us to lie low for the weekend, which means mind our own business until we're told what to do next. He was pretty pissed I wasn't at headquarters today though."

She pressed her palms to the table and peered at him over her laptop. "You can't hide out in the woods with me forever. You need to get back to VIPER. You're a government asset. You can't disappear."

"And if we don't find out who's behind this, I won't have VIPER to go back to. We'll lose all credibility and be disbanded. Remember? Linc said there are already rumors of the project's demise flying around headquarters."

The reminder of their situation felt like another rock added to the pile she already carried on her shoulders. "I remember."

"Relax. It's only Friday. We have the weekend ahead of us. I have faith your brilliant mind won't take long to figure this out."

"My mind's not a machine, Chris."

How many times had she itched to say those words to Henry? It felt good to finally say them to someone.

He covered her hand with his. "Sorry I'm putting pressure on you. I'm frustrated. I wish you could activate me. Then I'd know I'd be able to provide protection if we're found. Right now, I'm useless. Some fucking superhero."

"We'd already be found if you were activated. It would be like a neon arrow pointing the evil villains to our hideout. And you are on the opposite spectrum of useless." She curled her fingers under his palm. "You may not be saving the world, but you were my superhero last night."

He squeezed her hand before he withdrew it, a slight smile on his lips. "Anytime."

She rubbed her palms together, missing the heat from his touch. "What else did Linc have to say?"

"Thompson has everyone in your lab working around the clock on the breach."

"Why not all hands on deck? You and the team have skills to help find a traitor."

Chris shrugged. "Maybe Thompson's afraid we're too close to the investigation. Like if we discover a lead, we'll act first and think later. Or maybe he suspects our suspicions that he fed the hackers the code to get into the network and activate you."

She didn't want to consider the second scenario but couldn't blame Thompson for the first. Chris and the guys had acted last night when they'd gone against orders and gone to her townhome. "Doesn't matter how many people are searching for clues left in our network. If someone secured my retinal scan and the activation code, getting into our system would've been easy, like walking through a door someone left unlocked. It's a textbook example of insider threat."

"You spoke about insider threat at some cyber thing in London last year."

Scarlett cocked her head to the side. "You searched me online?"

"Damn straight I did. I had to be sure you were qualified to protect us."

"Did my qualifications meet your satisfaction?"

She held her breath as his gaze traveled from her eyes down to the hint of cleavage she bared and back up again.

He licked his lower lip. "And then some."

Time seemed to freeze in their cozy retreat, thoughts of traitors and danger forgotten in the intimate moment.

He leaned closer. "I know what insider threat is. I'm sure you can broaden my knowledge though."

Your mind, Scarlett. His motives may be honorable, but he wants your mind.

She redirected her thoughts to reality. "Simple. A network is only as secure as the people you trust with it. If someone betrays that trust, it doesn't matter what security measures you have in place. Your network is vulnerable."

"Tell me more about who has been privy to your environment control research besides Henry and James."

She stood and walked to the sink. "A handful of trusted colleagues, but James and Henry don't know about the advances I've made in the past several years." She twisted the faucet and scrubbed her hands under the water. The burn from this morning had faded, but the memory of being trapped against the sink by Chris's muscular arms flared hot and heavy in her veins.

He appeared next to her with a dish towel. "You mentioned James's family lost their fortune. Let me guess. James lost his inheritance?"

She muttered, "Thanks," and dried her hands. "I know what you're thinking. While it's true James would love nothing more than to profit from my research, it doesn't make him a suspect."

"Money is a fierce motivator."

"Thanks to Richardson Enterprises, he's more than tripled his family's previous worth. He has plenty of money now, and he wouldn't do anything to hurt me. Even though he can be a weasel sometimes, I believe he cares about me, at least on some level."

"Ever hear of 'crimes of passion?'"

She laughed. "Of the many things one might call James Samuels, passionate doesn't break the top ten. Unless it's about work. He spends nearly every Saturday in his office, sometimes into the night, trying to prove he's a better businessman than his father was."

Chris tossed his empty water bottle in the sink. The thud made her jump. "Everyone is a suspect. Don't you forget it."

NINETEEN

After Scarlett told Chris the names of everyone she could think of with knowledge of her work, they ate juicy hamburgers and potato salad capped off with the homemade cinnamon buns Billy's wife Marie had sent. Chris kept the conversation focused mostly on himself during dinner, as if sensing she needed an escape. She laughed as he entertained her with stories about riding in his father's police cruiser, playing on the precinct's flag football team, and his disastrous attempts to learn to play the bagpipes because women always swarmed the cops who played.

With the dishes finished, Chris grabbed her coat from a hook by the door. "Let's take a walk around the property before it gets dark. We won't go too far, and we'll keep the cabin in sight, but you need to be familiar with your surroundings in the event we need to flee on foot."

She shrugged into the jacket he held out, not surprised anymore by his sweet gestures.

Nothing surprised her anymore when it came to this man.

They stepped into the cool night. Shades of pink streamed from the final rays of sunlight and mingled with heavy clouds and a dark sky. She sucked in the crisp, cleansing air. A hawk glided overhead. "You have some beautiful property here."

"Thanks. It's only five acres, but I like it." He guided her onto a dirt path bordering the lush pine trees and bare oaks ringing the cabin. "It's probably not as nice as growing up in Henry Richardson's house though."

Scarlett snorted as she stepped around a pile of pinecones. "Don't let him hear you call his place a house. It's an estate. He'd love to refer to it as a castle and the grounds, his holdings, but even the great Henry Richardson would get laughed at for such nonsense."

"What was it like growing up at the *estate*?"

"Wouldn't really know." She stuffed her chilly hands into her pockets. "I only lived there for a short time with my mom. After she died, I lived at whatever school he sent me to, save for a few days around Christmas."

"Even during the summer?"

"According to Henry, 'One shouldn't miss the chance to prosper because the weather warms up,'" she said in gruff imitation. "There were no music lessons, failed or otherwise. I've never tossed a football around at a picnic or even been to a football game, but there were plenty of take-your-daughter-to-work days."

"What a dickhead. Did Henry have a stick up his ass all the time?"

"Put it this way, if you're a superhero, I was the princess locked in a tower."

"Sounds lonely."

"It was." Dried leaves crunched under their feet as they walked side by side. "I entered boarding school as a freshman in college. I was only twelve. Everyone else was eons older.

For years I was younger, smarter, and stranger than the other students, and usually one of few females." She refrained from telling Chris the other kids didn't talk to her because they were jealous. It sounded too much like bragging about being the smartest kid in school. "By the time I caught up in age to everyone else and the gender gap shrunk, I didn't know how to…" She kicked at the leaves with the toes of her sneakers. "Let's just say my Friday and Saturday nights weren't spent on dates."

He stopped and turned to her. "I'm sorry. I'll take you to a football game when this is over. Promise."

A flush crept up her cheeks at his thoughtfulness, and his pity. Her lack of independence—and a backbone—embarrassed her. She should have stood up for herself and said no to Henry's demands, at least when she'd turned eighteen, but she'd been programmed to do her duty. "Don't be sorry. Beth kept me in touch with the outside world. And she forces me to step out of my comfort zone by doing things like going dancing and trying tequila shots. And I have an outstanding education I'm finally getting to use to help others and my country."

Chris held out his left hand. "Then thank you for your service, ma'am."

Warm flesh enveloped hers in an awkward yet potent grip. "I, uh, thought you were a righty."

"I am." He held her gaze and squeezed.

White-hot heat flared up her arm. She'd experienced his steel touch many times: a handshake, his palm at the small of her back, his fingers tipping her chin. This was the first time she could recall him going out of his way to touch her with flesh and bone. She couldn't decide if man or machine made her hotter.

She studied a pinecone at her feet. A new subject and distance were in order. She was pleased she hadn't rambled, not even once since they'd arrived here. Time to quit while she was ahead and get him to do some sharing before she begged him to touch other places on her body—her naked body—this time with both hands. She turned from him and headed back toward the cabin. "You make a mean breakfast and even better burgers. Where did you learn to cook?"

"My dad. He wanted me to always have a warm meal when he was on the late shift. On the nights I didn't have a lot of homework, I'd make a big pot of spaghetti and meatballs or sometimes chili and bring it down to the station for him and the guys. I couldn't wait to turn eighteen and join the force and officially become part of the family."

"Where was your mom?"

He kicked a rock. "With whatever boyfriend she was screwing at the time. She couldn't handle motherhood. Even though I was only four, I remember her saying those exact words to my father the night before she left."

"I'm sorry. My dad took off when I was a few months old. I know how rough it must have been on you."

"It was at first, but my dad was awesome. He was all I needed."

"Did he…? I mean, your tattoo…?" She reached around to his back and brushed her fingertips over the spot he habitually rubbed when agitated. "You mentioned he died. Was it in the 9/11 attacks?"

The sadness in his eyes matched the melancholy in his voice. "He rescued two groups of people. When he ran back in for a third, the second tower collapsed. His body was found about a month later. At least we were able to have a proper funeral."

Oh, Chris.

She wasn't sure if she should continue with her questions, but she needed to know about the boy inside the man. "Is he the reason you decided to go to the Naval Academy? To fight back?"

He yanked off a brown leaf clinging to a low branch and crumpled it in his palm. "I wanted to be a cop like my dad, but in the space of a few hours, I vowed to single-handedly eliminate every terrorist on the planet. My plan was to enlist as soon as I graduated high school." His voice grew thicker as he continued his story. "It was my grandfather, his father, a crusty old Navy veteran who convinced me to go to college and become an officer."

"Did you live with your grandfather after your dad died?"

"Not right away." Bitterness laced his voice. "I was sent to live with my mom. After a few months of having me around, she took off for Mexico to marry her boyfriend and left me a plane ticket to Gramp's house."

Wetness pooled in her eyes. She didn't know what to say. A trite "I'm sorry" couldn't convey the heartache she felt for the boy who'd lost his father and had twice been abandoned by his mother. "Do you know when you get frustrated or uneasy, you touch your tattoo as if you're looking to your father for strength and guidance?"

"I don't do that." He reached across his chest with his steel and froze. A small gasp jumped from his lips as he dropped his hand. "Yeah. I guess I do. I didn't realize. Didn't know I needed to."

"Of course you need to." She stepped toward him, reached around his shoulder, and placed her hand over the ink beneath his shirt. "We all need someone."

He brushed her off and took a step back. "I don't need anyone. I'm made of steel, remember? I can take care of myself."

The sadness and anger he tried to hide with bravado pierced her as brutally as if he'd speared her with a branch. She knew the sorrow loneliness caused, but she'd always had

Beth. Always carried her mother in her heart and clung to the belief that someday she'd fall in love. Chris's confession about not needing anybody, like he'd given up all hope that somebody could care for him, killed her. Even sadder, she feared it might kill him someday.

For the first time since she was a kid, she acted without rational thought. Throwing her arms around his neck, she hugged him tight, tighter, until he pulled her against him and moaned into her hair.

"I take it back," he said into her ear, his breath ragged, as if he was resigning himself to something he didn't want to admit. "I do need someone. God help me. I need you, Scarlett."

TWENTY

Surprise stole all motor functions from Chris. He couldn't speak. Couldn't breathe. He only felt Scarlett's soft breasts pressed against his chest and the weight of his words hanging between them.

"I need you, Scarlett."

The confession had slipped as desire had overtaken him like oxygen to a flame. He should take it back. Needing her posed too much danger. A risk to them both, but he needed one more taste. He'd gone too long without a woman. Now the one who didn't look at him with fear and revulsion but awe clawed her fingers into his back as if she couldn't pull him close enough.

Bad idea. Let her go.

His body said, "fuck that," as he lashed his steel around her waist and flattened her against him. Her core collided with his cock. Smiling into her hair, he shifted his hips and left no doubt about where he planned to take her unexpected hug.

"Chris?"

The indecision clouding her voice pitted Red Dress Scarlett and Scientist Scarlett in a battle. He knew which woman he was laying his money on and would make damn sure she won. God knew how long they'd be alone in his cabin or when and if he'd see her again once this mess cleared up. But she was here now, in his arms, begging to be kissed. Cupping one cheek with his steel, the other with flesh, he lowered his mouth to hers. He brushed soft kisses against her warm lips, his tongue teasing, promising more.

Take it slow. Don't scare her.

"Chris."

This time, his name on her lips floated out like a plea instead of a question. Like a rogue commando hell-bent on a personal raid, he thrust through her cinnamon-laced lips and seized the opportunity to taste her again.

Sparks licked at his cock as her tongue darted out to meet his. A rough groan rumbled from his chest as she quickly retreated. Her tentative touch hit him like the clipped, one-word responses she'd offered him at headquarters. Thrilling because he savored any reaction from Scarlett, yet frustrating because he hungered for more.

Needed more.

Grasping a handful of her soft hair with his steel, he tugged her head back and launched an exploration of her delectable mouth. He teased, licked, and savored until her soft moans drowned out the wind whispering through the trees.

Her sensual surrender whizzed lightning bolts to the loaded torpedo pressed against her thigh. Grasping her hair tighter with his steel, he glided his other hand down her back.

Stop, his brain commanded as he reached her waist.

Too fast.

Again, he ignored reason and gathered up the round ass he'd only possessed in his dreams. As he pulled her flush against him, she scraped her teeth along his lower lip and gently bit down. He sucked in a breath, surprised, and thrilled by her boldness. "Fuck, you taste so good."

Her tongue tangled with his. "You too. So good. Oh my god. So, so good."

Like the words tumbling out of her mouth against his lips, her fingers rambled up his sides as if she wasn't sure where to touch first.

Blood racing, body buzzing, he plunged into his mission to claim his territory as her eager hands snuck under the hem of his T-shirt. With a frenzied touch, she skimmed his ribs. The dips and valleys of his abs. He shivered as she pressed her fingertips into the indents above his hip bones and he moaned her name. His heartbeat tripled in speed. It stopped short when her fingertips met in the middle and grazed the button of his jeans. Still, he didn't breathe, afraid a slight move would make the brazen woman disappear into herself.

Her fingernails raked his skin. The sweet pain ripped her name from his lips. Matching her animalistic fervor, he pushed her up against an oak nestled between two pines and pinned her to the rough bark.

Her eyes flew open.

Need as powerful as his own shimmered like the damp grass under the setting sun.

Cradling her head with his steel, he snaked his other hand inside her shirt and claimed her breast.

"You're full of surprises," he whispered in between wet kisses behind her earlobe. "No bra last night. Lace tonight." He pinched her nipple. A low moan rumbled in her throat. His need to be the lucky beast who satiated her hunger roared through him as he trailed his mouth to her neck and felt her soft, satisfied hum under his lips. The sounds and vibrations coming from her intensified to a husky plea as he rolled the hard nub under his palm. "What other surprises have you been hiding from me?"

***

Scarlett grabbed Chris's cheeks between her hands and gyrated her hips against his hard cock, seeking what she craved.

"That's the best surprise I've ever gotten, sweetheart," he groaned as he rocked with her.

The exquisite friction darted blistering sparks through her body, intense enough to start a forest fire.

He claimed her mouth and pulled her deep into a kiss, his lips consuming hers before she could take another breath. Grinding, pressing, they lost themselves in a moonlit carnal tango.

Panting, she yanked her lips from his and met his gaze, mesmerized by the dark pleasure blazing in his eyes. "More."

The hand in her hair shot down to cup her mound through her jeans. Trapping her between him and the oak, he answered her breathless plea with firm pressure. Closing her eyes, she dropped her head against the tree as she writhed against him like she'd die if he stopped touching her. She might because nothing on this earth should feel this good.

"Chris, please. I need...please." His cock pressing into her thigh grew harder than the cabin's stone chimney. She scraped her fingertips along his rigid length. Heat hotter than the sound of the sexy hiss sliding from his throat scorched her hand.

"I got you." He undid the snap on her jeans, yanked the zipper down, and kicked her feet apart. "Nice and wide, Scarlett."

She opened her legs to grant him access to anything and everything he wanted. Her wet heat met his fingers as he shoved his hand inside her lace and pushed apart her lips. She gasped as she sank her fingers into his muscled thighs. Like a sharpshooter, he zeroed in on the spot screaming for attention and plunged in.

"Oh god." Pleasure flooded her fast and hard. Wet heat dripped from between her legs like water from a damn about to burst while new, thrilling sensations spiraled up into her belly. She gripped his biceps and tried to close her knees against the sudden rush, but he braced her foot with his and blocked her retreat.

"Too much." Everything about him was too much, but God, she wanted more.

He growled loud enough to scare the wildlife. "Oh no, sweetheart. I'm the one pushing you out of your comfort zone now and I'm pushing hard. I need to feel you come, and you *will* scream my name."

The dirtiest words ever spoken to her instinctively pulled his name from her lips as she arched into his hand.

He pulled his fingers out of her sopping core and thrust them back in. "I said *scream.*"

The force lifted her to her toes. Her whimper cried on the wind as her breath caught. She'd never been touched like this before. Never so deeply. So demanding. Too much soared into too little as she bucked her hips against his and chased the kind of release she'd only heard about—no, dreamed about, from this man and this man only.

She pushed against his chest. "Chris, I don't…I can't…"

He rolled her nipple between his fingers. "Yes, you can. Shut off your brain and just feel."

Prickles of delicious pain danced under her skin. He moved his fingers inside her, and against her, in a masterful way that shut down her mind and left her libido in complete control. Rolling waves of pleasure, need, and many other powerful sensations she didn't know if science could define coursed through her in a torrent of wonder. But the need didn't abate. It only grew until the "more" she sought reduced her to a quivering beggar.

She burrowed her head into his neck. "Chris, please."

"Tell me what you want."

"I need to…"

He froze. "What, Scarlett? Tell me."

She arched against him. "Please don't stop."

"Say it." His hand controlling the sweet release she pleaded for gripped her from the inside out. "I need to hear the shy scientist beg me to make her come."

"For God's sake, just do it. Make me come. Now."

"Yes, ma'am." With a final twist of his fingers, he pulsed direct pressure to her clit and unleashed everything he'd built inside her. She bit into his neck as she rode out the waves and drowned in a tsunami of mind-numbing pleasure. As the molten crest burst into sharp crystals and pierced her body and soul with decadent, animalistic bliss, she finally screamed his name.

***

Chris felt the familiar high of a completed mission course through him. His target was at his mercy. His goal of learning what drove the writhing scientist in his arms to completely, unabashedly, come undone was complete.

He held Scarlett between him and the tree until her breathing slowed, his hand entrenched in her decadent bliss, not ready to break the connection and craving more.

Much more.

His cock pulsed a painful plea against his jeans. It would be easy to finish what they'd started. So easy, and not because she'd willingly given herself to him. He wanted her—no, he needed her more than he'd needed anything in his life.

"I need you, Scarlett."

The confession played on repeat in his head as if it needed to be recognized.

Understood.

He couldn't, wouldn't, say the words again. They were too raw. Too real. His driving desire to claim her as his safe harbor was too dangerous. Needing someone had always left him broken when they disappeared. He couldn't let himself need anyone again. He thought one kiss, one touch, would cure his terminal longing for Scarlett. He'd been wrong. He was at her mercy, and she held the power to destroy him.

If I don't destroy her first.

He closed his eyes and savored her for one more bitter-sweet moment before he yanked himself from the fairy tale forest and focused on the realistic dangers lurking beyond the trees.

And the dangers within me.

"I'm sorry; that shouldn't have happened." He made quick work of her zipper and button.

Long seconds passed as the blissful flush he'd put on her beautiful face drained.

"You're right. We need to keep things professional."

The steadiness of her voice surprised him. He'd expected her to break into a nervous ramble about boundaries, not agree wholeheartedly with his retreat. The easy resignation disappointed him more than he cared to admit.

She pointed to the cabin. "I have work to do."

He schooled his features to match her detached tone and stopped himself from rubbing his tattoo. Looking to his father's memory for strength would show weakness. He couldn't afford to be weak again when it came to Scarlett. "Yes. Work. It's the reason you're here, to save VIPER."

Her puffy lips opened in a wide circle. She nodded her agreement as she hurried toward the cabin. He almost claimed her lips to relight the blaze he'd kicked sand on. Instead, he stayed on course.

Pushing her away was smart.

It also sucked balls.

TWENTY-ONE

Once Scarlett reached the safety of the cabin, Chris braced his hands on his knees and pulled in gulps of air. A twig snapped behind him. He wheeled around, ready to fight. A young buck emerged from the trees. Chris exhaled a long sigh of relief. What if the creature had been the two-legged, gun-carrying sort? He cursed himself inside and out, and tacked on more because he deserved it. His actions were leading them down a selfish path fraught with emotional land mines and very real danger.

"Yeah, I know I'm an asshole. Wait until a cute doe comes around and see how you act."

Dammit, he was a Navy SEAL. He prided himself on his control. Apparently, all it took was one hug from Scarlett, and he regressed to the weak teenager he'd been during Plebe Summer at the Academy. What if he'd executed his plan to get her naked and lose himself inside of her? Would one round of sex be enough? Not a chance. He needed to cease his desired course of action before she got hurt. Any harm to one hair on her beautiful head, from the enemy or from him, was unacceptable.

But Christ, I was right.

He stomped over to the chopping block and placed a thick log in the center.

There is a sultry woman buried beneath the genius.

He picked up the ax. He shifted one hand to the base, the other to the neck, and studied the head.

Why do I have to be obsessed with meeting all the sides of Scarlett?

With straight arms, he swung the ax into the air and rose on his toes. A primordial grunt tore from his lungs as the ax carved through the night on his downswing. The solid log cracked in two with a sharp *thwack*. Each piece fell to the ground on either side of the block.

He threw the ax into the pine trees and crouched to pick up the sections of the halved log. With his body burning from exertion, he stayed in that position until his legs cramped. Embracing the discomfort was easier than addressing the raw ache in his heart. Scarlett would figure out what to do with the dormant sides of herself coming to life. Another man would have the pleasure of discovering the enticing, confident woman gradually emerging.

He wanted to be that man.

Raising his flesh-and-blood hand to his nose, he inhaled. God, he could still smell her. He yearned to barge into the cabin, strip her naked and revisit the spot—this time with his mouth—that he'd learned made her scream. To discover what made her moan softly in pleasure and what made her beg. To thrust his cock inside her and push her so far out of her comfort zone she'd never want to go back. And in between exploring every inch of her body with his lips and hands, he wanted to know every thought inside her beautiful, brilliant head.

He wanted to know it all.

Wanted her to be his home, but he wouldn't, couldn't set himself up for more disappointment.

After Natalie, he'd sworn he wouldn't fall in love again. He was a mercenary. He could come home from his next mission even more fucked up than he already was. Or he might not come home at all. Scarlett deserved a whole man, not a dangerous, damaged, or dead one.

He stood and picked up the ax again. His phone rang in his pocket as he prepared to swing. He threw down the ax and answered.

Nic chuckled on the other end. "Hello to you too, *mi hermano.*"

Chris ignored the insult Nic tacked on at the end of his greeting in Spanish. "Fucking talk, wiseass."

"I did some digging into Scarlett's ex and her stepfather. Richardson's lost some big government contracts lately, and the company's dipping in the stock market. Nothing drastic, but enough for Richardson to be looking for the next big idea to present to his stockholders. And this James Samuels guy seems like his lackey. Every article he's quoted in touts Richardson's virtues like he's a king or something. He seems like a wimpy dickhead."

A dickhead who's had his hands on Scarlett.

"Keep digging. They both stand to gain from our genius."

His genius.

"I'm on it. What's your take on King Richardson and his jester being connected to the hacking?"

"Scarlett doesn't want to think there's a connection, but I don't believe in coincidences."

"Neither do I, brother. Hold tight and be safe."

Chris hit the end button and shoved the phone back in his pocket. Tiny beads of rainwater dotted his sleeve. He yanked his shirt over his head, tossed it aside, and picked up the ax again.

I swear if James is behind this…

He swung the blade high into the air, picturing the piece of wood on the block as James's head.

***

Thwack!

Scarlett counted fifteen seconds.

Thwack!

Another twenty ticked off in her head.

Thwack!

She abandoned her laptop and rose from the table. Counting the time in between Chris's ax hitting wood wasn't tricking her brain into focusing. It was no use. She couldn't concentrate. Not with the taste of him fresh on her lips or his words ringing in her ears. Especially not with the knowledge he was outside her window chopping wood in the moonlight like Mr. November from a hunky lumberjack calendar.

She picked up the burner phone on the coffee table and punched in Beth's number.

"Scarlett. Are you okay? Is Chris taking good care of you?"

The heat in her body cranked up a few notches.

Oh, is he taking care of me.

When she hugged him outside, she hadn't meant to offer anything more than comfort. It certainly hadn't meant to evolve into a kiss. Or a heart-stopping orgasm. Who knew muscle contractions could feel so…

Even her genius mind couldn't find the right words.

"Scarlett, are you there?"

"Yeah. Sorry." She touched her fingers to her lips.

"What's wrong, sweetie?"

She fiddled with the hem of her sweatshirt. "I hugged Chris and he kissed me."

Beth let out a shriek. "Tell me everything."

She gave Beth a play-by-play of their encounter, leaving out the part about her orgasm against the tree. "And then he threw me away like a cracked test tube and told me to get back to work."

"Aw, honey, I'm gathering you think he only needs you for your brain."

"Doesn't he? Only difference is, he admitted it right off the bat instead of pretending to care for me."

"Listen, girl, I'm sure the rest of McSteely is as hard as his sexy arm. While you guys are holed up for whatever reasons you can't share, why not explore the blatant chemistry between the two of you? Think of it as a sexual attraction beta test."

An ache for more than Chris's hand between her thighs sprang to life. She clamped her legs to squash it. "Thanks, Dr. Love; now how about some rational advice?"

Beth groaned. "I knew you were going to say that."

"What else would I say? I'm not here to experiment with my sexual urges."

Beth snorted. "I beg to differ, but I'm your bestie, so I'll tell you the way it is. Chris probably does need your brain to figure out whatever is going on with VIPER, but he has other types of needs and so do you."

Man, do I ever.

Chris awoke desires she hadn't known needed satiating. The words of a psychology professor she knew danced on the edge of her psyche. How had she explained attraction?

"It's the instance our bodies comprehend what we want before our minds do."

"Now that makes sense," she muttered.

"Hallelujah." Beth sang the word two more times. "Of course what I'm saying makes sense. Chris wants you, and you want him. It's the truth, so stop fighting it."

After they hung up, Scarlett headed to the bedroom to get ready for bed. As she changed into yoga pants and a tank top, she examined the evidence she'd just gathered.

Reason had been the catalyst for her attraction to James. He'd been a safe and logical choice. Safety and logic had nothing to do with her attraction to Chris. She hadn't said, "Oh, Commander Daviani is handsome. Maybe I should let him kiss me." Every sizzling nerve ending in her body had initiated that conversation. There hadn't been any chemistry with James. It wasn't her fault neither one of them had been satisfied. Now she finally understood what had been missing.

Her head whipped to the *thwack* of Chris's ax striking wood again. She peeked out the window and gasped.

He stood shirtless under the rising moon's glow. Beads of sweat flew from his skin as solid muscle and steel crashed the ax into the log. When he raised the ax above his head to strike again, he was the god she'd thought him to be this morning when he'd stood in the doorway in nothing but a towel.

She looked away, the reasons why she should ignore the attraction between her and Chris listing in her mind like proofs on a whiteboard.

We're working together to catch a traitor.

He only needs me for my brain.

We're in the middle of a crisis, for God's sake.

She peeked out the window, allowing herself one more glimpse of the magnificent creature before she shut down her laptop and went to bed.

And in the morning, Chris will be a normal guy, and these distracting feelings will be gone.

He stood in the small clearing, the ax at his side and his eyes fixed on the grass. The clouds shifted, creating a chasm for the moonlight to beam down on his ripped body like a spotlight. Her eyes fixed on the viper inked on his chest. With every inhale and exhale, the snake seemed to writhe like a wild animal trying to claw its way to freedom. As he wielded the ax above his head and plunged it into the wood, he granted the snake the release it craved.

She jumped away from the window and leaned against the wall. Shaking, she slid to the floor.

The first time she'd met Chris, she'd closed her eyes and reasoned he'd be just another guy when she looked at him again. Her rationalization was as flawed then as it was now.

TWENTY-TWO

A scream tore Scarlett from sleep. She jerked upright in bed.

Chris?

Her hand crept to the side where he'd slept last night and met cold empty sheets. Holding her breath, she listened.

Silence.

Had she imagined the shriek that had woken her? Other than the melodic chirp of the birds saying good morning to the rising sun, it was quiet.

Peaceful.

A fear-laced moan interrupted the daybreak chorus. "Please, don't leave. Please."

She tossed back the covers and yanked the bedroom door open. Chris lay on the couch clad in the jeans and T-shirt he'd worn last night. His head thrashed from side to side as he cradled his steel arm across his belly like it was broken. A light sheen of sweat covered his face as it contorted in pain.

In three strides, she crossed the room. She stood in front of him, careful not to get too close. She knew enough about PTSD-triggered nightmares and about Chris's last mission to surmise that his mind had transported him back to a crumbling building, his arm pinned by debris, his team dead around him. If she tried to wake him, his traumatized brain could mistake her for the enemy. A cold shiver zipped down her spine. She was in danger, not from the traitor they chased but from the man she trusted most in this world.

"Chris. You're having a nightmare. Open your eyes." She yelled his name again, loud and firm from what she hoped was outside of his striking distance.

An anguished groan grumbled from deep within him. It pierced her soul to the marrow.

Please, God. Help him.

She took two steps closer and yelled louder. "Chris. Wake up."

His steel arm jerked against his body as if trying to reach out.

Visions of him laying helpless in the sand with crushed bones and severed nerves flashed before her eyes. Nausea gushed into her throat.

He bolted upright and screamed, his arm cradled tighter across his stomach, his eyes popping wide open. Relief flooded her for a moment until she realized the color wasn't returning to his face. He peered through her with cloudy, unfocused eyes. He was still there, experiencing the anguish and horror of being left for dead.

Desperation oozed from his words. "Come back. Help me."

Tears blurred her vision as she closed the distance between them, her heart shattering for the wounded warrior, damaged in body and mind. Crouching in front of him, she balanced on the balls of her feet.

"Chris, you're having a flashback." She shook his leg. "You're safe. Please come back to me."

His steel arm shot out. She rocked onto her heels to

avoid the blow but wasn't fast enough. Her ass hit the ground, her bare bicep stinging where he'd grazed her flesh with his knuckles.

"No, don't leave me again." He reached out toward her.

"I'm not leaving." She touched her fingertips to his. "I'm right here."

Her words must have flipped a switch in his brain because his gaze focused on her. A breath later, confusion replaced the fear in his eyes.

"Natalie?"

Chris buried his face in his hands. Although he could still feel the heat from the burning timbers raining down on him and his team in the godforsaken hovel in the Middle East, his body felt as cold as last night's rain. The faces of his buddies, charred from the fire, rotated in front of him like a sick kaleidoscope of death. As they faded into the smoky haze, Natalie's face blurred in his vision. He saw the revulsion in her eyes as she measured his deficient body. Heard her final words croak from her twisted lips before she left him alone and scared in a hospital bed without an arm.

Without hope.

Like a wild animal, he shook off Natalie's memory until her face shredded into the air. A comforting voice begging him to come back filtered through his ears. His vision cleared. Scarlett scooted toward him on the floor.

"Chris? Are you with me?"

He yanked her against him and covered her mouth with his, desperate to know the cruel mind tricks were over. Flesh met flesh. She was real. She was here.

She pushed against his chest. "Chris, I'm not—"

He ignored her objection and dove in like she was the

oxygen he needed to breathe. She was the air, the light, the hope he needed to *live* because nothing had ever made him feel whole again after a nightmare except waking up and smelling her honeysuckle scent.

Hearing her soothing voice.

Feeling her heart beat wild and strong against his.

"Chris." She shoved against him.

He held on tighter, wanting—no needing her as his anchor while the brimstone clouding his mind dissipated speck by fiery speck with each addicting taste of her mouth.

"Chris, stop."

With one last nip of her sweet lips, he collapsed against the couch and pulled his sweat-soaked T-shirt away from his skin.

She sat on her heels and rubbed her bicep. "Listen to me. I'm not Nat—"

His gaze followed her hand to a fresh bruise on her arm. *No. Please don't let me have hurt—*

Falling to his knees in front of her, he swatted her hand away. His stomach lurched as he examined the red spots about the size of his knuckles on her skin.

"Fuck." Last night, he'd done the right thing and had slept on the couch when all he'd wanted to do was crawl into bed and hold her in his arms. But dammit, he'd managed to hurt her from a room away.

His mind scrambled to remember what had happened while he'd slept. The familiar images came back in shocking clarity. His SEAL team slipping by his shattered body as their souls drifted into pain-free oblivion. His mother walking out the door again and again. His father, crushed under the rubble of the World Trade Center. And the final slide, always the last image he saw before he woke, the disappointment and disgust on Natalie's face as she left his hospital room.

Rage pushed up his throat. He swallowed the bitter taste.

"Dammit, Scarlett. How could you be so stupid?" He stood up and pointed to his head. "You know I'm fucked up, and you know better than to go near someone having a flashback."

She rubbed the bruise on her arm. "I'm fine. You barely hit me before I jumped away."

He paced like a trapped animal. "You should have stayed clear of me. I'm dangerous. I could have seriously hurt you." He held out his arm. "Or worse."

She rose from the floor. "I knew the risks of approaching you, but you were suffering."

"Didn't you hear me?" He pointed to the mark he'd left on her arm. "Stay away from me."

She took a step closer. "You didn't mean to hit me. It's not your fault."

He fled to the kitchen, afraid to see what she thought of him reflected in her eyes. As if the legs he'd been lucky enough to come home with couldn't bear the weight of his past anymore, he sank into a chair. "I'm tired of being told it's not my fault. It's my mind. My body. It's. My. Fault."

"No, it's not." She dropped to her knees in front of him.

He searched her face. Nothing but concern shone in her watery emerald eyes. How could she not despise him? He'd struck her. It *was* his fault. He'd signed on willingly for this existence, knowing full well the horrific shit he'd experience and the toll it would take. He'd sacrificed his sanity, his body, and almost his life. He wasn't going to sacrifice Scarlett's well-being too.

He pointed to the bedroom. "Go before I hurt you again."

She wrapped her hands around his knees. "I'm not going anywhere. I've lived most of my life being told what to do, and I'm tired of it."

The chair scraped the floor as he brushed off her touch

and rose. She didn't need to feel how bad his legs trembled from the nightmare. "For the last time, Scarlett. If you don't leave this room right now, I swear I will—"

She stood and rose on her toes to meet him nearly eye to eye. "You'll what?"

A shrill ring from the living room cut off his answer. He stalked to the coffee table. Scarlett followed behind him as he picked up the phone. "Yeah?"

An unnerving silence blanketed the cabin while he listened. "Hold on. I'm putting you on speaker."

Beth's voice filled the room. "Can you guys hear me?"

Scarlett perched on the edge of the couch. "Yes. What's up?"

"Something happened at your class this morning."

Chris's gaze snapped to Scarlett. "What class?"

"The coding course for beginners I teach at Georgetown."

"You teach a class on Saturday mornings?"

"It's a continuing education program for adults."

Chris shook his head. *Is there anything this woman can't do?* "Tell me what happened this morning, Beth."

"A hottie by the name of Ryan Bradley, as in, the governor's nephew, showed up."

Scarlett covered her lips with her fingers. "Oh no. I forgot I was supposed to meet him for coffee before class."

Chris's eyebrows shot up as high as his voice. "You had a *date* this morning?"

"Yes. Ryan and I were going to discuss the new federal cybersecurity mandate."

Beth let out a little whoop. "Way to go, girl. He sounds perfect for you."

Yeah, fucking perfect.

"Did I mention he's not only hot, but really nice too?" Beth sighed. "Anyway, Ryan said he didn't think Scarlett was the type to stand him up, so he came to her classroom to make sure she was okay."

Chris sat on the couch next to Scarlett. "What did you tell him?"

"I told him Scarlett was taking a much-needed vacation. When he asked me when she'd be back, I said I wasn't sure. Then he said his uncle was disappointed to hear about her resignation from VIPER."

Scarlett's chin jerked up. "What?"

"Yeah." Beth snorted. "Can you believe that? I set him straight on the resignation crap."

Chris leaned close to the phone. "What was his reaction?"

"He was surprised. Seems uncle and nephew think very highly of Scarlett. By the way, Ryan left his number with me. He wants her to call him as soon as she can."

Like hell she will. "Did you tell him anything else?"

"Nope, but there's more. After Ryan left, two men dressed all in black and as menacing as the goon in Scarlett's townhome walked in. When the substitute asked if he could help them, they said they were looking for Dr. Kerrigan."

Chris sat back into the cushions and ran his steel over his hair. "Sounds like hired hands. Ex-military, I'd bet."

"Are you sure you guys are safe?"

"Yes." He clenched his steel fist as he ended the call.

Scarlett rose and paced in front of the hearth. "What's going on? Thompson said Governor Bradley called for my termination. But if Bradley thought I resigned—"

She stopped in front of the fire and placed both hands over her heart. "No. It can't be true. Thompson said he believed in me. We were going to help people. Please tell me he hasn't betrayed VIPER."

Chris jumped in front of her. His vow to stay away crumbled as he took both of her hands in his and held them tight.

"I wish I could say he didn't, but Beth's information kicks up our suspicions a notch."

"There has to be a reason why he lied."

"I want to know why he lied too, but we have a whole agency of suspects to eliminate before we pin this on him."

But if we do, he's a dead man.

Curses flew out of Scarlett's mouth, one after the other. When she ran out of obscenities, she yanked her fingers out of Chris's grip and stepped back. Inhaling, she drew her shoulders up to her ears. A long exhale streamed from her lips as she rolled her shoulders down, slow and deliberate. When she looked at him, the panic was gone.

"Here's what we're going to do," she said. "You're going to make us a pot of coffee. I'm going to change. Then we're going to determine conclusively if Thompson betrayed his country."

He couldn't fathom how she planned to do that, and he didn't care. He'd thought Scientist Scarlett in her tailored suits was sexy. Red Dress Scarlett had stolen his breath, but this woman pacing before him was a perfect mixture of the two. Maybe she could handle him and his dark demons.

"Tell me, Dr. Kerrigan, are you this bossy with your students?" His gaze raked her body and landed on the top of her breasts peeking out of her skimpy tank top. "Because if you are, I might have to use my GI Bill to register for your class. Who knows? I might learn a thing or two."

She glared at him. "Not the time to tease me, Chris."

"Agreed." No more teasing. And no more being a coward. He took a deep breath and buried his fears deep down in the pile of crap life had thrown at him as he formulated a plan.

Protect Scarlett while she saved VIPER.

Get the girl without hurting her.

Easy, right? He was a superhero, after all. It was time he started acting like one.

TWENTY-THREE

"**H**e called me Natalie." Every detail from Chris's file was stored in her memory. She knew damn well Natalie was the ex–Mrs. Daviani.

God, what was wrong with her? Devising a plan to expose Thompson as the insider threat should be the only thing on her mind, but when she'd walked into the bedroom, an image of Chris tangled in the sheets with his ex-wife had sent every logical thought in her head flying out the window.

Groaning, she changed her clothes and tugged on her sneakers. She'd tried to tell Chris she wasn't Natalie, even got half the words out, but her attempt had been as useless as forgetting the hungry way he'd scrutinized her by the fire-place moments ago.

Despite his obvious desire, his harsh "stay away from me" rant had ripped her raw. She knew people with PTSD often lashed out at those closest to them. Since she was the only one around, it made sense she'd bear the brunt of Chris's jumbled emotions.

Her fingers froze on the laces of her sneakers. How jumbled had his emotions been? Had Natalie been in his nightmare? Was that why he'd said her name? Had he even known who he'd been hauling against him and kissing the ever-loving sense out of?

Jealousy swirled in her belly. This was different from the envy she'd experienced listening to Beth talk about the boy she'd kissed at the eighth-grade dance or her longing for the love of a family.

I have no reason to be jealous. He's not mine. Not. Mine.

She stalked into the bathroom and ran a brush through tangles born from a crazy night and an even crazier morning. Since she couldn't neatly categorize how she felt about the fantastical events, she focused on facts.

Fact number one? Chris wasn't hers.

Fact number two? Only the straightening iron she'd left at home would tame the wild mess on her head.

Brushing the hair from her eyes, she followed the smell of coffee into the main room. She looked to the left and found Chris standing in front of the fireplace staring into the flames.

He turned, a mug clutched in his steel, and nodded to another on the table in front of the couch.

"Thank you." She crossed the room and sat.

He bent at the waist in a mock bow. "When a woman orders me to make her coffee, I obey."

"I didn't order you."

"You did. And it was hot."

Heat from his audacious comment spread through her body and down to where his fingers had made her scream his name yesterday. She opened her mouth to ask if he'd thought he'd been kissing her or Natalie, but quickly shut it. What was she going to say? *Are you still in love with your ex-wife?* That might insinuate she was in love with him.

No, no, no. I'm not in love with Chris.

She raised the mug to her lips. Maybe the steam would provide a plausible reason for the flush in her cheeks.

"My biometric source got back to me a few minutes ago. He confirmed a prototype of the retinal scanner I described was purchased on the black market by an American entity in the last two weeks. He sent specs of what the device looks like. The infrared laser beam is only half a millimeter wide."

He put his mug down on the coffee table. "Whatever Thompson used to conceal the device, if, in fact, he's the insider threat, would have had to have a hole in it large enough for the laser to beam through."

"Yes. All we need to do is look through the footage, examine his outfit for pins or something to hide the device, and confirm a laser shot out of it."

He sat on the arm of the couch. "You're telling me you can discover what must be a thin beam of light on security footage from yards away? Is it even detectable to the human eye?"

"My source says it isn't."

"How the hell are you going to find a minuscule hole and an invisible laser in a grainy video feed?"

She sipped her coffee and swallowed. "I'll hack into the FBI's network and borrow their enhanced imaging software."

"You must have friends at the agency. Can't you ask someone to help you?"

She shrugged. "I could, but that's no fun?"

His lips crept into a smile. "You're a cyber badass, you know that?"

She tipped her mug in salute. Compliments about her work, she knew how to take. Badass ranked the best one she'd ever heard. "Thank you. And yes, I know."

With a nudge of his nose, he pushed her untamed hair from her face.. A shiver more satisfying than his compliment tingled down her spine as his warm breath skimmed her cheek.

"I thought you were adorable when you turned a dozen shades of red after I said you were 'hot. But the pride in your eyes when I said you were badass? That was sexier than your morning-after-an-orgasm-by-the-tree hair. Now get to work, professor. We have a traitor to catch."

After a quick cold shower, Chris marched out of the bedroom with a black duffel bag slung over his shoulder. Scarlett stared at him over her laptop screen, a satisfied smile lighting up her beautiful face.

"Find something?" he asked.

She hit a few more keys on her computer. "No. The hacker found us again."

"What?" The bag slid from his fingers. He bounded to her side. "Why are you smiling? This can't be a good thing."

"Actually, it is." She turned back to her computer. "After I initiated the retinal scan search, I accessed VIPER's network. I've been monitoring it since we got here, but this time I found evidence of a second breach."

"And?" He didn't bother asking how she'd hacked into the DOD network undetected. Somewhere over the last couple of days, his trust in her abilities and her loyalty had grown exponentially.

She cocked her head at the screen. "Nobody was compromised, but someone did get in to do some exploring, maybe to plan another attack like the one on the governor. I was able to find enough clues to program a trap."

"Nice job, but why did he—"

She pointed a finger at him. "Or she. Our hacker could be a woman."

He held up his hands in mock surrender. "Excuse me. I forgot you're not the only female cyber badass on the planet."

She smiled and raised her chin. "Not the only, just the best."

And sexy.

And smart.

And determined.

A lethal combination. "Why did he—or she leave a clue the second time but not the first?"

"The clue was there after the first breach. I would have eventually found it, but I didn't get to do a thorough search before Thompson fired me, and frankly, my analysts or anyone else back at headquarters aren't good enough to discover it."

His cock twitched at her confident statement. "Is that right?"

She smirked. "Not bragging. It's a fact."

Damn, if her smile didn't make him harder. "What did you find out?"

"Based on some digging I did last night and now this, I'm certain both breaches came from the same source. We need to let the team know the hacker returned."

"I'll make the call while you get your coat. Meet me outside."

"Outside?" She tapped the screen. "I have work to do right here."

"It can wait." He picked up the black duffel bag he'd dropped on the floor and peered out the tall windows next to the fireplace. His instincts were telling him they wouldn't be safe for much longer. "You may be a cyber badass, but your laptop isn't going to provide protection when men in black come gunning for you again. We have work to do. Now."

TWENTY-FOUR

Scarlett stood in the damp grass of the clearing. Clean, fresh air floated on the crisp wind. "You're going to teach me to shoot? But you said we were safe here."

He dropped his bag on the ground. "And you thought your network was safe, but it wasn't. I'd feel better knowing you know how to shoot a gun should the need arise."

He squatted and pulled out the black pistol she'd spotted on the nightstand the morning they'd arrived. "This is a 9mm semiautomatic." He ran his fingers over the barrel of the black weapon like it was a cherished childhood teddy bear. "It's the gun my dad taught me to shoot with when I was ten. Besides my arm, this bad boy is my favorite weapon in the world."

"It's a beauty. I mean, I guess, as far as guns go. What other toys do you have in there?"

He zipped up the bag. "No need to worry about it because you're not touching any of them. Only the 9mm."

"Yes, Commander." She touched her fingers to her head in a mock salute. Since he didn't ask if she knew how to handle a gun, she didn't offer any details. Authority with a good dose of cockiness looked damn sexy on him. Who was she to ruin his moment?

"That's your target." He pointed to the narrow run-down shed about fifteen yards away, on the edge of the tree line. "Aim for the black stain in the middle of the door."

A group of squirrels raced out from underneath. "You want me to shoot your shed?"

"I'm planning on tearing it down at some point. It leaks. Besides, you'll be lucky if you even hit it on the first lesson."

She shrugged and smiled. "Who knows. I might surprise you."

Chris stared at her with eyes the color of the dark clouds above. "Everything about you is a surprise. Now pay attention. First, we start with gun safety."

When he finished his lecture, his gaze traveled from her eyes to her toes. "Now let's talk about your stance. Feet shoulder width apart. Weight slightly forward on the balls of your feet."

She ignored the tingling his perusal triggered between her thighs and adjusted her body into the position. "Like this?"

He eyed her up and down again as he tucked his pistol into the back of his jeans. Stepping behind her, he gripped her shoulders and angled them a hair more toward the target. A pleasant tremor spiraled down her spine when his thighs brushed her backside. "Your stance is your shooting platform. It must be solid."

He kicked her feet wider apart like he had last night and molded his thighs to hers. "Right, solid. Got it."

My stance isn't the only thing solid around here.

"You must be stable and accurate."

"Stable and accurate."

Nothing's stable when he's this close.

He placed a steadying hand on her hip. "Are you nervous about shooting a gun?"

She shook her head.

"Then why do you keep repeating what I say?"

"I'm fine. What's next?"

He pulled the 9mm out of the back of his jeans. "Hold the gun as firmly as if you're shaking someone's hand, but no firmer."

He positioned the weapon in her grip. "Your weak hand supports the strong one. You need to completely encircle the gun so you can be in control of the recoil."

The recoil of the gun didn't scare her. The recoil of the lustful feelings she couldn't control did.

He held her hands in position. "Now form a straight line with the barrel of the weapon and your forearm."

She raised her arms and pointed the pistol at the shed.

"Good. Now, here's how you aim." He spread his legs on either side of hers and rested his calloused fingers on the curve of her waist. His steel settled over her grip as he molded the top of her body to his back.

Her sweatshirt and jacket hiked up as she fully straightened her arms. The ridged nail of his thumb tickled her flesh. She stared at their hands, mesmerized by the contrast of her soft skin encased between his lethal steel and the deadly metal of his gun.

Weak and strong.

Man and machine.

The two of them working together to achieve a common goal.

Protecting ourselves. Finding the enemy. Finding each other?

She heard him talk about rear and front sight and lining things up, but she wasn't listening.

Dropping his head, he grazed her ear with his lips. "Any questions before you shoot?"

She didn't answer, fearful if she breathed, if she felt Chris's arousal at her back for one more second or one more hot breath on her skin, she would explode like a bullet leaving the chamber.

She shrugged out of his embrace and stepped to the side. "Enough."

"What's wrong?" He raked his hand over his head with his steel. "Am I going too fast?"

Too fast? Too slow? She didn't know anymore, only knew the tension building within her needed to be released somehow, someway.

"I got this." She raised the gun with her right hand, flicked off the safety and cocked it with her left, and spun toward the target.

TWENTY-FIVE

Bull's-eye! Bull's-eye! Bull's-eye!

Chris gaped at the stain on his shed, now riddled with bullet holes. From his gun. Shot by Scarlett. All dead center.

She cocked her head at him, her wild hair blowing in the wind, an even wilder grin on her face as she fired off another three rounds. Wood splintered as her precise shots swallowed the stain.

"I was right. This gun is a beauty." She lowered the weapon to her side.

A smoking-hot beauty.

An image of Scarlett reaching into one of those dark suits she wore to work every day and whipping out a gun like a sexy secret agent had his cock twitching like her trigger finger.

She engaged the safety before dropping the empty weapon in the duffel bag and turned to the cabin. Without breaking her stride, she glanced at him over her shoulder. "I was on the pistol team in college. In case you were wondering."

It took Chris a full minute to recover from the hot-as-hell show she'd just staged. She'd played him, purposely letting him rattle on like a fool. "Get back here, Scarlett. We're not done."

She stopped at the steps to the porch and pointed over her shoulder to the shed. "I think we are. I can't get any more accurate than that."

"Your shooting isn't what I'm talking about, you little tease, and you know it."

She whirled around on her heel, almost slipping on the wet grass. Her eyes grew wide as she fought for balance. "A tease?"

He smiled, pleased to see her control snap along with the twigs under her feet. "Yes, Scarlett. Your little deception was a tease."

"If anyone's a tease, it's you. You kissed me. Twice. Then retreated. You've been asking about the woman inside since the day we met. Well, here I am." She stretched her arms out like an offering. "Just when I've found the courage to embrace everything you've been pulling out of me, you push me away."

He picked up the duffel, the rational part of his brain reminding him they needed to take this skirmish inside where it was secure. "You pushed me away this morning."

She backed up the stairs. "You thought you were kissing your ex-wife."

The bag slipped from his fingers. "What?"

"You said her name right before you kissed me."

Shame hit him square in the heart. Hurting Scarlett with his body was unforgivable. Knowing he'd hurt her with words flayed his wounds open and lashed him with a whip. Not even an hour ago, he'd vowed to protect and get the girl like a superhero. Who was he kidding? He'd done a piss-poor job of protecting Scarlett from himself, and in the end, the superhero never got the girl anyway.

He clasped the sides of his head and tried to crush the traumatic memories imprisoning his mind. "Natalie's in my dreams. Every. Single. Night."

Each word stabbed his brain with razor-edge clarity. He shook his skull, but the painful images didn't relent. "I'm trapped in a perpetual nightmare, and she's one of the stars of the show."

He held Scarlett's gaze as he prowled across the clearing. "Her face is always the last thing I see before I wake up, but this morning, it was your voice calling me back. I honestly don't remember saying her name. I do all sorts of horrible shit I don't want to remember when I revisit hell in my sleep, but you know what, Scarlett?"

The wind kicked up and blew scattered leaves around her legs. She didn't answer him. She just stared in wide-eyed mystification as if she were part of his dreams too.

He took the three porch steps at once and landed close enough to feel her breath on his face. She wasn't a dream, and he wouldn't make her another victim of his nightmares. "I'm not so fucked up that I didn't know I was kissing you."

"You're not fucked up." Her voice carried over the wind and the rustle of leaves. "You're the most honorable, smartest, toughest man I've ever met and not because of your enhancements."

He slammed his steel fist down on the railing. Wood splintered under the force of the blow. "This enhancement hurt you. I *hurt* you, thanks to all the guilt and regret and anger I carry inside me. Next time, I could hurt you as bad as I hurt Natalie. I threw her across the room when she tried to wake me from a nightmare."

He waited for his shameful words to register, but Scarlett didn't even bat an eyelash.

"You don't get it." He trapped her against the door and tapped his finger on her head. "I knocked her out so hard she got a brain injury, and that was before I had a steel arm. Do you want a concussion too? Because harm is about all I have to offer."

She gripped his wrist. "That's not all you have to—"

He shrugged off her touch, but the sympathy in her voice and the pity on her face clung to him like smoke. "I don't need or want you to feel sorry for me, but you need to understand this. I'm broken and not worthy."

Like a bomb, the sympathy on her face transformed into determination.

"Listen to me, *Commander*." She flattened her palms against his chest and pushed. "You're good at giving advice and barking orders, but you suck at taking them. You've been forcing me to realize that there's more to me than just a big brain. Well, it's time for you to get your head out of your ass and realize what I *see* inside of you."

He stared at the hellion before him. Something stirred in his gut he couldn't define, but it felt right. "Did you tell me to get my head out of my ass?"

"Yeah. I learned that phrase from you, so I suggest you start taking your own advice and smarten up." She gripped his chin. "I don't judge you for your pain or how it dictates your actions. You do."

Yeah, he did. And now he judged himself for his vulnerability. For confessing his darkest sin to the one person whose opinion he cared about. He glanced at her bicep, where the proof of his pain sullied her soft skin.

She jerked his chin back, giving him no choice but to meet her gaze. "I promised I wouldn't let you down, and I won't, so stop pushing me away because you're afraid of yourself. You're so much more than the scars you carry in body and mind and are worthy of everything good in this world."

The something in his gut he couldn't define identified itself.

Hope.

"And as for being worthy of *me*..." She ran her fingertip over his lower lip. "I'm the one who decides who is and isn't."

He met her gaze. The question lodged in his throat slipped out on the weight of his past and hope for the future. "Am I, Scarlett? Am I worthy of you?"

Scarlett didn't hesitate. She cupped Chris's cheeks in her hands and pressed her lips to his in a long, hard kiss, leaving no doubt about her answer.

"Thank fuck." He moaned low in his throat as his steel hand grasped her hip. The other snaked behind her neck and grabbed a fistful of hair. She squeaked in surprise at the sharp tug on her scalp and the primal need in his eyes. Tiny pricks of fear peppered her spine like voodoo-laced needles. She'd been in this position last night, but this felt more intense. More possessive. Darker and more...

Dangerous.

No doubt, Christopher Daviani was a lethal man, but the hazards of being this close to him had nothing to do with bodily harm and everything to do with her heart.

Another growl, grittier, deeper, rumbled from his throat as he flattened her against the door with his body. As he claimed her lips so quick, so forceful, she didn't have time to analyze the risks other than the thought of not ever knowing how it felt to be taken—no, devoured and possessed by this man. His kiss this morning had felt like an attack, but that had been a scuffle compared to this full-on assault of twisting tongues and wet, nuclear heat.

His grip at her waist tightened. The soft stubble on his

jaw scraped along her cheek as he licked the crease of her mouth. A moan floated out of her lips. He swallowed the satisfied sound with a sharp suck on her tongue. She reached her arms around his waist and pressed herself against his granite torso and tangled her legs with his. She needed to be closer. Didn't think she could ever be close enough to the powerful, magnificent man who'd introduced her to carnal magic she hadn't known existed.

Flames seemed to shoot up from the forest floor through the wooden porch, igniting an inferno. She clung to him tighter, rocking against his rigid length and seeking more of what he'd given her last night.

And what he hadn't.

He dipped his fingers inside the front of her jeans and burrowed inside the damp lace. "God help me, Scarlett, but I need all of you. Every. Fucking. Piece."

She shivered at the desire in his voice, ached at his desperation born from vulnerability and pain, and returned his kiss with the beautiful strength of his steel. She slid one of her hands under his sweatshirt and danced her fingers over the hard ridges and deep valleys of his abs. Her other hand traveled between their heated bodies. She smiled at his sharp inhalation as she grazed his thigh. Reveled in his muttered curse when she brushed her knuckles against the thick proof of his wild need.

His fist tightened in her hair. "You're completely oblivious about what you do to me. Aren't you?"

She smiled against his lips, his animalistic reaction igniting an exhilarating charge of confidence. With her palm, she stroked him upward and pressed her fingers into the thick tissue of his cock.

"Jesus Christ." His hand covered hers against the rock-hard length straining against his jeans. "Feel what you do to me. I've been like this since we met."

She drew her head back, her eyes widening in surprise.

"That's right, Dr. Kerrigan. You've made me hard since day one." He tugged her away from the door and yanked it open with his steel. "Inside. Now."

She didn't need the encouragement of his slight shove across the threshold.

Behind her, the door slammed shut with a bang. The sound signaled the start of something she knew she could never come back from.

Quivering with anticipation, she stepped toward the bedroom and what would surely be the most memorable moments of her life. She'd commit every touch, every sensation, every moan from his mouth and feel of his body to memory. It might be all she had of him when this crisis was over.

He followed her, his hand at the small of her back, only breaking contact with her body to peel off his jacket and drop it to the floor. At the edge of the bed, she stopped and turned. The intensity of the blazing fire in his gaze stole her breath. Last night by the tree, with the sun setting and emotion clouding her judgment, she hadn't had time to think about what she lacked in sexual prowess. And outside just now, she'd been full of adrenaline from shooting the shed and making him see the man she respected.

And desired.

But here, inside the cabin with too much time to think between the short walk from the porch to the bedroom, self-doubt poked at her bravado. Could she deliver on her bold actions?

What if I disappoint him?

Without her permission, her brain shifted into scientific mode, assessing the variables, and presenting expectations. "I should tell you I've only been with one other man." She warned herself to shut up, but her mind didn't listen. "You've probably been with lots of women. I mean, look at you." She eyed his beautiful body from head to toe. "But the feedback from my last partner concluded my skills were, uh…" Her gaze dropped to the floor. "He said they were lacking."

"Was it that James asshole?"

She nodded.

"He's an idiot." He pressed a steel finger against her lips. "Now stop rambling and take your clothes off so I can give you an experience I promise both of us will find most satisfying."

For a long moment, she held his gaze. The order that promised everything she'd been dreaming about since she'd met him played in her mind before she dropped her eyes to the floor.

He captured her chin in his hand and forced her to look at him. "What are you afraid of?"

She studied his face, searching for the disappointment she'd grown accustomed to seeing from the men in her life. What she saw in his warm eyes, fighting for space along with blatant desire, was patience. He'd always known who she was. From the moment they'd met, he'd pushed, teased, and even begged her to unlock the woman buried inside. He'd recognized all along there was more to her than just a big brain. Confident he'd meant it when he'd said he wanted to know *all* of her, she voiced her fear. "I'm afraid of failing at this."

"You didn't fail yesterday. Your genius brain caught on quick when you were riding my hand against a tree."

Heat rushed to her cheeks. She tried to look away from the fire in his eyes before it burned her, but he wouldn't allow it.

"Watching you come was the most erotic moment of my life." His grip on her chin softened to a caress. "The only way you can fail is by not having the courage to go after what you want." He snuck his steel hand under her shirt and skimmed his fingers up her rib cage.

Trembling, she arched her back.

"Do you want me, Scarlett?" Cool fingers teased the outer side of her breast as his heavy breathing turned ragged. "Do you?"

His heated question and her nipples that ached to feel the pressure of his steel charred the brain cells controlling rational thought. She knew what his hand could do. She'd programmed it and witnessed the destruction it could cause. Now she wanted to experience the sinful pleasure it could ignite on the most sensitive parts of her body. To feel his warm, heavy breaths against her lips.

On her breasts.

Between her legs as she screamed his name again and again.

Shrugging out of her jacket, she let it fall to the floor behind her. The ashes of her doubts followed. She searched his face again before pulling her sweatshirt over her head. Contrary to his urgent words, his gaze held patience. The calmness didn't last for long though, as a storm nearly as dark as the satin and lace bra she revealed brewed in his gaze.

Her pulse sped up as he skirted both his hands down the sides of her breasts.

"I knew there was more to you than just suits." With a fluid motion, he unclasped her bra and slid it past her shoulders.

Taking his command to get naked seriously, she toed off her sneakers as she unsnapped her jeans. He halted her motions with his hands.

"My job." He covered her lips in a demanding kiss while his fingers skated up her torso, along the planes of her back, and around to the curve of her breasts. His cool caresses left a trail of delicious goose bumps on her skin, along with a bone-melting tenderness that made her forget his hand was a deadly weapon.

She moaned his name as she scraped her nipples against his shirt. Pain and pleasure ricocheted through her stomach as he enclosed her hard nub between his fingers. How he knew exactly what amount of pressure to exert to drive her wild was a phenomenon she looked forward to exploring.

A devious smile quirked his lips. "You like that?"

The question danced over her skin along with breath-stealing sparks. She managed to nod.

"You want more?"

A moan accompanied another nod. "God, yes."

"Good. Now that you've come out to play, you're mine. I won't ask permission to touch you again."

He gripped her tight around the waist and jerked her against him as he trailed warm, wet bites down her neck. Gasping, she sunk her teeth into his shoulder as he pulled down the zipper of her jeans, slow and measured, building a delightful pressure with every tooth that came undone. When his sweet torture was complete, he stepped back and peeled her jeans down her quivering thighs. Her stomach tightened as he sucked in a breath. Licking his lips, he pressed his mouth to her soaked panties and breathed her name.

Her hips twisted under his hands against the storm building between her thighs. "Hell, Chris. That feels incredible."

"Drives me crazy when curses come out of your sweet mouth." He peeked up with a smirk as he pulled her jeans down the rest of the way.

She stepped out on trembling legs and sighed "Yes," again as his fingers glided up her calves to her thighs and finally inside her soaked panties.

"Curse for me again, Scarlett."

"Fuck," she whispered. A scream followed as he plunged his fingers inside her wet heat. Her knees buckled from the intense intrusion. Backing her up while working his magic, he pressed her onto the bed.

A hedonistic buzz burned through her body. With wide eyes and heavy breaths, she watched him remove her panties and toss them aside, never taking his gaze off her. Every inch of her flesh, from her face to her toes and every part in between, became electrified under his reverence.

Pride surged through her as she lay naked in front of him with no hint of embarrassment. As she begged him to touch her, she had no doubt that sexual chemistry was a subject she was about to master.

TWENTY-SIX

C hris tore his shirt off. His plan to be naked on top of Scarlett in t-minus three seconds unraveled as she scrambled to the edge of the bed. "Where do you think you're going?"

She rose on her knees, a wicked glint in her eye and answered his question with a kiss to the head of his viper tattoo. Her tongue traced the snake, her fingers gliding along the wet trail of her kisses. "So beautiful."

He sucked in oxygen, holding on tight to his control while she feasted on the symbol of the deadly creature he had become. Like a snake, he hissed.

"So hard." Her tongue glided up to his shoulder. Her hands followed, caressing the spot where his arm had been severed clean off. The scarred seam where flesh and metal joined came alive under her touch, as she dipped her head and straddled the juncture of man and machine with her lips. Soothing yet scorching heat penetrated his flesh and steel, replacing all the pain he'd endured with a blinding beam of hope.

"You're perfect." She wrapped her arms around his neck and pressed her lips to his.

His hands dropped to cup her ass. Dragging her hard against him, he dug his fingers into her bare cheeks and took control of the kiss. The friction of their heated skin fanned his simmering desire into an uncontainable firestorm he never wanted to be rescued from.

With an urgent edge to her voice, she moaned his name and wriggled out of his grip. A cold chill spread down his spine.

Did I hurt her again?

He spun her around. Red marks from his bionic fingers marred her creamy skin. "Sorry. You're the first woman I've touched like this with my steel." He'd played with her nipple somewhat roughly earlier but had been in control. There had been nothing controlled about the way he'd just grabbed her delicate ass.

She turned to him and placed a finger to his lips. "You didn't hurt me. And don't apologize for your strength. It's who you are."

He watched her fumble with the button on his jeans as his dick grew harder than his super arm. "It's who you made me."

"Even without the cool accessory, you're the most beautiful man I've ever met. Now, take your clothes off, Commander."

"Yes, ma'am."

Within seconds, he stood nearly naked before her. He held back a laugh at her little yelp of surprise as he freed his erection from his boxers. A caveman-like urge to beat at his chest overtook him. With a guttural groan, he urged her legs apart with his knee and pushed her onto the bed.

A throaty hum rumbled from her throat.

Like a lion ready to pounce, he crawled onto the edge of

the mattress and ran his fingers over the light-blonde curls at her apex. Her purr sounded like hot fudge pouring over him, sweet and indulgent as he ran his fingers up the insides of her thighs.

She thrust her hips up and he smiled. "You're beautiful, Scarlett." He bent his head and hovered his lips over the glistening spot he'd dreamed about tasting. "Open wider for me so I can finally devour you."

Slowly, she started to oblige with a groan; it wasn't quick enough for the insatiable appetite he'd developed for his beautiful genius. He grabbed her thighs and spread them wide. Dipping his head, he ran his tongue up her slick center. Now that he knew the woman hidden beneath the reserved scientist could handle his strength, he led a voracious attack on her body.

A whimper emerged from the back of her throat as a series of sexy-as-hell moans tumbled from her lips. He slid his steel underneath her ass and lifted her to his hungry mouth, ecstatic his fantasies about Scarlett writhing beneath him were finally coming true.

In awe that she found him beautiful and worthy.

The intensity of the ache to be inside her exceeded painful, but he wasn't done demonstrating the decadent things he could do between her gorgeous legs. As he plunged a finger into her tight wetness, he smiled against her slick lips at her whimper. Tense nerves under her heady-tasting flesh trembled against his tongue as he indulged himself in the taste and feel of everything Scarlett.

"God, yes." Her back arched off the bed and pressed against his eager mouth.

Adding another finger, he joined them in a twisty dance that sent his blood thrumming through his cock and pulsing in unison with the spasms of her tight walls.

He raised his head. "Look at me."

She peered at him from hooded lids.

"Keep your eyes on me while I make you come."

He gently squeezed her swollen clit with his steel fingers. Tremors vibrated against his digits lodged deep inside his idea of heaven on earth as a scream tore from her throat.

As her angelic face twisted in pleasure, he swore he'd never seen anything more breathtaking.

He played with the beautiful gift of her body, licking, squeezing, teasing until every wall she'd built around herself and every insecurity she harbored crumbled under his touch and she begged him to let her come.

As he sucked hard on her sweet spot, she screamed her release—and his name—over and over.

He crawled off her to reach for his jeans where he'd tossed them by the side of the bed and found a condom in his wallet. Quickly, he rolled it on and kneeled between her thighs.

She stared up at him with bright eyes. "I never knew." She glanced away from him as she repeated the words in a breathy stutter.

"Never knew what?" His cock pounded with the urge to thrust into her, but he placed a finger under her chin. "Tell me."

Her eyes widened. Wonder sparkled in their endless depths. "It felt so, so good. I mean, the one you gave me yesterday was spectacular, but this one was…groundbreaking."

"Your orgasms? You've never had one?" Surprise doubled him over. He caught himself on his elbows and braced them next to her head. "Did I give you your first one yesterday?"

Without waiting for an answer because the hitch of her breath said it all, he eased into her. Her muscles tightened at the intrusion.

"You okay?" Beads of sweat broke out on his hairline.

He was big, and she was sinfully tight, but knowing he'd been the first to make her body sing like a siren made it nearly impossible to hold back from slamming into her all at once.

Her hands clamped on his hips. "Yes."

Need thrummed through his veins, but he harnessed the ache and gritted his teeth. "I don't want to hurt you."

He never wanted to hurt her.

Ever.

She shook her head. "You won't."

But he'd hurt her this morning. Hell, she already had bruises on her ass from when he'd grabbed her, and there were probably more on her inner thigh from his steel. Gentle hadn't been on his mind when he'd pulled her legs apart to feast. "I could."

"I don't care if you do." She wrapped her legs around his waist and dug her heels into his back. "I need all of you."

Her hips jerked up from the bed and banged against his. The thin wire holding his tension at bay snapped as the woman he'd unearthed turned wild.

"Oh god," Scarlett screamed as Chris drove into her with the abandon of a starved man.

The headboard slammed against the wall. He stilled inside of her. "You okay?" Concern edged his tight voice that shook as much as his arms, braced by her head.

"Stop worrying." The command sizzled from her lips on a surge of exquisite pain and the promise of indescribable pleasure. "Move. Now."

She contracted her muscles around his cock.

His eyes rolled back into his head. "Fuck." The curse snapped out of his mouth, along with his control.

Another thrust, and another fully seated him in her so tight not a molecule of air could fit between their bodies. Gripping his hips, she urged him to move. "Don't stop. I can take it."

"I know you can." He lowered his head to brush a soft kiss across her lips as he pulled out. Without giving her time to catch a breath, he plunged back into her without restraint.

She closed her eyes and rode the wave his pulsing cock ignited in her muscles. "Do it again."

"That's my beautiful badass." He reached down and hooked his arm under her leg. With a shove, he raised her knee up to her shoulder and pushed deeper inside.

She cried out as the sudden force rocked pleasure through her belly. The wet slap of their bodies slamming together filled the room as she matched him thrust for thrust.

Relentlessly, he tunneled in and out in a punishing rhythm she greedily accepted. Surely, she'd have more marks on her body from *both* of his hands, but she didn't care. She felt more freedom imprisoned in his arms and pinned to the bed by his unyielding strength than she'd ever experienced in her life.

Somehow, she knew she'd never be the same again.

Each powerful punch of his hips contracted her slick muscles tighter around his rigid cock. An image of him smashing his way through a battlefield popped into her mind. She quickly shut it out. Of all people, she knew the hazards in his future, but right now, she would experience all the pleasure this dangerous man could give.

Clasping his face in her hands, she yanked his head down for a kiss. Their tongues met in a fierce dance that matched the savage union of their bodies and the primal smell of sex in the room. Grabbing his hips, she sank her fingers into his skin and pulled him closer.

Deeper.

The building tension strained her muscles until she felt she might snap.

"Chris." His name grated from her throat, begging for release.

Rising on his haunches, he pulled her onto his lap and impaled her on his cock. "Straddle me."

She wrapped her legs around him without hesitation.

"Tighter, and don't you fucking dare let go," he growled as he grabbed her ass and yanked her harder against him. She'd thought he'd filled her before, but this angle left her seeing stars. Before she could catch her breath, he toppled her onto the sheets. Grasping the headboard, he ground against her, his cock grating against the sensitive spot he'd sucked earlier.

More stars flashed in front of her eyes as her orgasm ruptured through her in a blustering surge. His name ripped from her throat, urging him to chase his own release harder.

She held on to his biceps for dear life while he rode out his own firestorm. As his body tensed above her, he screamed her name with a curse before he claimed her lips in a searing kiss she feared she might never experience again. Holding her superhero tight, she prayed fate would give them a little more time together before the mission brought them back to cold reality.

TWENTY-SEVEN

When their breathing returned to a somewhat normal state, Chris gathered Scarlett in his arms and rolled onto his back, his cock still half-erect inside her. The cabin stood quiet, save for their heavy breaths and the muted hiss of the fire from the main room.

Calmness washed over him more intensely than in any of his fantasies. He smiled into her hair and kissed the top of her head. Honeysuckle mingled with sweat teased his nose. He inhaled deeply, bottling her fragrance inside of him so he could recall it when the darkness invaded.

She shivered in his arms. He pulled the comforter over them as his dick twitched inside of her. With a gasp, she raised her head off his chest, her gaze a heady combination of blissful contentment and unabashed desire. "Does that mean we can do it again?"

He wanted to do it again and again, forever, but he couldn't promise her anything more than this fragment of time. Instinct told him danger would find them soon and they needed to be prepared.

The pot-belly stove at the foot of the bed and the fire in the main room needed more wood. He needed to check in with the team. Scarlett needed to monitor the imaging scan on her laptop. And he needed to do some digging into Thompson. God help the man if he proved to be the traitor.

Despite his dark thoughts, he smiled. Once they were done with those tasks, the whole night lay ahead of them. Alone. In the woods. Besides, giving Scarlett more orgasms to make up for the ones she'd missed when she'd been with her ex-asshole would be the honorable thing to do.

"Yeah, we can do it again after—" He pressed his fingers to her lips and listened. "That's a helicopter. Get dressed." He rolled her off him and jumped to his feet.

She scrambled out of bed. "Do you think we've been found?"

"Yes. Now move."

"Maybe it's a news helicopter." She picked up her jeans and bra.

"Do you hear the beat of the two blades slicing the air? A commercial helicopter doesn't sound like that when it lands. That bird is military-grade and coming for us."

She pointed a finger toward the ceiling. "Land where? There's nowhere to set it down unless you have a helipad on the roof."

"There's a clearing near Billy's clinic the medivac choppers use to pick up critical patients." He yanked on his boxers. "The landing site is less than a half mile from here."

He watched her naked ass disappear into the bathroom. Cursing to himself, he tugged on his jeans and shoes. While he tied the laces, he scanned the room for his duffel bag.

His gut dropped to the floor. He pounded his fist into his thigh and looked out the window. The bag of weapons sat open near the shed. How could he have been so careless? He was supposed to be keeping Scarlett safe, not putting her in greater danger. His breath hissed out long and harsh. "Wrong head in the game."

He pushed open the bathroom door without knocking. Scarlett's hands froze on the clasp of her bra. With her jeans unbuttoned, her hair messed up, and her lips swollen pink, she looked like a woman who'd been fucked good and hard and loved every minute of it.

Focus!

"I'm going outside to get the weapons. Lock this door and stay put. Don't come out unless it's me on the other side."

He pulled the door closed behind him. Scarlett stopped it with her hand. "You can't go out there unarmed."

"I have no choice."

"Yes, you do." She ran to her laptop bag sitting next to her suitcase on the floor, unzipped a side compartment, and took out a pistol.

"You packed a gun?" He stared, certain Scarlett brandishing a weapon in curve-hugging jeans and a white lacy bra was the sexiest sight he'd ever seen.

"What else would I pack to hide out in the woods from bad guys? A curling iron?" She placed the weapon on the bed and reached down into her open suitcase. "You can take the gun. Or I'll cover you." She pulled a tank top, followed by a sweatshirt, over her head. "Which plan do you like better?"

He didn't like either. If he took the gun and wound up getting shot out there, she would be alone *and* unarmed. If she fired a shot while covering him, she would give away her position, but at least she'd be able to protect herself. Everything about this situation sucked.

He pointed to her weapon. "Ready to cover me?"

She pulled on her sneakers and straightened. "As I'll ever be."

He grasped her chin in his steel. "Remember. Do everything I tell you without question."

The tense set of her jaw gave away her fear, but the spark of determination in her eyes gave him hope. He prayed it would be enough to get her through whatever mayhem was coming their way.

He walked through the main room, his eyes on the windows while he schooled his mind into combat mode. He could assume whoever attacked would not kill Scarlett. They needed her mind. It didn't mean they would leave her unharmed.

"My path to the bag will be that way." He painted a zigzag pattern with his finger along the side of the house, across to Grandma Darren's Buick, and over to the duffel bag where he'd dropped it to the ground. "Once I secure the weapons, I'll assess the situation and return. Don't shoot at anyone if they don't have a gun. Understand?"

"Yes." Her clipped word sounded intense and sure. "Be careful."

"I will. You too. Be right back."

He skirted around the side of the cabin and listened. No sound of approaching cars or feet and no gunshots. Praying all remained quiet, he sprinted to the car and crouched behind the front tire. Pausing, he swiveled his head before he dashed to the bag. Without stopping, he scooped it up and ran back to the porch, hoping the familiar burn of a bullet didn't pierce his skin.

Once inside, he pulled a semiautomatic out of the duffel, loaded it, and strapped it to his chest. "If whoever is in the helo gets past me and you need to shoot, don't aim to kill. We don't need to blow this place up and attract every cop within twenty miles, nor add manslaughter to the list of laws we're breaking out here. Our goal is to incapacitate, get to safety, and regroup, but do what you must. Understand?"

In a whir of blonde hair and soft curves, she zipped by him to the kitchen and typed on her laptop.

He held his position by the window. "What are you doing?"

"Increasing our chances of survival."

"Take cover in the bedroom doorway. Now."

"One more minute."

Each *click-clack* of her fingers on the keyboard felt like an eternity while he waited for her to obey his command. "I mean it, Scarlett. Back in position."

"Thirty more seconds."

The calmness in her voice increased the tension in his. "Dammit, step away from the laptop. That's an order."

She slammed her finger into the keys one last time. "Done."

With heaving breaths, like she'd been the one to sprint to the bag and back, she pulled his arm's fail-safe device out of her laptop bag and ran over to him. She jerked back his thumb and popped open the manual override compartment. "God, I hope I'm doing the right thing," she said as she inserted the device and gave it a twist.

"You activated me?" He held up his hand in front of his face. The familiar sting raced down his neck and into his shoulder.

"I told you I'd let you know when it was time for steel and V-Strikes." Her chest rose and fell with each breath. "It's time."

"You're fucking amazing." He meant every word. "Now get in position."

She shoved her laptop and the device into her bag and zipped it up.

Chris welcomed the current coursing through his arm. "I thought you needed a code and a retinal scan to activate me?"

"I should." She dropped the laptop bag inside the bedroom. "But the hacker's latest visit left a back door wide open. There's one problem though. By activating you, I may have given away our location. Yesterday I built in precautions to cloak us in the event of something happening like this but use your V-Strikes only if necessary. The more you fire, the quicker we could be found."

A thud sounded on the porch. "I'd say someone already knows where we are."

TWENTY-EIGHT

Something heavy rammed the door. Scarlett bit back a scream as the force struck again and the cabin shook. A shaft of sunlight filtered through the wood. A boot encasing a beefy leg burst through the fissure. Before a body could follow, Chris fired a V-Strike from his wrist.

The man attached to the black thigh jerked back. "Fuck."

Silence followed. A moment later, the eerie calm shattered as a second man jumped through. Tall and wide. Short hair. Dressed in black, like the goons Beth had described.

Before the goon could recover, Chris delivered an uppercut to his chin, followed by a sharp hook to the nose. The goon's head snapped to the side. An orange tiger tattooed on his neck caught the light. It faded into shadows as he crumpled to the floor.

Scarlett winced at the crack of his skull on the hardwood. She heaved in a deep breath. Before she could take another, an overgrown goon with skin as pale as his clothes were dark burst through the shattered door and tackled Chris into the corner. Like two possessed ninjas, they grappled and threw fists and knees, each gaining the advantage, only to lose it again.

A scream rose in her throat, but she choked it back. *Don't give away my position.* She pressed her back into the door-frame and yelled a silent, "Way to go," as Chris rolled on top of his attacker and pinned him to the floor. The overgrown goon heaved his upper body to gain the advantage, but Chris knocked him out with a punch to his jaw with his flesh-and-blood fist.

She silently cheered again. A growl from the kitchen killed her pep squad debut. Tiger Tattoo rose. He spit out blood. A flash of metal caught the sunlight.

"Gun," She yelled the word, but the sound lodged in her throat.

Tiger Tattoo leveled his weapon at Chris. A bone-chilling surge heightened her focus and flipped fear to intent. She took aim and squeezed the trigger. The gun flew out of his hands. Surprise shrieked from her throat.

Tiger Tattoo screamed his own surprise and cradled his arm. Limp fingers dangled from his wrist. He snarled and lunged at Scarlett.

She shifted her gun to shoot again. Chris jumped between them and shoved him away.

Steel met flesh and bone with a sickening crunch as Chris jabbed like a heavyweight at Tiger Tattoo's face. The force sent his prey hurling across the main room and into the kitchen table. Its legs gave way under his weight and buckled. Table and goon crashed to the floor.

Chris stared back at her with an open jaw. His eyes held hers for a second, surprise and fury flaming in his stormy, sapphire gaze. "Nice shot."

A groan from the overgrown goon he'd grappled with under the window halted her thanks.

Chris whipped around and fired a V-Strike into his stomach. "That'll keep him down for a while."

Relief rushed from Scarlett in a long, choppy breath. Footsteps pounded up the front stairs.

Chris jumped behind the couch and crouched on his haunches. "Get back in the bedroom doorway and cover the rear. Shoot again if you have to."

Shoot a man? Again? She gripped the gun in her hand tighter, the instinct to protect herself and the man she was falling in love with more fervent than her fear.

Before she could jump back into position, another goon in black barreled through the broken front door. She raised her gun to shoot.

Chris yelled from behind the couch. "Cover the rear."

She spun around as another body crashed through the window next to the fireplace; she fired. This time, she missed.

Shit, shit, shit.

Scarlett followed the trajectory of the short, stout body as it hit the floor. She leveled the gun to take another shot when the goon's arm snaked out and grabbed her ankle. Her right side slammed into the hardwood behind the couch. The impact sent her pistol flying from her hand and out of reach.

She kicked against the goon with both legs. "Let me go."

"Sorry, sweetheart. You're coming with me." He wrapped a beefy hand around her calf.

She kicked again and again, screaming every insult she'd learned from the team.

Shorty gripped her calf tighter. "The boss told me you were a helpless little thing, but I like your spirit. Too bad it won't do you any good."

She stopped fighting and went slack.

A smirk twisted his fat lips. "Good girl."

With a vicious twist, she wrenched her leg from his grip and rammed her heel into his jaw. "Fuck you, asshole."

She scurried away on her bottom as Chris tackled Shorty. The goon stumbled into the wall and collapsed in a heap of black.

She snatched her gun from the floor and rose on shaky legs.

Christ!

The cabin resembled a crime scene right out of prime time. Chris stood over a bloody goon like the heroic star of the show. More unconscious bodies littered the floor. The beaten door hung on its hinges. She willed the goons to get up and head to lunch while the set was readied for the next take, but this wasn't television.

The guns were real.

So was the blood.

A sob broke from deep within. "Please don't let these men be dead."

"They're not. I held back." Chris grabbed her hand. "We've got to get out of here."

She nodded and followed him, stepping over prone bodies, and froze when she spotted Tiger Tattoo sitting among the rubble with a gun pointed at her chest.

Chris snapped his head to the weapon trained on Scarlett. Out of the corner of his eye, he saw her pistol rise. She didn't have a chance against a trained mercenary.

He threw his body against hers and reached for the semi-automatic strapped to his torso. He was done merely subduing the enemy. This time he was going old school with intent to kill.

A gunshot rang in his ears. The bullet meant for Scarlett slammed into his bicep. He pulled her down with him. The familiar pain penetrated his shoulder. As they fell to the floor, he aimed his own gun and squeezed the trigger. The stunned asshole clutched his arm as he tumbled over. Before his upper body hit the ground, Chris fired a V-Strike to his chest.

"Ain't getting back up now." Chris closed his eyes and breathed through the pain.

Scarlett scrambled to his side. "No, no. No."

He heard the floor creak. A heartbeat later he felt her warm body next to his. He sighed when she laid her head on his chest and he inhaled honeysuckle. "I'm not dead."

"Thank God." She dropped her gun, tore off her sweatshirt, and held it against the blood seeping from his arm.

A hiss slithered through his teeth. He'd forgotten how much gunshot wounds hurt. He'd been hit a few years ago in the leg. The experience sucked as much as he remembered.

Jackhammers banged against his head as he raised it off the floor to assess the aftermath. The goon with the tattoo on his neck lay motionless on the ground. Another lay sprawled under the window next to the latecomer he'd quickly subdued with a well-placed kick to the head. The short asshole who'd tried to take Scarlett was slumped against the wall by the bedroom. All were unconscious. And bloody.

He looked at Scarlett. With a gun in one hand, she applied pressure to his wound with the other. Damn, she had handled a pistol like a pro, and he couldn't be prouder, but he knew shooting another human being would take a toll on her mind. He wished he could hold her and make the darkness go away, but they needed to leave.

Now.

A voice bellowed from the porch. "What in the blazes?"

Scarlett's head snapped up with her gun. A tall man with dark-red hair, dressed in medical scrubs and toting a rifle, stood in the doorway.

Chris squinted to make sure he wasn't seeing things. "It's

okay. It's Billy." He tipped the barrel of her pistol away from his buddy.

"Did my invitation to this little party get lost in the mail?" Billy hurried across the room, dropped to his knees, and looked at Scarlett. "What do we have here?"

"He's been shot."

Chris hissed through his teeth as Billy peeked under the sweatshirt bandage. "We were ambushed. Long story. We need to get out of here and to the clinic. Quick."

"You think?" Billy rolled his eyes as he set down the rifle he carried. "Does your partner know how to shoot a gun?"

Chris cut off whatever his brave genius was about to say with a wink. "She's fucking Annie Oakley, but you can call her Scarlett."

Billy pulled some gauze out of his pocket and wrapped it around Chris's wound. "You got hit with a nice shot, brother."

"No shit."

"Don't get your panties in a bunch. The bullet only grazed you, but it did take out a big chunk of skin." He secured the bandage with white tape. Standing, he wiped his bloody hands on his thighs before he grabbed his patient under the armpits.

"I can stand myself." Chris rose, cursing his way to his feet on his own. He'd once run two miles with a bullet lodged in his leg. He didn't need a babysitter for a mere flesh wound.

Billy backed off. "Your shiny arm doesn't make you invincible, you know."

"I know, but it can beat you senseless if you don't stop being a jackass."

Scarlett's gaze trained on the blood already seeping through the gauze. "Let him help you."

Chris glared at her too. "The only thing we need to worry about right now is getting out of here. These mercenaries might have more friends. Once we get outside, you shoot anything that moves. Understand?"

TWENTY-NINE

S carlett swayed at the sight of her blood-stained fingers gripping the gun. Her hands shook. She breathed like her coach had taught her to do in competition and tried to block out the voice in her head.

They came for me.

This is all my fault.

Billy stepped through the broken door first and into the gloomy afternoon. He scanned the clearing in front of the cabin. A moment later he motioned for Scarlett to proceed.

She grabbed her laptop bag from inside the bedroom door and slung it over her head and across her body. Carefully, she stepped around the battered goons and made her way to the porch. She spared a backward glance at Shorty and hoped his jaw hurt like hell when he woke up.

Billy touched her shoulder. "Remember, shoot anything that moves."

She gulped at the directive she'd heard too many times today. Crisp air flowed into her lungs. The clean mountain scent did nothing to calm her roiling stomach.

Don't throw up.

She pulled in more air to try and calm her nerves as she followed the gun-carrying doctor down the steps.

Chris closed in behind her. "Stay close to Billy. I'm right here."

She found his hand and squeezed as she started down the steps. The stench of blood and sweat clung to him and seeped into her nose. His warm breath on the nape of her neck reassured her they were alive. Every inhale, every exhale slowed her racing heart.

"I was finishing up at an accident scene down the road when I heard the chopper." Billy talked fast as he led them across the grass in the clearing. "I could tell it wasn't tourists, so I figured you got your ass into trouble. I drove straight here, ditched the truck, and hoofed it in. Sorry I was too late to join in the fun."

"No worries, man." Chris placed his hand on Scarlett's shoulder. "She took out one and I got the others. Just wish I had been fast enough with my gun before the bastard shot me. It hurts like a son of a bitch."

Scarlett looked over her shoulder. "You would have been fast enough if you weren't protecting me. I could have made that shot."

"Or maybe we both would have been hit, and you'd be trussed up with a bunch of goons in a helicopter heading God knows where." Chris dipped his head to her ear as he pressed against the small of her back to nudge her to move faster. "I said I didn't want to hurt you, and I meant it. That includes making sure you don't get kidnapped. Or shot. Or killed, so enough with the would've, could've, should've bullshit."

Billy angled his head to a wall of pines in front of them. "The truck is behind those trees. Hang in there, bro."

Chris snarled. "I'm fine."

Billy spread the thick branches with both hands. "I can tell since you're being an ass in front of a lady."

"He's always an ass." Scarlett spun her head to Chris again. "And you're not fine. You got shot."

"It's okay." He stepped next to her and grabbed her elbow with his steel. "It's what I do."

"But it's not what I do." Her tenuous hold on sanity weakened with every reminder she'd shot a man, might have to shoot another, and had almost been kidnapped because someone wanted her brain and the things she'd created.

Sensing a hysterical ramble coming on, she shut her mouth and walked sideways through the branches. Pine needles scraped her face and arms. She matched her breaths to Chris's and listened for more goons as they hurried to Billy's truck.

The forest stood quiet as she climbed into the back seat. Chris scrambled in next to her and took her hand. His hard squeeze eased the panic careening through her mind like a clown car in a circus ring, but just a bit.

Billy started the engine. Her body jerked toward Chris as the truck lurched forward. Her laptop bag bumped his wounded arm.

"Crap. I'm sorry." She tugged the bag to her other hip.

He set his jaw. "It's okay."

"No, it's not."

She studied his bandaged wound. Crimson stains seeped through the white gauze.

"Hurry, Billy." She pulled the laptop bag closer so it didn't bump him again and remembered the fail-safe device inside. "Oh my god. You're still active. If the hacker is in the network, he could hijack your weapons systems and make you fire."

Billy peeked over his shoulder. "No firing of anything in my truck. I just got it detailed."

As Scarlett manually deactivated Chris, she willed a portal to another plane to appear so she could drag him through it and back to the warm bed they'd shared not even an hour ago. Instead, a log structure similar in look to Chris's cabin but four times as long appeared around a bend in the road.

Billy halted the truck at a side entrance with a sign above the door that read, "Urgent Care Clinic." Before the vehicle stopped, Chris threw open the door and jumped out with more grace than a man who had just been hit with a bullet had a right to possess.

"Move," he said as he grabbed her hand and slid her toward him. Ignoring her plea to take it easy, he pulled her from the vehicle and set her feet on the ground. Her toes barely touched the gravel before he shoved her toward the clinic entrance.

Once inside, she spun on him and fixed her gaze on the bandage stained with even more of his blood. "I knew you'd make yourself bleed more."

He strode past the chairs and the cluttered desk in the cramped waiting area and opened a door marked, "Exam Room." As he crossed the threshold, he glanced over his shoulder at his steel. "Don't worry. I've handled much worse."

The thought of the "much worse" he'd endured and what could have happened today if the goon's bullet had found a fatal mark launched her stomach into violent spasms.

Clutching her belly, she shook her head. "*I* can't handle much worse."

Her life had gone from an orderly computer lab to a bloody battlefield in less than three days. The threat hadn't been stopped, which could only mean the worst was yet to come.

She speared her other hand into her hair. Tears flooded

her eyes. "I can't handle more guns and blood." She stared at Chris's gunshot wound. "I can't handle you…"

God, she couldn't handle him getting hurt again while he protected her.

Her hand flew to her mouth. She swallowed her puke and prayed the ajar door next to the desk was a bathroom.

As she ran toward it, she heard the exam room door slam. Heard Billy calling her name. She ignored him and raced to the toilet. Spasms rocked her body as she gripped the edge of the porcelain seat and retched. When there was nothing left in her except an empty chill, she scooted against the wall and leaned her head next to the toilet paper holder.

A soft knock sounded at the door. Billy poked his head in. "Are you okay?"

"Yeah. How's Chris?"

"On the phone with someone named Kane." He pushed inside and closed the door behind him. "I stopped most of the bleeding. When he's done barking orders, I'll stitch him up and he'll be good as new."

Good as new.

Just in time for him to throw himself in front of another bullet for me.

She picked at Chris's blood under her fingernails. "Those goons at the cabin were after me. Do you think they'll come here?"

"No. I heard their helo take off while you were puking. My guess is the least injured hostile dragged the others out. I called a retired law enforcement buddy and asked him to check the cabin and make sure they're gone. My security system will alert us if any more hostiles come near my property. You're safe."

"I am, but Chris was shot protecting me."

"Stop right there." Billy lowered himself to the tile floor and sat cross-legged in front of her. "Chris is fine. He was made for situations like today, even before VIPER turned him into the bionic man. I don't know what his cool-as-shit arm can do, but I know it wasn't designed for a mere security detail. I'm guessing you're responsible for the top-secret things he can't tell me based on the tinkering you did to his hand when we were in the truck."

She shrugged. "I'm responsible for some of it."

"Thank you." He placed his hand on her knee. "Really, Scarlett. Thanks."

"For what?"

"Everything was taken from him when he lost his arm. *Everything.* But VIPER gave him a reason to live." His voice cracked. "I was afraid I was going to lose him to all the dark shit he'd endured, but you gave him a purpose again. I can't thank you enough for that."

She didn't know what to say. She knew VIPER was important to Chris. She hadn't realized how much.

And it's in danger of being disbanded because of me.

Somebody wanted her.

Not Chris.

Not the team.

Maybe not even control of the VIPER program.

The longer she stayed with Chris, the more danger he was in. If she eliminated herself from the equation, he'd be safe.

She wiped her nose with the back of her hand, frightened, yet satisfied with her logic. Besides, they couldn't keep living as fugitives. Every day he stayed with her and didn't return to VIPER headquarters, put his job—his purpose—in jeopardy.

This madness had to end now.

She peered down at her blood-sprayed, vomit-speckled tank top. "Is there a place I can clean up?"

Billy rose from the floor and leaned against the pale-blue

wall. "The door on the other side of the office leads to my home. My wife Marie and the kids are at her sister's house for the weekend, so nobody will bother you. There's a guest room upstairs with its own bathroom. Last door on the left. Marie keeps extra toothbrushes and stuff in there. In a basket in the closet are clothes she's giving away. Grab yourself a clean shirt."

Scarlett stood and placed a kiss on his cheek. "Thank you. Take good care of Chris while I'm gone."

She waited for Billy to leave the bathroom before she skirted the few wooden chairs in the reception area and headed for the entrance to Billy's residence. On her way, she paused by the closed exam room door. How she'd managed to fall in love with the beautiful, damaged hero on the other side would be a mystery she'd never unlock. And how it had happened so fast baffled her even more.

She did know one thing though. She had a mission to complete on her own.

Fifteen minutes later, Scarlett started the compact car sitting in the driveway on the side of the house opposite Billy's clinic. She'd scribbled a note apologizing to him for "borrowing" the keys she found on a hook by the garage, along with a promise to return his vehicle soon.

Taking a deep breath, she pulled onto the road with blood-free hands, fresh breath, and a clean shirt courtesy of Marie's toiletries and hand-me-down pile.

Everything I need to find a traitor.

Except a plan.

The only direction she had was Washington, DC. That's where the threat had started. Instinct told her it would end there, but where should she go when she arrived? Going to the higher-ups at the DOD wasn't an option. She didn't know who she could trust, and they certainly didn't trust her. Involving the local police was a viable route, but by the time she explained everything, the hacker could strike again.

Or more goons with guns could find me.

But not for the next few hours.

She'd used her hacking skills back at Billy's house to ensure she wouldn't be caught by any surveillance cameras from here to DC. She'd also worked some magic to protect Chris from being found again. Despite her precautionary efforts, her reckless plan ranked a solid ten on the stupid scale. Being with Chris had proven to be even more dangerous though.

He threw himself in front of a bullet for me.

Maybe he did value more than her brain and desire more than her body.

Her heart warmed and hope soared. She tamped both down. Getting all gooey over a man had never made sense to her. Logic did, and she needed some now.

THIRTY

Chris jumped off the exam table as Billy entered the room. "Where's Scarlett?"

"Gone."

Blood roared in Chris's ears. "What do you mean she's gone?"

Billy leaned against the wall inside the door next to a poster of the skeletal system. "As in, I went to check what was taking her so long to clean up and change—like you just insisted I do— and she's not there to check on."

In three strides, Chris crossed the small room and leaned over the computer monitor tracking Billy's surveillance system. "How did they—"

Billy clasped Chris on the shoulder. "The bad guys didn't take her. She stole my car."

"What?" Chris spun around.

"She took off while I was stitching you up."

"How? We would have heard her."

"The car is on the other side of the house and we're close enough to the road to have mistaken her getaway for passing traffic. She was nice enough to leave a note."

Billy handed him a piece of paper.

> *Sorry I borrowed your car without asking.*
> *I promise I'll return it.*
> *Please tell Chris I'll handle the situation on my*
> *own and that I'm really sorry.*

The final words screeched through his mind like a banshee.

I'm sorry.

That's what Natalie had said when she'd left him in the hospital after he'd lost his arm,

He crushed Scarlett's note in his steel fist and launched it at a container of latex gloves attached to the wall. Disappointment tore a hole in the future he'd begun to believe they could have. He and Scarlett were supposed to be partners in crime. Their story would be a tempest of passion, danger, excitement and, dare he believe, a happy ending after she saved VIPER and he got the girl.

So much for that fractured fairy tale.

She was like the rest of the women in his life who left because they couldn't "handle" being around him. He hadn't expected her to bail while mercenaries were after her though.

"Damn stupid woman." He pulled the burner phone from his back pocket and dialed the number of the one he'd given her. No answer. He hung up with a curse. "You wouldn't happen to have a tracker on your car?"

"Me?" Billy sat on a rolling stool. "No way. I'm a quiet country doctor these days."

"You didn't look like one when you showed up at my door with a hunting rifle." He held out his hand. "Give me your truck keys. I'm going after her."

"Bad idea. She's got at least a thirty-minute head start.

The better course of action—and you know it—is to wait for your team to get here and devise a plan to go after your woman."

Chris scrubbed his steel hand over his face. Billy was right. The team would be here soon in the helicopter Linc borrowed from a buddy. Once they arrived, Nic could hack into traffic feeds and track Scarlett's location. And once they found her, Chris would…

What? Beg her to learn how to handle me?

He had no right to do that. She'd done well defending herself at the cabin against the goons, but if he attacked her during a nightmare again, she'd fail miserably.

Maybe fatally.

His muscles tensed. He winced as pain shot through his arm and into his heart. "Scarlett's not my woman."

Billy pushed up from the stool. The force sent it rolling back into the white wall. "You can lie to yourself, but you can't bullshit me. I saw the way you two looked at each other. Did you have sex with her yet?"

Chris looked out the window. What they'd shared at his cabin just beyond the trees had been more than sex. More than a quick, convenient fuck. It had been—

"It doesn't matter. She left. What's important now is finding her and figuring out who is responsible for the attack so she can get back to work and I can get back to shooting shit out of my—" He cut himself off before he spilled the details about what he could do with his arm.

Billy eyed Chris's steel. "Someday you'll have to tell me more about the "shooting shit" part. Right now, how about telling me what's going on between you and Annie Oakley?"

"Nothing."

Billy crossed his arms over his chest like they had all day to gossip about women.

Chris sighed. "Nothing anymore. You heard her say she

can't handle me."

"She isn't Natalie."

"This isn't about my ex."

"There you go again, lying to yourself. It is about her and your mom. They may have ditched you, but Scarlett didn't."

"She isn't here, is she?"

"My guess is she's taking matters into her own hands because she doesn't want you to get hurt again."

Chris shook his head. "That's a noble excuse with a big flaw. Why would she leave when she's still in danger?"

Billy bent down and picked up the bloodied, bullet-torn shirt he'd cut off Chris and threw it in the trash. "Because she's terrified and worried about you. Didn't you hear her puking her guts out while you were on the phone with your team? Sounds like she's protecting you because she cares, but you're too stubborn to see it."

Chris ran his hand over his bare chest and rubbed the back of his shoulder. "If she cared about me, why didn't she stay so we could figure out a plan?"

Together.

He slapped himself upside the head at his own naivety. And then what? Would he sit around and wait for her to leave when more danger struck? Maybe when he lashed out at her during the night and hurt her again? Or maybe when she realized life with a super soldier wasn't so super after all?

Billy leaned against a tall cabinet and shrugged. "Sometimes the heart doesn't listen to the brain."

"Enough with the wisdom and find me something to wear."

Billy rummaged through a cabinet. "Are you in love with her?" He tossed a shirt at Chris.

He caught the shirt in his steel and squeezed it tight. Examining that loaded question was a path he needed to avoid like a land mine.

THIRTY-ONE

"Think!" Scarlett gripped the steering wheel tighter as she approached the DC metro area. Several hours on the road with nothing but time hadn't brought any ideas about who she could trust to ask for help. If only she could trust Thompson. She still found it hard to believe he'd betray VIPER.

She chewed on her lower lip. Maybe he had a good reason for lying about her termination. Maybe she could march into VIPER headquarters, update him about the situation, and close herself in her office while he handled it.

The traffic light ahead turned yellow. She sped up and blew through it. Yanking the wheel, she turned hard into a gas station. There was only one way to determine if she could trust him. Pulling out her laptop, she prayed the enhanced imaging program she'd run to determine his complicity or innocence was almost done.

As if someone heard her prayers from above, the alert she'd set to signal the program's completion chimed as she yanked out her laptop. Her heart beat so hard, she thought it would burst out of her body and splatter all over the steering wheel as she flipped the screen up.

"No!"

She brought the laptop closer to her face. A tiny hole in Thompson's American flag pin and the faint flash of light shooting through it confirmed he'd stolen her retinal signature the night of the governor's gala. Her last thread of hope he wasn't the traitor disappeared, along with the sun that had sunk hours ago.

She had to let the team know but couldn't call them. Like most of her acting-before-thinking decisions today, she'd left her burner phone in the cabin. Instead of calling, she used a text messaging app on her laptop to send the details of her discovery to Chris and the team.

After stowing her laptop in her bag, she pulled into traffic and gripped the steering wheel tight. At least the proof of Thompson's treachery at the governor's gala had given her an idea of who to ask for help—Governor Bradley himself.

He was the only person close to VIPER she could trust, considering he hadn't wanted her fired and was a big supporter of the project. She needed to speak to him, tell him about Thompson's betrayal, and beg him to help her figure out what to do next to stop this insanity.

It sounded like a good plan, her only plan, but with one big obstacle. Calling the governor's mansion and demanding to speak to Bradley about a life-or-death matter wasn't feasible. Whoever answered the phone would laugh at her and hang up. She thought about calling his nephew and asking him to get a message to his uncle but entangling Ryan in this mess would only put him in danger as well.

That left only one other option she didn't like at all.

Thirty minutes later, she pulled up to the gates of Henry's mansion in Chevy Chase, Maryland. A state-of-the-art security system and concrete walls secured the two-acre grounds.

No gun-toting goons are getting into this place.

Henry could get her message to Governor Bradley. He had a personal relationship with the man and loads of money donated to his presidential campaign.

She smiled at the guard at the gatehouse. "How are you today, Ernie?"

"Dr. Kerrigan. Haven't seen you in a while. New car?"

"It's a rental while mine's in the shop. Is Henry home?"

"He sure is. I'll call up and let him know you're here."

She tapped her fingers on the steering wheel while the familiar gates carved with an ornate *R* granted her entrance.

"He'll help me," she muttered as she drove through the pretentious barrier erected to keep out the riffraff. She was certain if she begged Henry to call someone as important as the governor for a favor, he would say yes simply because it would inflate his ego.

After a quick hello to the housekeeper, she entered Henry's office. She glanced down, surprised her footsteps weren't permanently imprinted on the oriental carpet. She couldn't count how many times she'd waited for Henry in this very spot, pacing back and forth, hoping her grades pleased him or praying he wouldn't be angry because she'd dared take time away from her studies by doing something like joining the pistol team.

Thank God he never found out about that.

She peered around the massive room. The heavy mahogany desk in front of the bay window gleamed as always. The temperature set to a cool sixty-eight degrees and never a fraction less or more caused a shiver. The blinds, which opened on a timer to illuminate Henry when he sat behind his desk, were drawn against the dark. Henry controlled every aspect of his lair. Even her, right up until the day she'd left Richardson Enterprises.

The day he'd told her she'd failed him as a daughter.

Sweat coated her palms. She wiped them on her laptop bag slung across her body.

Crap, he's still controlling me.

The heavy latch of the double doors clicked. She took a deep breath.

It ends tonight.

Henry pushed into his office with a flourish befitting royalty.

Unimpressed, she stood tall. She'd seen the "Henry is better than mere mortals" show dozens of times.

He stretched out both arms as if he expected a hug. "To what do I owe this pleasure?"

She held up her hand. "I need your help."

Henry sighed and strolled over to the minibar. "You've gotten yourself in over your head, little girl, haven't you? I've been expecting you to crawl back and grovel for my assistance."

She ignored his insults. "I need you to get me on the phone with Governor Bradley."

Henry poured himself a tumbler of bourbon from a crystal decanter. "Why?"

"It's about a matter of national security. Please, Henry, call him. It's important."

He smiled as he hit the intercom button on the wall. "Send him in."

Bitter-tasting bile flooded Chris's throat. Fuck, his arm hurt. He'd barely held the contents of his stomach down in the helicopter after Linc and the team had picked him up at Billy's cabin. The ride in Kane's SUV from the private airfield to the DC business district wasn't much better.

The painkiller Billy had shot him up with had worn off.

Worry had compounded the pain when they'd received Scarlett's email confirming their suspicions about Thompson's betrayal, but Nic wasn't able to discern her location thanks to "glitches" in the city's surveillance network.

Wonder who made those glitches?

He growled as he pictured Scarlett typing at the speed of light to ensure she couldn't be found. And for what? To keep him safe? He growled again. It was his job to keep *her* safe, goddammit. He'd failed in spectacular fashion since he didn't know where she was.

Beth hadn't known her whereabouts either. The security feeds from Scarlett's townhome showed she wasn't there, and the security on her laptop was so tight Nic couldn't ping its location.

Linc ended a call as he leaned through the front seats from his place in the back. "Still no sign of Scarlett at VIPER headquarters, according to Patience."

"Good." Chris curled his fingers into a fist. "I don't want her anywhere near Thompson."

Kane honked the horn at a double-parked taxi. "I can't believe our shy genius stole a car. And shot a guy."

Nic punched Chris's steel shoulder. "I can't believe she snuck away from you."

Chris raised his flesh-and-blood hand to give Nic the finger. The tiny motion stirred enough pain to remind him how close Scarlett had come to being shot and he cursed. Did she care about him enough to risk her own life to protect him? If so, leaving him had been the most beautiful thing anybody had ever done for him.

Kane merged into traffic. A few miles later, he jockeyed for a spot in front of Richardson Enterprises headquarters. Even though it wasn't a workday, a few people still exited the brightly lit office building. Scarlett had said James worked most Saturdays, sometimes into the evening. As Chris eased out of the vehicle and met the team on the curb, he prayed the asshole was still inside.

Linc peered up at the tall glass walls. "Do you think James will know where Scarlett is?"

Chris shrugged. "Not sure, but we'll find out."

He'd suspected all along that James had a hand in this. The information Nic uncovered this afternoon about JS Holdings, the dummy corporation that had staked out Scarlett's place, added even more reason. Chris was happy to give the asshole a chance to confirm or deny during a not-so-friendly visit.

A security guard with white hair seated near the entrance peered up from a magazine. The young woman at the reception desk smiled as they entered the lobby. She fixed her eyes on them as their boots thumped on the cream-colored tile.

Nic smiled at the pretty redhead, who sent a sultry grin his way. "I got this."

A few minutes and a phone number later, they waited for the elevator to take them up to the thirty-fifth floor. Chris hit the call button again. "Remember the plan. We don't hurt James. The plan is to scare the shit out of him until he tells us everything he knows about Scarlett."

Nic punched his palm with his fist. "Can we hurt him if he doesn't cooperate?"

"Yes."

When the elevator doors opened, James stepped out. He looked up from his phone and froze.

"Hello, Jerry." Chris smiled as he intentionally called him by the wrong name. "Thanks for saving us a trip upstairs."

THIRTY-TWO

Dread, the soul-stealing kind she'd felt when Henry had summoned her to his office after the ambulance had taken her mother away, seized Scarlett. As she spun to see who Henry had called into his lair, every muscle in her body tensed like a bowstring.

The knob turned.

The clicking latch popped like a gunshot.

She stopped breathing as the doors slowly opened.

"You?" The tension in her burst like a cork as she gaped at Director Thompson. His gaze didn't meet hers as he stepped into the room and closed the door behind him. The slump of his shoulders solidified his guilt.

"I'm sorry." He didn't bother to wipe the sweat from his head as it dripped onto the expensive carpet. "I never meant for anyone to get hurt."

Tears welled in her eyes as she balled her fingers into fists. "People did get hurt."

This man, who'd said he'd believed in her, whom she'd trusted, whom Chris and the team trusted with their lives, let it happen.

He finally met her gaze and cleared his throat. "We weren't supposed to let it get this far."

"We?" The puzzle pieces jammed into place. She'd suspected Thompson as the insider threat, but she'd never once thought…

Scarlett whipped around to Henry. "You paid him to leak the activation codes, didn't you?" The perpetually cool air in the room rocketed to an unbearable degree. Sweat ran down her back. Henry didn't make a move from where he leaned on the minibar, but she hugged her laptop bag against her like a shield. "You sent those men to my house."

She knew he wasn't above morally gray business deals, but she'd never thought he'd betray his country—or her, at least to this extent. She'd been so naive to think he cared for her at all. "It was you all along. You hired someone to hack into VIPER. Sent the goons to my house. Ambushed the cabin. Tracked me here so you could stage this sick confessional."

"I didn't track you here, my dear. You did a fine job of cloaking yourself after you left your hideout. Thanks for showing up and saving me the trouble of sending out more of my men to retrieve you."

"You deranged sicko. You were behind everything."

He didn't utter a word. His victorious smirk provided all the confirmation she needed.

Run!

Chris's voice screamed the command in her head. She spun and yanked the door open. Shorty filled the doorway. He didn't speak. Instead, he wiped his bruised jaw as if to say, "You're not going anywhere."

A half scream, half gasp jumped from her throat. She reached into her laptop bag. Before she could get a grip on her pistol, he wrapped his big hand around her wrist and yanked her to face him. She yelped, more from surprise than pain. "Let go of me."

His grip tightened. "Not this time.

She raised her knee and tried to slam it into his groin. He twisted and laughed as her attack hit his solid thigh. The smug amusement left him unguarded long enough for her fist to land squarely in his stomach. His soft *umph* echoed in her ears as he whipped her backside to his front and manacled his arm around her waist. "That's enough, bitch."

"Next time, my fist hits your broken jaw."

Henry cleared his throat like he was calling a board meeting to order. "Calm down, girl." He sipped his bourbon as he sauntered away from the minibar to his desk. "It wasn't like I sent him to kill you."

She struggled against Shorty's hold. "You think your actions were justified because you weren't planning to murder me?"

Henry slammed his hand onto the back of his chair. "Stop being dramatic, like Jacquelyn was for the better part of our marriage. She's lucky I didn't divorce her for all the times I had to hear, 'Oh Henry, we'll ruin Scarlett's childhood if we send her away to school.'" He continued mimicking a feminine voice. "Scarlett needs friends. Scarlett needs normalcy. Scarlett needs her family." He leaned forward. "I'm the one who knew what you needed. She was as ungrateful as you are."

Over a decade's worth of fury dripped into Scarlett's words. "Don't talk about my mother."

His constant calm cracked. "Sit down."

Shorty pushed her forward. She stumbled but caught herself before her knees hit the rug. She'd never be on her knees in front of Henry again. Figuratively or literally. "Screw sitting. I've been sitting in front of you for half my life. I'm done."

She looked at Thompson. Perspiration poured off him like a shower. A tear coursed down his cheek. Sympathy welled in her chest. She shoved it down. She knew how manipulative Henry could be. But Thompson wasn't a scared twelve-year-old eager for someone to love him. He'd had choices and had made a terrible one by aligning himself with her stepfather. "Henry doesn't have the skills to compromise VIPER on his own, so I'm assuming he paid you to help. Why?"

Thompson unclenched his hand and held out a photo. More tears fell from his dark, troubled eyes. "That's my daughter, Callie, and my son-in-law, Brian."

Her eyes fixed on the beautiful young woman with brown skin and curly hair and the boyish-looking blond with a despondent smile.

More tears choked Thompson's words. "They want to start a family, but Brian is falling so deep into depression, he won't even talk to her."

Scarlett didn't look up. She couldn't take her eyes off the dejected young man in the wheelchair. One, two, three limbs were missing from his body.

Thompson sniffed. "And even if Callie did get pregnant, how can she care for Brian and a baby? When I heard about Project VIPER, I lobbied hard for the director job. I thought if I headed up the program, I could get Brian in. It made me so angry when the government, who sent him home without an arm and two legs, decided he wasn't a viable candidate."

"Why didn't you tell me about him?" Her eyes remained glued to the young couple. "I could have helped."

"I appreciate that." He closed the photo in his fist. "But anything you could have done costs an astronomical amount of money."

"That's where I come in." Henry set his drink on the desk as he sat in the plush leather chair. "When I found out you were working for my old fraternity buddy, Thompson, we got to talking and realized we both needed you, so we formed an alliance of sorts."

Fear pricked down her spine. "What kind of alliance?"

Henry sat back, opened a glossy wooden box, and took his time choosing a cigar. "I'd engineer an unfortunate scenario to give Thompson a plausible reason to terminate you from VIPER in disgrace and shake you up a bit with some good old-fashioned burglary."

"Good old-fashioned? Are you insane? Do you think there's any *good* in what you did?"

Like a king on his throne with his staff, he pointed the cigar at her. "It was a good plan, but you didn't do your part. You were supposed to get scared and run back to the safety of your family. To me, James, and Richardson Enterprises. In return, I committed to paying for the materials for you to outfit Thompson's son-in-law with prostheses so cutting-edge, the man could win a marathon."

She stalked to the desk and slammed her palms on the glass top protecting the expensive wood. "How could you get me fired from a job I loved? Where I was making a difference?"

He rose from his chair. "I needed you back here." His shout rattled the crystal chandelier above his desk. "I invested a lot of time and money in your future. You embarrassed me by taking a job as a *public servant.*"

"You're a traitor to your country." She glared at Thompson, who sat slumped in a chair near the door. "You're both a disgrace."

Spittle formed at the corners of Henry's mouth. "Forget about this patriotism drivel. Do you know how many foreign governments will pay for what's in your brain? I don't appreciate you keeping what you've been working on to yourself like a selfish brat. It's high time you shared."

"Why do you need more money?" She swept her arm around the room. "You already have everything."

Angry bourbon-capped waves rolled from his breath. "You don't know the first thing about business, girl. It's not about the money; it's about the game. I've come very close to losing this one. Since you didn't play along, I had no choice but to revert to plan *B*."

She didn't think it possible for her blood to grow any colder. Sticking around for plan *B* wasn't an option, but she didn't see an escape.

Henry blocked the doors to the patio behind him. Thompson slumped in a chair by the door. He didn't look like much of a threat, but she'd already underestimated him. Shorty guarded the only other exit. She touched the outline of the pistol in her bag. Shooting all three of them and making a getaway would be impossible.

Henry walked around his desk. He leaned against it and folded his hands on his stomach. "Here's the plan, little girl, and pay attention. I'm tired of the feds not awarding us contracts because they prefer low cost over quality. It's time we took our business to a government that appreciates our knowledge and expertise."

She shuddered. "Us? We? Ours?" Did he think she was on board with whatever he'd planned?

He smiled like he always had when dictating her next project. "Yes, dear daughter. You're coming with me. You'll have your own lab with unlimited funds and resources in a palace with a staff to attend to your every whim."

Her fingers gripped the strap of her bag. "And where might this palace be?"

"Far, far away from here." He waved his hands through the air like he was telling a fairy tale. "Let's just say there's plenty of sand. It should remind you of your mom. She always did like to build sandcastles. It's a shame she'll never get to visit your new home."

"Don't ever talk about my mother again." She sucked in a huge gulp of air as she pulled her arm back and drove her fist into his jaw.

Chris stood back from the elevator bank and enjoyed the fear in James's eyes.

The weasel tried to duck around Linc and Nic, but they boxed him under a gigantic potted palm in the corner. A small squeak jumped from James's throat as a frond brushed his cheek. "What do you want?"

Chris stepped in front of him. It took monumental effort to rein in his wrath for the weasel who'd fed Scarlett's self-doubt instead of treating her like the most beautiful, desirable woman in the universe. "Tell me where Scarlett is, and we'll leave."

James's eyes darted toward the silent elevators and the near-deserted lobby. "I'm calling security."

Nic flicked his thumb to the guard reading a newspaper. "Do you really think Grandpa over there is any match for us? And Tiffany at the desk is having drinks with me tomorrow night. Wonder who she'll side with if you start crying like a baby."

Chris closed in on the weasel. "Scarlett's gone missing. Right after hired guns tried to kidnap her. Tell me what you know."

James backed farther against the palm tree. "I don't know where she is."

"You *will* regret it if you don't talk. To be fair, I won't beat you with my steel hand." Chris nodded toward his other arm. "I'll use the human one instead."

"Okay, okay." James held up his shaky palms. "All I know is Henry assured me he was putting a plan in motion to get Scarlett back to work. Very soon."

In motion.

That meant it wasn't over. He gripped James's palm in his steel like a handshake and squeezed hard enough to bruise skin but not break bone. "What else did he say?"

James stared at their clasped hands. His lips twisted in agony. "That's your bionic one."

Chris smiled and squeezed a smidge harder. "I said I wouldn't beat you with it. No promises about anything else."

James gagged and covered his mouth. Chris released his grip. He didn't want puke on his shoes. "Swallow your shit and talk."

James cradled his hand against his suit jacket. "That's all I know."

"We discovered someone with license plates tied to a company called JS Holdings has been staking out her place. Those are your initials."

"I don't know anything about such a company."

"But you were there when her house was being broken into."

"Henry sent me. He thought after the fiasco at the governor's gala, she'd be scared and would come running back to her family. I didn't know anybody had broken into her house. I swear."

Nic hissed. "You're so not her *familia*. We are."

Chris nodded in agreement without taking his eyes off James. "Are you missing her, or are dollar signs the only thing you see when you look at Scarlett?"

James tilted his head. "You fucked her, didn't you?"

Chris grabbed him by the throat. "Say that again, and I'll rip your tongue out." He dipped his head and lowered his voice to an ominous whisper. "And just so we're clear, I satisfied her so thoroughly she doesn't remember your name. Now tell me where she is so I can make sure she screams *my* name for the rest of her life."

Chris shoved him into the tree and let go.

James rubbed his neck. "Mine and Scarlett's engagement was more like a business deal to keep her tied to the company. But I do care about her and haven't given up hope that someday she'll become Dr. Jacquelyn Scarlett Kerrigan Samuels."

"Jacquelyn Scarlett?" Realization blasted through Chris. Jacquelyn was her mother's name.

He spun to face his brothers. "I know who's behind JS Holdings."

THIRTY-THREE

S horty gripped Scarlett's upper arms and pulled her away from Henry. She threw her head back. The crack of her skull against the goon's nose reverberated in her brain. Bright lights flashed in her vision as her knees hit the carpet.

Henry laughed. "See what happens when you don't behave, little girl? You get yourself hurt, like the time I told you not to join the track team and you sprained your ankle."

She pulled air into her nose and fought nausea. Showing any more weakness wasn't an option. A moment later, she opened her eyes. The red mark on Henry's face fired her strength and she rose. She hoped the blow she'd delivered hurt as much as the back of her head.

Shorty grabbed her bicep. She bent her elbow and aimed for his bloody nose. He twisted her arm behind her back. A cry rushed from her lips. She bit her tongue. Hard.

"Let her go." Henry rubbed his jaw. "She knows better than to hit her father again, don't you?"

Scarlett jumped away from Shorty but didn't get far. He

stayed so close she could feel his breath on her neck. "You aren't my father."

Henry rubbed his jaw as he pointed to her left hand. "Did I mention you're going to marry James to keep the business in the family? The wedding will be fit for a princess. Again, a shame your mother won't be there."

"I said not to talk about my mother." She gritted out the words and swallowed blood.

Henry leaned against his desk and crossed his ankles, as relaxed as if they were discussing a wedding she actually wanted to take place.

To a man she loved.

Chris.

God, she loved that stubborn, beautiful, dangerous warrior.

Henry lifted his tumbler of bourbon off the desk and took a sip. "Let's talk about Daviani. Using his ex-wife's place as a hideout was smart. Too bad he'd mentioned the place to Thompson a few months back. Did you get cozy at the cabin with your super man?"

"Don't talk about him either." Her mom was lost to her forever, but as long as Scarlett breathed, Chris wasn't. "And you're nuts if you think I'm going to marry James and live in some palace. Does he know about your plan?"

"It doesn't matter. All you need to know is that James agreed to marry you and go wherever I need him. There were several foreign governments who wanted you. The bidding went higher than I'd ever anticipated."

Bidding?

Was this his sick idea of a joke? She searched his eyes for a sign of humor. The maniacal truth had her stumbling back into Shorty. "You really sold me to the highest bidder?"

Henry sighed and shook his head. "Don't make the trans-action sound so distasteful. I didn't actually sell you. I leased your expertise. When the contract is up, I'll see where you are needed next. Thompson's son-in-law will meet you at your new home. Once you and your new colleagues are finished with him, you'll start working for our new client."

"Do you have any idea what atrocities can be committed if technology like mine is sold to terrorists?" She swallowed. "If *I'm* sold to terrorists?"

"Not my problem once the deal is done."

"You're insane. I could have died today. Chris got shot trying to protect me."

He slammed down his tumbler. The glass cover on the mahogany desktop cracked. "I gave strict orders you were not to get hurt. And your lover is of no consequence."

"He's not my lover."

He's so much more.

She lunged at her stepfather. "I hate you."

Shorty yanked her back.

Henry rubbed his reddened jaw. "Seems you've picked up some bad behavior at VIPER."

She struggled against the goon's hold. "Fuck off."

Henry nodded. Something sharp pricked her neck.

I should have never left Chris, she thought before darkness consumed her.

Chris banged his steel on the dashboard as they drove away from Henry's house. "I can't believe we just missed him. How do we know the guard at the gate wasn't lying to us?"

James fidgeted in his spot, sandwiched between Linc and Nic in the back seat of Kane's pickup truck. "I've known Ernie most of my life. He has no reason not to be honest with me. If he said Henry left by himself, that's what happened."

"Doesn't mean Ernie wasn't instructed to lie to you."

"Can I go now. I got you into Henry's house like you demanded. And just because this company you say was staking out Scarlett's house has the same initials as her mother doesn't mean Henry is behind her alleged disappearance."

"Shut up," Chris growled. Where the hell was Scarlett? His hope that she was at Henry's quickly died when a search proved she wasn't there. Billy's car wasn't there either, but that didn't mean someone hadn't moved evidence of her arrival.

Chris glared at James. "Have you come up with any bright ideas about where Henry took her?"

The weasel shook his head.

"Think harder before I decide to use you as target practice."

Fucking douchebags. He and Richardson. They thought Scarlett's brain was their ticket to something big and planned to cash in. "Nic, any luck finding Henry or Thompson?"

"No pings on their phones. I'm trying to hack into the city traffic cameras and the surveillance feeds at Henry's house, but no luck yet."

"Keep trying. We need to understand the connection between those two assholes."

"I'm with you, *hermano*. What good are our superpowers if we can't find the enemy?"

Scarlett's words echoed in his head.

"Cyber is my battlefield. When I need steel and V-Strikes, I'll let you know."

The memory of her voice, passionate and confident, slowed down his racing pulse. She'd been right. This wasn't his battlefield. At least not yet. "We'll get to kick some ass soon, but first, we need some serious cyber power. Now."

Nic stuck his head between the seats. "How? Scarlett's not here."

"No, she's not, but I know someone else who can help us. Kane, call Beth."

"Why? She works for one of the health agencies. She's not a cyber expert."

"But she can get in touch with someone who is."

THIRTY-FOUR

The drumbeat in Scarlett's head banged a steady rhythm against her brain. She opened her eyes. Mist clouded her vision.

Where am I?

Through the fuzz, she could discern two identical goons sitting in front of her in folding chairs. They didn't look as beefy or as tall as the overgrown ones from the cabin, but they still appeared plenty formidable. The white bandages over their busted noses added to their hired mercenary aura. She squinted. Both goons merged into one, only to separate again when she relaxed her vision.

Acid from the greasy drive-through burger she'd scarfed down on the way to DC coated her throat. The nasty taste hurled her into reality.

Thompson. Henry.

She squeezed her eyelids shut. The nausea wouldn't abate. She held back a sob, but a single tear threatened to make a break for it.

Think strong, like Chris.

He'd thrown himself in front of a bullet to protect her

and remained steady and sure despite the terrors haunting him in the dark. She imagined his powerful arms wrapped around her, holding her securely in his steel embrace.

His voice telling her she was sexy and badass and funny filtered through her mind. She opened her eyes. Her vision cleared. The tears dried. Her breath pushed out in a soft whoosh as she surveyed the stark room. She had no idea where she was, but it didn't take a genius to figure out the gun and the zip ties on the card table next to Buster the Goon meant she was a prisoner.

Somewhere, but where?

Buster looked up from his phone. A dimple in his jaw winked. "Sit still and nothing will get messy."

She swung her legs over the cot and leaned back. The cold, hard wall behind her offered relief to her feverish body.

"I said don't move." He nudged the zip ties with his fingers. "I've been instructed to tie you to the cot if you give me a hard time."

She held up her hands in surrender and sniffed. "Sorry."

Stop crying.

Facts, not tears, would help her devise an escape plan before Henry shipped her to a prison palace. She rubbed her eyes. As her vision cleared, she examined the tiny dim room. To her left, a thick crowbar secured the only door. Moonlight filtered through a window on her right, not nearly big enough to crawl through. Below it, another card table held a coffeepot and disposable cups. Based on the beverage station and the comfort and cleanliness of the cot, she guessed she was in a break room.

Scarlett surveyed Buster, praying a conscience lived underneath his light-brown buzz cut. How unscrupulous could a guy with such a cute dimple be? She hoped not too bad because without his help, she didn't see any way to escape. "Please tell me where I am."

He dropped his gaze to his phone. Whatever he looked at conjured a smile.

"Can you tell me what time it is?" She rubbed her stomach. "I'm hungry."

He sighed as he raised his gaze. "It's way past dinner."

Sadness, not malice, appeared to lurk in his gray eyes. And she'd caught him smiling a moment ago. He didn't look as deadly as the goons from the cabin, although the tight black long-sleeve shirt he wore didn't hide his lean muscle.

She tilted her head to the window and sniffed. The scent of grass tickled her nose. She strained her ears to listen. A plane engine roared to life. Was she near Reagan National Airport? Or Dulles? No, it couldn't be. That wasn't a commercial jet engine. That had to be a commuter plane, which meant she was likely in a hangar at an airstrip.

A sharp rap on the door made her jump.

"Let me in."

She stiffened at Henry's voice. As Buster removed the crowbar, she resisted the urge to sink into the wall. She'd be damned if she'd let him know his stepfather-gone-batshit-crazy transformation terrified her.

Henry stepped into the moonbeam. "Glad to see you've woken up from your nap. I thought I'd stop by and see how you were doing on my way to talk to my pilot."

She didn't dare get up and gouge her fingers into his eyes, or rip his tongue out of his vile mouth like she wanted. Henry was so unhinged he wouldn't think twice about having Buster carry through with his threat to tie her up. Now that she had a clue where she was, she had to keep Henry talking. "Did you get a new plane?"

"Why, yes. She's a beauty."

"Are we at the airfield by your mansion?"

"Don't worry about the details. I've got the trip all arranged. Our new client is eager to meet you. He has an entire army of soldiers waiting to be blessed with your genius."

"What is your client planning to do? Cut off limbs so I can give the soldiers weaponized ones?"

"Among other things. There was talk about thought-detonated bombs." He shrugged. "What the client does with my product is none of my business."

She jumped to her feet. "*Your* product?"

He stepped in front of her, his face so close she could smell the bourbon on his breath. "Yes. My product. Everything in your remarkable mind belongs to me."

The cool head she needed to prevail fumed to near boiling. "It doesn't matter what you think. VIPER *will* find me, and you and Thompson *will* go to jail for betraying your country."

"Don't be so sure. You're not the only one who can hack into surveillance cameras. I have a team of two dozen making sure your friends can't track you here." He took his phone out of his pocket and glanced at it. "And I've received confirmation from Thompson that, as per the deputy secretary of defense, Project VIPER was disbanded due to—"

He held his phone away from his face and made a show of scrutinizing the message. "Oh yes, here it is. Due to, 'potentially dangerous insecurities in the technology and its management.'"

"No." She wouldn't accept defeat.

He held up his arm like a scarecrow on a post and dangled it back and forth. "Soon, your boys will be the only security guards with shiny, useless toys hanging from their bodies." He stepped to the door, a satisfied smile on his face. "Rest up, princess. We leave for the Middle East within the hour."

*   .   ⊕   *   *

Chris met Governor Bradley and his nephew Ryan in the underground parking garage at VIPER headquarters. "Thank you for coming."

Bradley shook his hand. "Ryan was dropping me off at the airport when Scarlett's friend called to say you needed his help. We got here as soon as we could."

Ryan slung the laptop bag in his hand over his shoulder. "Any updates on Scarlett's location? I knew something was off when she didn't meet me for coffee this morning before her class. She'd seemed really excited at the gala to discuss the new federal cybersecurity mandate."

Chris shook Ryan's hand a bit too hard at the reminder of how perfect he was for Scarlett. "No updates. We're hoping you can help with that."

"I can." Ryan headed for the elevator. "Let's go find our genius."

Chris fired a glare at his back with the intensity of a V-Strike.

Scarlett was *his* genius.

Bradley raised his eyebrows. Chris swallowed his jealousy. Ryan was a respected cyber expert, according to the articles written about him, and he'd dropped everything when Beth had called. He'd even been in the military. Yet, it killed Chris a little to ask Scarlett's admirer for help.

Minutes later, they arrived at the briefing room. He nodded to the team seated at the table while he watched security escort James to another conference room for further questioning about Henry's plan to get Scarlett back to work. Sweat dripped down the weasel's face. He's lucky it wasn't blood. Chris cracked his flesh-and-bone knuckles, half-proud he'd shown restraint when James had spoken about Scarlett like she was an object and half-pissed that he hadn't put a permanent curve in the guy's straight nose with his steel.

Chris nodded to the team seated at the table as Admiral

Edgar appeared in the doorway. "Nice of you to show up to work, Daviani?"

Before Chris could answer, the admiral spotted the governor. His crusty demeanor softened. "What are you doing here, Bradley? I thought you were on your way to meet Kathleen in the Bahamas?"

"Looks like my wife's going to have to wait until this mess is cleared up."

Edgar tugged at his mustache. "You want to talk about a mess? I was at the White House when I got a call about VIPER going to hell. The president's not happy the Joint Chiefs of Staff are suggesting Project VIPER be disbanded."

Kane shoved back from the table and stood. "Disbanded?"

Nic punched his hand into his other fist. "No. Oh, fuck no. VIPER can't be disbanded. I haven't kicked any terrorist ass with my super leg yet."

"And I was promised a plane," Linc whined like a moody teenager. "Some opportunity to be superheroes this turned out to be."

Fear snaked through Chris. VIPER couldn't be dissolved. He needed the program— No, he needed a purpose to get out of bed every morning and do something meaningful, like he needed water to exist. He couldn't let his thoughts go to the dark place he'd inhabit if he didn't have VIPER in his life.

Or Scarlett.

His arms snapped to his sides at attention. "Admiral, we can explain everything."

"Damn right you'll explain. Starting with where you've been, why Thompson is MIA, and why Dr. Kerrigan set a trap in VIPER's network to catch the hacker, even though she's no longer employed here."

Hope jumped in Chris's chest. "Did her trap work?"

THIRTY-FIVE

Scarlett eyed Buster. She didn't know how many muscled goons Henry employed, but this one was her only chance of escape. "Can I get up and stretch? I'm a bit sore."

He grabbed the pistol with one hand and touched his swollen nose with the other. "Fine, but standing only. No steps."

"Did Henry send you to ambush the cabin? Is that how you busted your face?" She didn't remember seeing him among the bloody bodies, but focusing on staying alive could make a girl miss things.

He rubbed his wrist. "Be quiet."

She knew riling up the man with the gun didn't fuel her plan, but her panic-laced, anger-fueled adrenaline needed an outlet. "Sorry. It must hurt your face to talk, so I'll leave you alone while I stretch."

She stood and craned her neck toward the window. A sleek white plane sat on a grassy runway. Two men bustled about as if they were readying it for a flight.

To a place far, far away.

Her hands shook. If she got on that plane, she'd never see Chris again.

Never get to tell him I love him.

Despite her chilling situation, warmth surged into her heart. It felt wonderful to say the words, even in her head, but she didn't have time to explore her new feelings.

Buster waved his hand. "Enough. Sit down."

One more stretch wouldn't yield any information. Frustration burned her already bloodshot eyes. She wouldn't cry again.

Be strong, confident like I felt when I wore the red... Wait. Numbers. On the tail.

"Got it."

Buster's eyes narrowed. "What did you say?"

"Nothing." She didn't know how yet, but those tail numbers would help her escape.

Buster rubbed the inside of his wrist. Since she'd woken up, she'd noticed him rubbing the spot, much like Chris rubbed his 9/11 ink when he was uneasy or upset. She leaned closer. Sure enough, a dark-red mark peeked out from under his cuff.

"Is that a tattoo of your girlfriend's name? Or maybe your wife's?"

He pinned her with a hard stare. A moment later, his features softened. "My daughter's."

So, the goon's a daddy.

His menacing factor slid down another notch.

She matched her tone to his, sensing life wasn't all sunshine and unicorns for Buster and his child. "What's her name?"

"Lucy. She's seven." He touched his nose. "I got this playing softball with her. She's going to be one hell of a pitcher."

Scarlett sat on the cot and leaned toward him. "What a pretty name. Does she look like you?"

He chuckled. "Thank heavens, no. She looks like her mother. She was so beautiful."

Scarlett's heart constricted at the past tense. "I'm sorry."

His eyes drifted to another place. "She was Army. So was I until breast cancer took her and I became a single dad."

"I also lost my mom when I was young." She wouldn't wish that on anyone. Thank God the girl had a father who loved her. "Tell me more about Lucy."

"She's amazing. Smart and sassy, with a big heart that wraps you up like a warm, fuzzy blanket. She's my reason to get up of bed in the morning and who I look forward to snuggling each night."

Scarlett hugged herself, recalling how it felt to wrap her arms around her own mother.

Buster rubbed his wrist. "We were doing okay, going to therapy together and making a new life for the two of us."

"That's smart of you to see a therapist. I have an excellent colleague, Dr. Airis, if you need a referral."

"It's kind of you to offer." His gray eyes turned stormy. "Lucy is struggling with more than losing her mother. Richardson said you're a famous genius. You can no doubt hook us up with the best, but I can't afford the kind of doctors you know."

Scarlett's scientific instincts kicked in. "Tell me what happened."

Buster glanced at the door. "I shouldn't be talking to you. I'm supposed to keep you locked down and quiet. According to Richardson, your hyperintelligence makes you unstable and you fly into rages."

She laughed. "If anyone in this family is unstable, it's my stepfather. Trust me, we'll hear Henry coming if he checks on us. He likes to make a big entrance."

"Weak men do that."

He smirked and his harsh, angular features took on a playful quality she found handsome.

"You seem like a good guy. Why are you working for a criminal?"

"I started working as a security guard a week ago. I'm catching on that Henry isn't a good man, but I can't leave until I get another night job because I need to be home with Lucy."

He pulled in a deep breath. His broad shoulders slumped as he exhaled. "She doesn't speak anymore. There was a shooting in the park across the street from our apartment. Every day my baby must look out our kitchen window and see the spot where she watched her friend die. I can't afford to move. And I can't afford the specialist our therapist has recommended."

Scarlett leaned forward and touched the back of his hand. "I'm so sorry. Watching your baby suffer and not being able to do anything about it must tear you up inside."

She placed her hand over her heart where it broke for him and Lucy and still ached for her own loss. "You and Lucy need to get in to see Dr. Airis right away. The quicker they can start the intake process and gather information, the quicker they can formulate a plan of care."

"But—"

She gripped his hand. "Don't worry about the money. Dr. Airis will help Lucy because she's a good person. But I can't make that happen if Henry ships me off to a foreign country. You need to help me get out of here."

Chris rubbed his 9/11 ink as Admiral Edgar's aide relayed an update about the location of the hacker. "The coordinates lead to an abandoned apartment building outside of DC. A TAC team is raiding the place now."

"She did it." Scarlett found the bad guy. At least one of them. He couldn't wait to tell her how proud he was. First, he had to find her.

"Good." Edgar turned to Daviani. "Brief me on what's happened since you shot the governor."

By the time Chris finished relaying the details, Edgar's ears flamed as red as the stripes on the American flag hanging in the corner. He motioned to his aide. "Send someone to interrogate this James guy. I want to know everything he knows about Richardson right up until the last shit he took."

He pointed to Ryan Bradley. "Find Richardson and Thompson. I'm giving you a battlefield promotion to VIPER support, effective now."

The sound of fingers slamming into keys chimed like a symphony in Chris's ears.

Edgar took a break from barking orders and clapped the governor on the shoulder. "I'm sorry about VIPER going bad at your expense."

Bradley sighed. "Not Scarlett's or Daviani's fault, or anyone else's at VIPER. Except Thompson's. I thought he was one of the good guys."

Chris watched the exchange, impressed with the admiral's assertiveness and the governor's compassion. The boulder on his chest crumbled a little. Their cyber plan was in motion, but the slight progress only eased his tension by a fraction. He still didn't know where Scarlett was. They were banking on her being with Richardson, but what if they were wrong? What if a third party was involved, or someone else besides Thompson was behind the hacking?

Doing nothing was slowly driving him mad. He had to get out there and search for Scarlett. "When can we expect word from the TAC team?"

Edgar tapped on the computer console built into the table. "Any minute. If the hacker's there, we'll get him."

"Or she. Our hacker could be a woman."

Scarlett's words from the cabin echoed in his head. The memory of her voice slowed his heartbeat a notch.

Edgar's aide poked his head into the room. "Sir, the TAC team lead is on the line."

A video feed from the raid location popped up on the screen on the other side of the room.

Jealousy raced through Chris. He'd been engineered to use his strength, not harness it, while he waited for someone else to deliver results.

The TAC team lead came into focus. "I'm sorry, sir." He stepped aside to reveal an empty loft, except for a folding table and a tangle of wires. "We're too late."

A litany of curses bounced around the conference space.

Chris slammed his steel onto the table hard enough to rattle the mugs scattered about.

Ryan sliced a hand through his wavy hair. "I can't work if you flood my laptop with coffee."

"Hey." Kane jumped up and waved a burner phone in his hand. "It's Beth. She got a cryptic text from Scarlett."

Hope pressed against the fear swirling inside Chris like a dam against a raging river. "Put her on speaker."

Edgar's bushy eyebrows furrowed. "Are there any more characters in this show I need to know about?"

Chris ignored him. "Go ahead, Beth."

"I got a text from a number I didn't recognize a few minutes ago. I called but got a busy signal. Scarlett's in danger, isn't she?"

"I need you to calm down and read me the message."

"It says, 'Won't make dinner tonight. Needed a little vacation, so took a nap. Lunch tomorrow at the Middle

Eastern place on the corner of N and Eighth at six forty-five? Bring *V* and *S*.'"

He leaned over the phone. "Did you have plans to meet her tonight?"

"No."

"The message is clearly not about dinner because no such intersection exists," Nic pointed out.

"And Scarlett hates Middle Eastern food, and she never takes naps. Or vacations," Beth said.

Nap?

Fear wound its way around Chris's spine and slithered into his arms. He could even feel it in his steel. "Could 'take a nap' mean kidnapped?'"

"To the Middle East?" Linc shook his head. "She hasn't been gone long enough."

"Or whoever kidnapped her is planning on taking her to the Middle East. On a plane because—"

Linc speared his hand into his spiky hair. "You take vacations on a plane, and every plane has a tail number."

Governor Bradley slapped his leg. "N and eighth at six forty-five. She's telling us the plane's registration number is N8645. That woman really is an honest-to-goodness genius."

Pride surged through Chris.

My genius.

Edgar pointed to Ryan. "Find me that plane."

"Wait." Nic held up his steel hand. "What does *V* and *S* mean?"

Chris's lips twitched up at the corners. "Steel and V-Strikes, baby. That's us."

Kane rubbed his leg. "We've got the *S*."

"Now we need the *V*." Chris turned to the two men who could help them get it. "Can one of you ask the president to activate us?"

Governor Bradley pushed the phone on the table to Admiral Edgar. "Would you like to be the one to call our esteemed classmate?"

"No, you do it. She always did like you better."

THIRTY-SIX

C hris paced like a caged animal on the roof of
VIPER headquarters. The helicopter to take them
to Scarlett's location sat ready to go on the helipad.

Ryan had found the plane registered to the tail number
in Scarlett's text message in a matter of minutes. In another
few, they'd be in the air. Once Chris found Scarlett, he'd
shoot Richardson in the balls. And if he'd hurt one hair on
her beautiful head, he'd cut the fried balls off the degenerate's
body.

A hand clamped on his shoulder. "Daviani."

He spun. "Yes, sir?"

Bradley met him eye to eye. "Are you up for this?"

"Why wouldn't I be?"

Because I'm going on a mission to save the woman I love.

The truth hit him like a V-Strike. He must love her
because he couldn't remember anything scaring him as much
as the paralyzing fear of putting his trust and his heart in the
hands of a woman again.

Bradley narrowed his eyes. "I ain't blind, son. You have
feelings for her. Feelings that could compromise the mission."

Chris swore under his breath. Could everyone see how he felt about Scarlett? "I can handle it."

He dropped his gaze to the ground. What he couldn't handle was being the one left behind to worry. Was this how Natalie had felt when he'd deployed? He'd understood her fears on a logical level but never in his heart. How would Scarlett feel when he left for a mission? If she were with a man like Ryan Bradley, she wouldn't have to handle any of it.

Or handle me.

Someone yelled a two-minute warning to takeoff. Chris raised his gaze and met the governor eye to eye. "I got this, sir. I'll bring her back."

Bradley clapped Chris on the shoulder. "Good luck, son." A low chuckle rumbled from his chest. "You're going to need it."

As Chris loped toward the helicopter, he somehow knew Bradley was wishing him luck with more than the mission.

A short ride later, Linc set the helo down in a clearing a half mile out from the airfield where they surmised Scarlett was being held.

Ryan's clipped voice cracked in his ears. "I've taken care of the security cameras. Sending entry points to your comms now. Your video feeds are live. We'll have eyes on you the whole time. The trauma surgeon VIPER just hired is en route as medical support."

"Listen up." Edgar's voice boomed over the line. "Don't make the new guy work too hard on his first day. And remember the plan. Secure Dr. Kerrigan and apprehend Richardson. Alive."

Minutes later, Chris and the team crouched in the bushes at the perimeter of the airfield. Although Ryan had confirmed the plane was still on the runway, he breathed easier when he viewed the tail numbers through his binoculars.

Nic pointed to the armed guards. "There are the men Ryan reported seeing on the aerial surveillance."

Linc studied the aircraft. "The fucker's got good taste in planes. Looks like the pilot's already in the cockpit doing a preflight check."

Chris held up his steel and gave the command to move.

Kane fanned out to the front of the hangar on the far side of the airstrip. Chris followed Nic and Linc under a gap in the fence Ryan had identified. After they reported their status to headquarters, they ran into the night, their dark clothes blending into the shadows. Chris fired a V-Strike meant to incapacitate and not kill to the abdomen of an armed guard standing at the tail end of the plane. Nic shot the same force to the guard near the nose. The two stationed outside the hangar entrance suffered the same fate. Chris smiled as they collapsed to the ground.

He scanned the area for more hostiles. "All clear."

Kane confirmed his area was clear too.

While Chris took cover behind the wheel and Nic behind a small shed near the entrance of the hangar, Linc climbed aboard the aircraft to overtake the pilot.

Sweat gathered under the cap Chris wore low on his forehead.

Come on, Scarlett. Let me know you're here.

He didn't have to wait long. Scarlett and a man in black emerged through the hangar doors and onto the grassy airfield. Red blotches peppered the whites of her eyes under the moonlight. No tears fell, but her lower lip quivered. The guard, who was only a few inches taller than Scarlett but packed plenty of muscle, held a pistol to her side and grasped her like a prisoner.

If he hurts her, he's a dead man.

Chris started toward them, but the voice of one of his SEAL instructors rang in his ears.

"Hold your position no matter what."

He commanded his feet to stop moving. As his pulse accelerated and his patience plummeted, he locked his gaze on the woman he loved.

Come on, sweetheart. Stay tough.

Seconds later, Richardson strode out, his chin in the air like he was the president boarding Air Force One. He pointed to the tail of the plane. "What the hell happened to my security guards?"

Chris growled as he bent low and barreled toward him. The man holding Scarlett whisked her out of the way as Chris slammed Richardson to the ground and planted his boot on his chest. "It's over. Your men have been neutralized. Our pilot has commandeered the plane."

Richardson wrapped his hands around Chris's ankle and shoved. "Get off me, or I'll have my man shoot her."

"No, you won't. You need her mind."

"The human body is funny like that." Richardson's voice remained steady despite his attempts to dislodge Chris's foot from his chest. "It's amazing what it can endure and still manage to function. What do you think, Daviani? How much pain can *she* withstand?"

Chris grabbed Richardson by the throat and yanked him up. "She's withstood a lot of pain living with you. Question is, how much can *you* take?"

The color drained from Richardson's face.

A biofeedback alert vibrated from Chris's comms. "Keep your cool, Daviani. We need him alive."

He cursed at Edgar's command to control his rage, but he loosened his grip.

Richardson stuffed his hands in his pockets as he nodded

to the man holding Scarlett. "Gage, show Commander Daviani I mean business."

"Oh, no." Gage lowered his weapon. "I'm not shooting anybody. Except you, maybe. She's right about you being the unstable one in the *familia.*"

Nic crept up behind Henry. "Like I told that fucker James, you're not her family. We are." He grabbed Henry's fisted hands from his pockets and forced them behind his back. "And you don't have the balls to kill anyone. Even your own man turned on you."

Henry laughed as Nic zip-tied his hands. "I killed her mother. Why wouldn't I kill her?"

Chris whipped his head to Scarlett.

The color drained from her face. "You…you what?"

"Jacquelyn wasn't on board with my plan for your future. She even had the audacity to ask for a divorce and take you away from me so I did what any good businessman would do. I alleviated the barrier to my goal. A swipe of my hand and her inhaler on the nightstand fell to places unknown."

"You murdered my mother because of…me?"

She trembled as thick tears rolled down her cheeks. Gage pulled her into his chest.

Richardson shrugged. "Sometimes we have to make sacrifices for the greater good."

Chris shoved Richardson back. Screw taking him alive.

He visualized his target.

Dead center in the heart.

"Stand down, *hermano,*" Nic said.

Gage agreed. "Dead men can't pay for their crimes."

Chris's body vibrated with the need to end Richardson and gather Scarlett in his arms, but hell, Nic and their new ally were right. Bradley had been too. He'd almost let his feelings for Scarlett compromise the mission.

"Military police are two minutes out," Ryan said through the comms.

"Roger that." Chris repeated the information to Gage and Scarlett.

A sinister smile crossed Henry's lips. "They won't make it in time."

A firecracker on steroids popped from the plane. Chris whirled as a deafening bang sliced the atmosphere and vibrated the air. The explosion propelled him onto his ass. Scarlett's muffled scream filtered into his ears. As he jumped to his feet, the aircraft's wing erupted in flames.

When his eyes focused a half second later, he spotted Henry sitting in the grass. His laugh carried over the roar of the blaze as he rolled onto his side and splayed out his cuffed hands. A black device rolled onto the ground.

A detonator.

Henry looked him in the eye and mouthed, "Kaboom."

Fuck the plan. Chris visualized his target and fired. A satisfying current pulsed out of his bicep and shot into Henry's dick.

"Psychopath," he spat as Henry howled.

Chris searched for Scarlett and spotted her on the ground a few feet away. Gage sat up next to her.

"Fuel tank's been hit," Ryan shouted. "Get Linc out of the cockpit."

Chris spotted Nic sprinting toward the aircraft.

He looked at Gage. "Get her to safety." The blaze toasted Chris's skin as he ran into the fire. Black smoke streamed out the cabin door and obscured the gangplank steps. "Linc, what's your status?"

"I'm…" Linc coughed hard as a biofeedback alert sounded. A ragged wheeze followed. "I'm trapped in the cockpit. Gonna bust out of here."

"Hang on, we're coming."

Chris jumped up and grabbed the nose of the plane with both hands. Agony tore through his stitched-up arm as he swung his legs like he was dangling from a rope and hoisted himself up.

The hiss of the fire nearly drowned out Ryan's voice. "Kane, what's your status?"

"Headed to Scarlett."

Hold on, baby, Chris begged as he shimmied up the slope of the nose and joined Nic at the windshield. Thick smoke consumed the cockpit. He strained his eyes against the undulating heat waves distorting his vision. "Come on, buddy, where are you?" The sole of a booted foot smashed into the windshield from the inside. "Found him."

Chris wrangled the urge to shatter the glass with a V-Strike. Instead of upsetting the aircraft's already volatile structural status, he took a deep breath and visualized a hole big enough for Linc to fit through. Concentrating, he harnessed the current ripping into his arm with the precision of a surgeon and cut into the windshield.

"Can't...breathe," Linc wheezed through the comms.

"Hold on." Chris held his breath as the V-Strike finished scoring a circular fissure. He heaved out a breath as he pushed through the glass. The frame buckled from the heat as Linc's hand burst through the broken window. Nic tore off pieces of metal threatening to collapse into the cockpit as Chris grabbed Linc's hand.

As he pulled him from the fiery cockpit, a second blast tore through the night.

Scarlett screamed but couldn't hear herself over the roar of the thunderous explosion. A wall of sweltering heat rose before her as Chris, Nic and Linc tumbled from the nose of the plane and onto the scorched earth.

"Help them," she yelled to Kane as he rushed toward her. She grabbed the gun from Gage. "You too."

He looked at Henry wiggling on the ground and hesitated.

"I got this." She cocked the gun. "Go."

She watched the two men run into the fire as she pointed the gun at her stepfather. "Sit still."

Despite the V-Strike to his crotch, the murdering bastard still moved.

She kept one eye on him, the other on the wall of flames and held her breath. Long seconds passed as she waited for Chris and the team to walk through fire. She sobbed in half relief, half dread when Gage and Kane stumbled through the curtain of thick smoke with Linc supported between them. Next came Chris, his steel arm supporting Nic, who limped on his flesh-and-bone leg.

Breathing came easier now that she had eyes on Chris. She turned her full attention to Henry.

He peered at her through glossy eyes. "That bomb was my plan C in case plan B went awry. Good thing I have a plan D."

She looked down the barrel of the gun at him. "I don't care if you have a whole alphabet of plans. Shut up."

"No, my dear. Time for me to shut *you* up." With a smug smile, he yanked his arms from behind his back.

Her gaze snapped to the pocketknife he'd used to cut his zip ties. The small pistol in his other hand glinted in the moonlight as he aimed it at her.

She squeezed the trigger. A loud pop rang in her ears. The gun slipped from her hand. Confusion paralyzed her for a split second before her brain reacted to the excruciating inferno spiraling in her chest. She felt her ribs crack. Felt the breath rush out of her lungs as she hit the ground.

"I'm sorry it had to come to this," she heard Henry say. "But if I can't benefit from your genius mind, nobody else will either."

Chris spun toward the gunshots. Scarlett's stunned eyes met his as the force of a bullet thrust her back. He roared her name as he jumped past Nic and fired a V-Strike at Henry's hand. As Chris slid on his knees to Scarlett's side, he heard Henry scream.

"No." Blood oozed through her shirt from a bullet hole below her right breast. "Wake up, goddammit."

Her lips didn't move, and her eyes remained shut.

Behind him, Henry bellowed at Gage and Kane to release him.

"Help," Chris screamed as he pressed both hands to her wound. Where was the medical support Ryan had said would be on-site? He stared at Scarlett's pale face and willed her eyes to open. "Don't you dare leave me again, do you hear me? Don't you dare."

Someone dropped next to him.

Chris spun his head. "Langley? You're our medical support?"

"Yup, and what a first day I'm having."

Chris had never been so happy to see an old friend. "I thought you retired after…"

"I saved you from bleeding out?" He unhooked a pair of scissors from his backpack and snipped the neckline of Scarlett's shirt. "I did retire, but I heard you and your super soldier posse needed a super doctor on their team, so here I am." He tapped Chris's steel hand with the scissors. "Nice upgrade from the one you left back in the Middle East. Now move and let me do my job."

Every instinct told Chris not to let her go, but if he could trust anyone with Scarlett's life, it was Dr. Hudson Langley.

Slowly, he pulled his hands off Scarlett's wound. Blood stained his palms. His own blood dripped down his arm inside his jacket. His reopened stitches would have to wait while the man who saved his life back in the military field hospital in the Middle East now saved the life of the woman he loved.

Gripping Scarlett's hand, he held on tight and silently begged her to wake up and start rambling about something.

Anything.

He blocked out Henry's angry shouts and the blare of sirens and lowered his head to Scarlett's ear. "Come on, baby. Wake up. I've got something to tell you, but I need you to be awake when I say it."

Gage dropped to his knees at her other side. "How is she?"

Langley didn't look up as he packed her wound. "Alive."

"That's one determined woman. She didn't give up on convincing me to help her. She'll survive this."

Chris jerked his gaze to Gage's. "You helped her?"

"Yeah. She said you guys would come for her if I let her send a text from my phone. It was pretty clever how she coded the message in case Richardson somehow found it, don't you think?"

Chris's heart beat against his rib cage like a wrecking ball as he pressed his lips to Scarlett's. "That's my genius."

Her mouth stirred against his. "Chris."

He jerked his head up.

From under hooded lids, Scarlett held his gaze. "I knew you'd come for me."

The wrecking ball in his chest changed its beat to a

victory tune. The dam holding back his tears cracked. He sniffed them into submission as he wiped the sweat from her brow. "Steel and V-Strikes, baby. Always."

Her pale lips tilted up. The sweat on her forehead thickened as her smile drooped and her eyes rolled back into her head.

THIRTY-SEVEN

S carlett awoke to a warm hand in hers and a familiar forest-after-a-rain-shower scent.

Chris.

The pain in her torso and the pounding in her head amplified as she fought to open her eyes. She blinked until his face came into focus.

"You're awake. Thank God." Chris scooted his chair next to her and gently brushed hair away from her forehead. Deep lines fanned from his eyes and tears welled in their blue depths. He dropped his lips on her cheek. "I thought I lost you."

Tears formed in her own eyes. She closed them and let his scent and strength and everything Chris seep into her tired, achy body. "I'm right here."

He cupped her cheek. "How are you feeling?"

"Like I've been…"

Pain roared through her as she bolted into a sitting position. "Shot. I was shot." She touched her midsection. An ache thumped under her hand. Through the thin hospital gown, she felt a bandage. "How did this happen?"

Boring scientists like her didn't get shot.

Warriors like Chris got shot.

Lying, cheating bastards like Henry got shot.

Chris gently eased her back onto the pillows. He entwined his fingers with hers. "You don't remember?"

"Yeah, I do." She squeezed his hand as it all came into focus in sickening clarity.

"Are you okay?" She ran her gaze over his body. A white bandage peeked out from the sleeve of his T-shirt. A scabbed-over cut hugged his hairline, and an angry red burn marred his cheek.

"Now that you're awake, I'm fine." He stroked his thumb along her jaw.

"And the team?"

"All good. Patience plied us with some concoction to help us heal faster."

"Thank God." The memory of them running into the blast and falling from the burning nose of the plane would remain ingrained in her mind forever. "Where are they?"

"In a briefing, where I'm supposed to be." He brushed a kiss on her lips. His hand remained in hers as he straightened.

She rubbed her stinging eyes. "How long have I been out?"

"Nearly thirty-six hours. We found you at the airfield Saturday night and it's Monday morning." Emotion thickened his voice. "The bullet caused internal bleeding and you needed surgery. Patience gave you a hefty sedative to give your body time to rest."

"Am I in MedLab?" If she weren't hooked up to a monitor that beeped incessantly, she'd think she was in a hotel suite. Photos of Washington, DC's monuments graced pale-blue walls. An open door led to a bathroom. A large flat-screen television sat in the middle of a narrow wooden dresser-like cabinet that spanned the other side of the room. A vase of daisies sat next to it, and the bed she lay in was big enough for two.

"Yeah. I've been here since we brought you in, waiting for you to wake up, except for when Edgar contained me in a debrief."

"You stayed with me?"

The hitch in her breathing had nothing to do with her injuries and everything to do with the flood of emotions coursing through her sore chest. She was safe now. Everyone she cared about was safe.

Except for her mother.

Tears leaked out of the corners of her eyes. She could see her beautiful mom reaching for her inhaler, frantically searching her bedroom while her breaths grew short and her skin pale. Could hear the wheeze of her breathing as her airway constricted. Scarlett clutched her throat. She used to imagine what her mother had felt when she'd taken her final breaths. Now she was experiencing it.

Tears streamed down her cheeks. She didn't bother to wipe them away.

Chris gathered her in his arms. "I'm so sorry."

A sob wrenched from deep inside her soul. Unchecked and unashamed, she let herself cry, each tear a measure of each day she'd felt lonely.

Lost.

Unloved.

Grieving for her mother once was hard enough. She shouldn't have to relive it all over again.

Damn Henry.

Damn her mother for inviting the monster into their lives.

No, no. no. I'm sorry, Mom. This isn't your fault. It's my fault. All my fault.

Her genius mind was to blame. It was the reason Henry had tried to sell her to the highest bidder. The reason he'd killed her mother. But the harm her gift had caused didn't end there. The federal government had trusted her to protect VIPER from threats, not to bring hackers and goons with guns to their doorstep. Chris had been shot. The entire team had been caught in an explosion. It was a wonder nobody died.

She sniffed as she pulled away from Chris. "Where's Henry?"

"In a holding cell in the building. So is James. Seems he knows more about Henry's plans than he let on. Neither one of them is giving up information about who Henry sold you to."

She hoped they were both suffering under interrogation. "What about Thompson?"

Chris shook his head. "He took his own life. They found him in a closet at the airport, gun still in his hand."

Don't throw up.

Don't. Throw. Up.

She turned her head and fixed her gaze on a photo of the Washington Monument at sunset until the nausea passed. Thompson was a criminal. A traitor to his country. He deserved to face justice for the crimes he'd committed. He hadn't deserved to die though. And his daughter? The loss of a parent was a sentence she wouldn't wish on her worst enemy.

Chris nudged her cheek to face him. "You don't look too good. I'll get Patience."

He pulled away, but she tugged him back. "I'm fine. Is VIPER still intact? Henry said it was disbanded. Please, *please* tell me he was lying."

"We were put on hiatus, but we've been reinstated." He kissed her on the middle of her forehead. "Thank you."

Another kind of ache seized her torso. This one in her heart. "It's my job."

Was her job. "I need to see Edgar. He needs to reinstate *me* so I can secure—"

"The only thing you need to do is rest." Chris gently squeezed her shoulders. "Edgar told me your reinstatement will happen. Ryan Bradley is assuming your cybersecurity role until Patience clears you to return to work."

"Ryan Bradley? How did he get involved with VIPER?"

"His help was invaluable after you went missing."

"How so?" Scarlett slurred the last word as fatigue overtook her.

"I'll tell you all about it later." He smoothed his hand over her brow. "For now, he said to tell you that he understands why you stood him up for coffee and will take a rain check."

She smiled. Some of the tension eased from her body as a memory skittered into her mind. "After I got shot, I think I heard you say that you had something to tell me."

The door opened. A man she didn't recognize, with striking features and a head of thick wavy brown hair, poked his head in. "Hi, Dr. Kerrigan. Glad to see you awake." He stepped inside the room. "I'm Dr. Hudson Langley. I treated you at the airfield and did your surgery back here in MedLab. How are you feeling?"

"Like she doesn't want to be interrupted by you." Chris waved him away. "Give us a minute."

Dr. Langley chuckled as he backed to the door. "Better make it quick. Edgar wants you in the briefing, and I need to examine Scarlett."

"Is that our trauma surgeon?"

"Yes. We go way back. Don't believe anything he says about me." Chris dropped a kiss on her lips. "Rest up. Edgar is itching to debrief you and *we* have a lot to talk about. Do you need anything before I go?"

She shook her head and yawned. "I need clothes. I'll ask Beth to drop some off."

"Okay." He kissed her again. "I'll be back as soon as I can."

"Hurry," she said as the door shut. Now that she had answers about VIPER, she needed one from Chris that had nothing to do with the project and everything to do with her heart.

THIRTY-EIGHT

Chris paced in the hallway outside of Scarlett's room in MedLab. Twenty-four hours ago, he'd kissed her with a promise to be back soon. Since he'd left, he'd snuck away twice from the army of scientists who had run tests on him and the team to see how their bodies had reacted to the active V-Strike technology. Both times he'd been barred from entering her room because Edgar was debriefing her.

When the testing had finally ended late last night, he'd raced to see her. Edgar was gone, but she'd been asleep.

Now it was the next morning and Scarlett still slept.

In the big bed.

By herself.

He'd wanted to climb in next to her and sleep in the haven they'd found at the cabin, but he didn't dare.

Thank God he hadn't.

When he'd finally fallen asleep, his nightly freak show had poisoned his slumber. Except last night's fucked up dream had included a bonus scene tacked on at the end.

Scarlett, covered in blood as red as her name, had begged him to leave her alone.

The impact of his steel punching the wall had woken him up.

He wiped sweat from his brow despite the cool temperature in the hallway. A beep sounded from his comms. A message about a high-priority briefing with Edgar in thirty minutes flashed on the screen. Did that mean VIPER had been cleared for missions?

Footsteps sounded behind him.

He spun and came face to face with Governor Bradley. "Good morning, sir."

Bradley held out a to-go cup. "I met Ryan for coffee earlier and took one for the road, but you look like you need this more than me."

Chris accepted the caffeine. "Thanks."

"How's Scarlett?"

"Still asleep."

"Well, please tell her I stopped by to see how she was feeling." He clamped a hand on Chris's shoulder. "Now, you tell me why you are out here in the cold instead of in there holding the woman you love."

Chris choked on the coffee he'd just sipped. "Excuse me?"

"Well?" Bradley laced his hands in front of him and waited.

Chris leaned against the wall and rubbed his 9/11 ink. "It doesn't matter if I love her." The truth burned like acid on his tongue. "She doesn't deserve a man like me. I could come home maimed again. Or not at all." He held out his steel. "And I'm a weapon I can't control. I can't take the chance of hurting her."

"Like you did your ex-wife?"

Shame slithered up Chris's spine. He straightened from the wall. "How do you know about that?"

"You might not remember all the times I visited you in the hospital because you were out of it. I know what you scream about in your sleep. I know everything about you. What happened to Natalie wasn't your fault, but you don't get it."

"It was my fault. My fucked up mind can't distinguish between reality and a dream. I was a danger before I lost my arm. Now I'm new and improved, and once I get back in action, I'll be seeing and doing things so wrong in the name of making things right I won't want to remember any of it, but I will."

His voice cracked. Guilt and fear seeped out like a scourge. "I'll remember it in all my dreams. Every. Single. Night. I've learned you can't forget even when you try. And I'd be bringing it all home to Scarlett. It's not fair to ask her to live with my ghosts."

Bradley poked him in the chest. "Did you forget your SEAL training already, boy? Pain is weakness leaving the body. If you don't let it out, the weakness will stay inside. When I got home from combat, I didn't recognize my PTSD symptoms. They didn't stay hidden for long though. One night, the festering memories exploded. I thought my wife was the enemy. I grabbed her. Snapped her arm in two."

Chris's gut twisted at Bradley's honest, raw misery. This kind, smart man who might be his next president battled the same demons.

Bradley pulled in a ragged breath, the memory clearly hard to talk about after all these years. "But my Kathleen, she was my angel. She stood by me. She held our family together and never gave up, even when I did awful things to push her away. From what I've heard about Scarlett, she's not the giving-up kind. Not like your mother, who left you, and not like your ex-wife. When you find an incredible woman like that, you don't let her go."

He reached over Chris's shoulder and tapped the tattoo under his shirt. "Your father, God rest his brave soul, wasn't the giving up kind either. He ran into the fire when others ran to safety. Question is, which way are you going to run?"

The door to Scarlett's room clicked open. "Chris?"

Like an angel beckoned by his deepest desires, she stood in the doorway, dressed in nothing but a Navy T-shirt that came to her mid-thigh.

My T-shirt.

He lost his breath at the beautiful sight.

She noticed Bradley. That mouth he needed to claim dropped open.

The governor blushed as he backed down the hallway. "Good to see you looking so, uh, healthy. I'll leave you two alone."

Chris closed the distance between him and Scarlett and fingered the hem of her shirt. Smooth skin met his touch. Desire pulsed up his arms in desperate waves and ricocheted through his body. "Where did you get this?"

More heat flooded her cheeks. "Patience may have procured it from your locker. I, ah, couldn't sleep after you left yesterday, so I thought about how good I slept with you our first night at the cabin, and I needed something until we could..." She crossed her arms over her chest. "Your shirt smells like you."

"Good, I hope." He gently took her wrists and tugged her arms away from her body.

She leaned into him. "Yes, very good."

Suddenly, everything Bradley had said made sense. Scarlett was a thousand times stronger and more selfless than his mom and eons different from Natalie. She hadn't bailed when he'd tried to push her away. She'd sneaked away to protect *him*. And yesterday, when duty had called and he'd left her alone, injured, emotional, and needing answers, she didn't seem to be holding it against him. She'd waited in his shirt until he'd returned.

As he pulled his beautiful, rambling genius into his arms and claimed her mouth, he raced into the fire.

THIRTY-NINE

Chris held her against him. The tenderness in his touch made her eyes tear, but his kiss was anything but gentle as he backed her into the room. With deep strokes of his tongue and a passion that lit her body on fire, he drank her in like a soldier going off to war.

The super soldier she'd created.

"Chris." She pulled her mouth away from his with a breathy sigh. "I need to get dressed."

"No, you don't. In fact, my shirt should be the only thing you wear. Ever."

He sank his teeth into her lower lip as he burrowed his steel under her panties and gripped her ass cheek.

The delicious bite of his teeth sinking into her mouth and his steel fingers branding her bottom zinged flaming arrows between her legs. Despite her protests, she opened for him and tried to nudge his hand to where she burned for him to touch and make her explode.

"Chris, I accepted my job back during my pre-brief with Edgar yesterday. He just called me into a meeting in thirty minutes."

"Me too." He kicked the door behind him. It slammed closed. "Looks like we're not going to make it in time."

"But…"

"Edgar can wait."

Heat simmered in her belly as she watched his eyes darken to almost black.

He gripped her bottom lip between two fingers. "I thought you learned at the cabin not to listen to your doubts."

The intensity in his gaze sent his sexiness quotient soaring to an incalculable level. "That's the problem. I can't think when you're near."

"Good." He shifted his steel hand from her ass to her hot core and slipped a finger inside. "I don't want you to think, except if you're thinking about me."

She pressed her hips against his welcome invasion. Strong and deep, he set to conquering her. An ache flared in her gunshot wound. She ignored it along with every reason she should stop him and confess her feelings before she fell so hard, so deep for this man she'd never recover if she lost him.

He murmured her name against her lips as he dove into her mouth. Her body bowed into his on instinct, and she stopped thinking completely.

"Easy, sweetheart." He set her back. "I don't want to cause you any more pain than you're already in."

A moan rumbled in her throat. She liked the feral sound. "You're going to leave me in more pain if you don't touch me like I want you to." She laid her palm on the bulge in his black tactical pants and squeezed.

He groaned, and she liked the savage sound of that even better.

"Scarlett, I don't want to hurt you."

She pressed two fingers to his lips to silence his sweet,

jagged protest. "I convinced Patience to give me some of the super-healing stuff she gave you and the team."

"Are you sure you're okay?" He nipped at her fingers.

"Yes." She squeezed his cock harder. "See how strong I am already?"

His smile burned hot enough to be declared a lethal weapon. "You think you're a badass in the bedroom now, too?"

"I guess being shot made me lose my inhibitions."

"Promise me you'll never find them again." His lips crashed down on hers once more as he lifted her up. Wrapping her legs around him, she hung on tight as he crossed the room and deposited her on the cabinet. The ache from her wound and the pounding of her heart strung her tight between a fine line of pleasure and pain.

She needed him to snap it.

Hard.

"Chris." She shimmied out of her panties and opened her knees for him.

He kept his smoky gaze on her wet center and made quick work of his belt and zipper. Desire simmered in his eyes as he raised his head. His nostrils flared, and the sound that grated from his throat as he growled her name would haunt her dreams in the most pleasurable way.

"Sorry we can't…" He looked toward the bed as he fisted the base of his cock. "We don't have a lot of time."

"Stop apologizing and fuck me, for God's sake."

In one smooth move, he entered her fully. With a groan, he nipped at her ear. "Drives me crazy when the shy scientist talks dirty."

She bit her lip as the swift intrusion stretched her body and mind. Who knew she could talk like that?

He had.

She'd taken the job with VIPER to help change the world

over time. In the space of a few days, he'd changed her, and good God, she liked the new Scarlett who grabbed the man she wanted by the balls and asked him to fuck her.

He gathered his hands under her ass and pulled her toward him. "You tell me if something hurts. Understand?"

She gasped as his cock slid even deeper. "I feel perfect." She wrapped her arms around his neck and held him tight. Even if their blissful union broke every rib in her body, she'd be better than perfect. "Don't stop."

Locking her legs around his waist, she pulled him closer until unchecked desire suctioned their bodies together. The sweet smell of sex and his earthy scent filled the sterile room. His neck under her lips tasted like sweat and pure male.

"God, Scarlett, you feel like the kind of dream I never want to wake up from." He pulled his hips back and slid halfway out. With a savage growl, he shoved back into her center.

The force pushed her into the wall. She cried out in plea-sure. Pain she'd feel later. Lots of it. Not just from her phys-ical wounds but from loss. They'd only had two days alone in the woods and it had left her wanting so much more. If Edgar's meeting meant what she thought it did, Chris would leave soon.

And might never return.

She lifted her lips from his neck and captured his gaze as he pulled out and slammed back into her. Her slick muscles contracted around his cock, and she moaned his name. "Remember this when the bad dreams come." She caught her breath as the first tremor of an orgasm rippled through her core. "Remember how we feel together. Promise me you'll remember."

He stilled. Something in his eyes shifted. "I'll remember." He repeated his vow as he set a heavenly rhythm of long, deep, slow strokes that touched every hidden place in her soul.

Closing her eyes, she soared until she floated off the cabinet.

"Look at me." He gripped her hair and yanked her gaze to his. "I want to remember how breathtaking you look when I'm deep inside your beautiful body."

He dropped his hand between them and teased her clit. She jerked, and he groaned. "How you melt when I touch you."

Panting, she bucked her hips against his and trapped his touch where she wanted—no, needed with every particle of her soul.

"Chris, please."

Her efforts weren't a match for his determination as he slid his hand out.

"I want to remember how you taste, Scarlett." He gripped her hair harder as he brought his fingers, glistening with her arousal, to his lips.

Even if he hadn't held her immobilized, she couldn't, wouldn't, look away. "God, that's…" Her brain couldn't conjure words to describe the wicked satisfaction she got from watching him lick his fingers, like her arousal was the most decadent treat he'd ever savored.

"Heaven." He slid out and teased her sensitive clit with the head of his cock. "You taste and feel like heaven."

Grabbing his ass cheeks, she dug her nails into his hard muscles and pled for her own satisfaction. "Take more. *I* need more."

A sinful grin amplified his groan as he notched himself at her pulsing center. "Yeah baby; beg for me so I can remember how you sound when you give me, and only me, everything."

Without constraint, he pounded back into her with laser-focused determination. "I want your body."

Again, he rammed into her. "Your heart."

She felt his powerful need and unfettered truth blaze through her like a match to gasoline.

He pulled out again and stilled. "I want your beautiful soul."

She screamed as he thrust into her so deep they became one. As she exploded into dazzling flames, a glow lit within her and beamed like a newly discovered bioluminescence species forging from the depths. For she *was* a new species. A badass scientist in love with a super soldier.

With a guttural cry, he pressed her into the wall as he found his release. Bodies shuddering, faces buried in each other's necks, they clung to each other in their stolen moment.

As their breathing returned to normal, she took his steel hand in her shaky one and kissed his palm. The question she didn't want an answer to but had to ask slid from her mouth. "Do you think Edgar's meeting has to do with the clearance you've been waiting for?"

"Maybe. But understand this." He cupped her cheeks in his hands and held on tight. "*This* is the moment I've been waiting for. The moment you gave me what you've given no other man. All of you."

Her breathing and heart stuttered in tandem. Did that mean he wanted all of her? Forever? She tried to harness her emotions but couldn't keep her voice from trembling. "It still doesn't make sense how we fit so perfectly together when we're worlds apart, but I—"

A reminder alert from Chris's comms unit about the meeting stopped her from making the most illogical, bravest, potentially heartbreaking statement of her life.

FORTY

Edgar entered the briefing room and stalked to the head of the table, his gaze darting from Scarlett to Chris. "The rest of the team will be here in a few minutes, but I wanted to talk to the two of you before they arrived."

Scarlett gripped the edges of her seat. "Has VIPER been cleared for active missions?"

"No, but soon."

She relaxed in her chair as she stole a glance at Chris seated next to her. He *would* leave, but not today. She pushed her laptop bag to the corner of the table and smoothed her hands down the skirt of the new outfit Beth had dropped off. The note attached to the deep-red suit had said, "Wear it like a rock star." The hungry gazes Chris shot her way made her feel more like a goddess.

Edgar braced his hands on the table and leaned toward them. "There's going to need to be some changes around here if you two are in a relationship."

Scarlett glanced at Chris. He didn't flinch at Edgar's "relationship" comment. Her stomach did though. A happy flip-flop a hundred times over. "Understood, sir. And I have an idea about how we can manage things."

Chris growled next to her. "It better not entail you leaving me."

She squeezed his knee under the table.

"Calm down, Daviani." Edgar straightened and pinned his gaze on Scarlett. "I also have an idea about how we can keep you on board, but first, we have a much bigger issue to discuss. Ryan Bradley has been working to shore up our network while you recovered. There's still more work to do before we are as near to one-hundred percent secure as we can get, but he's done a tremendous job so far. As of this morning, he's part of Project VIPER. He's already proven we made a good choice in hiring him because an hour ago, he unearthed intel about the group Richardson sold you to."

Chris gripped her hand hard. "They want what they paid for, don't they?"

"No." Scarlett shook her head. "Just no."

"The intel is credible, Scarlett. I'm sorry." Edgar focused on Chris. "I want her under protection until we catch these guys or get them off her tail. You and the team can work out a rotating schedule. And Sergeant Gage McAllister, who helped Scarlett contact us when she was being held by Richardson, is in the building and being interviewed for a VIPER support position as we speak. Once he's vetted and hired, he can join the rotation."

"Understood, sir." Chris rose from his chair. "She'll be safe with me."

She jumped up next to him. "Oh no. I'm not going to spend the next God knows how long letting Henry's diabolical plans dictate my life. And I'm not letting you take another bullet for me. Your safety is equally important."

The team and the new trauma surgeon, what was his name—Langley—walked into the room.

She ignored them. "I can't go on like this. We need to end it. Now."

Langley snickered. "Breaking up with Daviani already?"

Chris tugged her to his side. "She better not since she's moving in with me."

Moving in?

Her heart soared at the idea, but a beat later understood the reason for his quick proposal. She shoved him away as her elation plummeted into a nosedive. "We're not moving in together."

"Didn't you hear Edgar? There are terrorists searching for you." He gave the team a quick rundown of the situation. "Moving in with me is the most logical way to keep you safe."

"Logical? You want to live together because it's logical?"

"You, of all people, should understand how much sense it makes."

She did understand, but she also understood the risks of sharing his home, his bed, his life, and falling deeper in love only to find out he didn't feel the same way about her.

"I don't want it to make sense. I want..." She speared her hands in her hair. For the first time in her life, she didn't need numbers and facts to guide her decisions. Why was he so focused on logic? Was her safety the only reason he wanted to be with her?

Kane sat at the table. "This is more entertaining than the drive-in theater in my hometown. Anyone got popcorn?"

Langley dropped next to him. "A beer would be nice while we watch Daviani get his ass handed to him."

Scarlett glared at her audience. "Maybe the two of you can tell your buddy what he doesn't seem to get."

Edgar banged his fists on the table. "Enough." He pointed at Scarlett. "I want to hear your ideas about how to end this since it's your life on the line."

She straightened her jacket and drew strength from her power color. "Henry is in custody in this building. Is his lawyer here?"

"His team arrived five minutes ago."

"Maybe we can work with them on some sort of deal to coax Henry into sending a message to the buyers about a time and a place where they can, uh, collect me. If we can't convince him, maybe James will give up the information. Either way, we need to set a trap to apprehend my buyers. End of story."

Chris slammed his steel onto the table. "No fucking way. Henry deserves all the jail time he gets, and you aren't bait."

A vein throbbed in Edgar's neck. "Sit down, Daviani."

"No." He turned to Scarlett and gripped the back of her head with his steel. She gasped in surprise, but he didn't relent. "I love you and will protect you with my life. Are those logical enough reasons for you to move in with me?"

Chris held his breath. Time narrowed as he faced the woman in his arms and the "I love you" he'd had every intention of saying later when they were alone.

He stared at her wide eyes and waited for her to say something.

Sirens blared through the room and swallowed the air. He shoved Scarlett behind him. For a moment, the room was still except for the emergency lights spinning like a disco ball.

"There's been a breach." Edgar picked up the phone in the computer console and barked orders for the team to be activated.

Chris felt the sting of activation as Scarlett pushed past him and ran to Edgar's side. He positioned himself between her and the door and embraced the current coursing through his body.

The team stood and waited for direction.

Edgar pointed to Nic and Linc. "Secure underground." He swiveled his head to Kane and Langley. "You two. Second level. Daviani, secure this room."

Damn straight I'm securing this room.

"Confirm activation." Ryan's voice filled Chris's ear.

"Activated."

The team echoed their status as Chris slipped into battle mode.

Scarlett and Edgar shoved earpieces into their ears. She leaned over and hit the keys in the console.

Edgar flanked her. "What's the status, Bradley?"

"Four hostiles entered through the main lobby posing as Richardson's law team. In Meeting Room B, they shot the guards and took Richardson."

Chris stole a glance at Scarlett as he covered the door.

The blood drained from her face, but she kept typing. "They're in our system."

"I know." Ryan cursed. "Richardson and two hostiles were spotted heading down the east stairwell thirty seconds ago. The other two were spotted coming your way. Someone is remotely trying to scramble our internal video feeds. For each camera I get back on, they turn another off."

"Thompson must have given up the schematics of headquarters to Henry." Scarlett dropped into the chair behind her without missing a beat on the keyboard. "Crap. They got through another layer of security. Video is down in the whole building."

"Stay here." Chris edged to the door. If a fight was coming, he'd meet it head-on in the hall instead of having it reach Scarlett. He reached for the door handle as it burst open. A man in a suit held Gage around the throat with a gun pressed to his temple.

Chris paced back to block Scarlett. He calculated the odds of shooting a V-Strike before the hostile pulled the trigger. The odds were in his favor, but he couldn't take the chance with Scarlett in the room. "Let him go."

The hostile shoved into the room with Gage as a shield. Another in a suit blocked the door. "Give us Dr. Kerrigan, and you can have him."

"Let. Him. Go. This is your last warning." Chris caught Gage's eye. The guy nodded, completely in control despite the boiling fury in his gaze.

The hostile laughed. "If you try and take me down with one of your high-tech lasers, I'll give the command to my buddy to shoot his daughter." He pressed his gun harder into Gage's temple. "We've got our sights trained on his kid as we speak."

"No," Scarlett cried.

Chris tuned her out and reevaluated his options. This mission had just gotten a hell of a lot more complicated.

"Please don't hurt Lucy." Gage sniffed back tears. "Please leave my baby alone to enjoy the day at my sister's house. Please let her be."

Chris barely heard Scarlett whisper through her comms, "Check Gage's military records for an emergency contact."

"On it," Ryan said.

Edgar stepped in front of Scarlett. "What did you do with Richardson's lawyers?"

The hostile sneered. "They'll be needing some sick leave."

"Got the address," Ryan said. "Local PD has a unit in the area. They're on their way to secure the child. Keep the hostile talking."

The hostile pressed the gun harder into Gage's head. "Give us the girl, or he *and* his daughter die."

Gage flinched. "Please tell your sniper not to take my daughter out. Please."

The hostile gave the gun a twist. "If I tell him to shoot, he will without hesitation."

"Hostile confirmed there's only one sniper," Ryan said.

The hostile's gaze shot back to Scarlett. "You have five seconds to give yourself up." He glanced over his shoulder at his accomplice. "And if we meet any resistance while we exit the building, the kid dies."

"Local PD is two minutes out," Ryan said.

Scarlett held up both hands. "Okay, okay. I'll go with you."

"Sit down," Chris growled. He wouldn't let her leave him in death like his father.

She eased to the back corner of the table. "He won't kill me. Henry needs my brain." She held her hands up and cocked her head to her laptop bag. "I can't complete the work Henry's buyers want me to do without the hard drive in there."

The hostile tightened his hold on Gage. "I don't care about your work. I was hired to deliver you and Richardson to my client. End of story."

"The underground level and level two are secure," Kane said through his comms. "Linc and Nic have Henry and the two hostiles cornered in the stairwell. Henry's been injured. Langley is attending to him."

Scarlett's face didn't show any emotion. Damn if she hadn't proven him wrong several times when he'd questioned if she'd be able to keep it together when shit got real. A child's life in danger was as real as it got.

Edgar edged close to her side. Chris breathed a bit easier.

No doubt, the man would take a bullet for her. He held his position and prayed the situation wouldn't come to what he figured Scarlett had up her sleeve.

Brave, foolish woman.

God, he loved her.

Scarlett shrugged. "I guess I have no choice but to go with you and leave the hard drive behind. But when the buyers get angry because they didn't get everything they paid for, they'll come after you."

The hostile cocked his head to the bag. "Get it. But only the drive. Leave the bag here."

Scarlett held up a hand and pulled at the zipper with the other. Slowly, as if she had all the time in the world instead of buying it, she eased her hand inside. "The drive is like a bullet, and I'm the gun. Neither works without the other."

"Girl is secure," Ryan said.

Chris held back a whoop as he nodded to Gage.

"Please don't hurt my baby." Gage sobbed and sagged in the hostile's arms.

The hostile stumbled to catch his weight. Gage spun and tackled him to the side.

"Get down," Scarlett yelled from behind Chris.

A shot rang in his ears as he dropped to the floor and fired a V-Strike at the second hostile in the doorway. The man clutched the wound on his shoulder, not from a V-Strike but from a bullet, and crumpled to the floor.

Chris sprung to his feet and spun toward Scarlett. The sight of her holding a gun that she'd taken down a mercenary with filled him with pride.

And fear.

She lowered her weapon and placed it on the table. Chris crushed her against him as Edgar helped Gage secure the hostiles. "That was amazing. Don't ever do it again." He pulled away from her and cupped her face in his hands. "From now on, I'm do the shooting in this relationship, understand?"

"No promises." Her voice shook along with her body. "We both know this isn't over. Next time someone comes after me, I won't hesitate to shoot them."

"There won't be a next time. I'll make sure of it."

"How?" She gripped his biceps. "Since we've met, you've been hacked, shot, and caught in an explosion. Now head-quarters has been infiltrated—all because of me." She pointed into the hallway to amplify her point. "Are you sure moving in together is a good idea? I may be the death of you."

"Then I'll die a happy man." He gathered her hands in his and tugged her close. "I meant it when I said I love you. *All* of you. Forever. I have a lot of messed-up issues to work through, and I'll be gone a lot. If I could trade the danger for a guaranteed lifetime of safety, I would, but—"

She touched her finger to his lips. Tears brimmed in her eyes as a smile lit her face. "I love you too, exactly the way you are."

Awe, at her words, and his belief in them, nearly burst his heart. Any doubts he'd had about her ability to handle him bugged out as fast as his demons did when she was near.

He touched his forehead to hers. "We'll find a way to end this threat and any others that come our way. I can't lose you."

"You won't. I'm a badass, remember? The hidden parts of me you've brought out—and the awkward, boring scientist I am most of the time aren't going anywhere." She raised her hand, joined with his steel and placed it over his heart. "I promise. You have all of me, and I love all of you exactly the way you are.

His grin spread as wide as the joy illuminating the dark parts of his mind. "I'm a superhero who got the girl."

"You got that right, Commander Daviani, but you didn't get just any girl. You got the one who will love you for the rest of your life."

"Yes, ma'am. I believe you will."

EPILOGUE

One Month Later

The referee on the football field raised both hands in the air.

"Touchdown," Nic screamed along with the crowd.

"Dammit," Chris's breath puffed out into the cold December afternoon.

"Score is tied, *hermano.* Won't be long before Army puts more points up on that board and beats Navy's ass."

Scarlett pointed a gloved finger at the scoreboard. "There are only ten more seconds in the second quarter. We still have a full half to beat you, and based on the numbers, the probability of Navy coming back is quite favorable."

"Check out my girl talking football and math at the same time." Chris wrapped his arm around her and brushed his mouth against her ear. "And your trash talk is making me hard."

Scarlett snuggled closer to his warmth. Despite the bright sun and the thousands of bodies packed into the stadium in Baltimore, Maryland, her teeth chattered. She didn't mind the near freezing temperatures though. Her heart was warm. She was with the man she loved, her best friend, and her team. Her family.

"Hey." Ryan held up his phone. "My uncle wants us to come up to one of the suites."

The timer on the scoreboard hit zero as they filed out with the crowd into the concourse and into an elevator, where a security guard granted them access. Scarlett breathed in the warm air and took off her gloves. As soon as her hands were bare, Chris wound his fingers around hers and squeezed.

He nuzzled his face into her shoulder. "Having fun on our football date?"

Tingles raced down her back. After a month of living together, going on dates like today's game to make up for the experiences she'd missed, and sharing their hopes and fears in therapy, he still held the power to electrify her. Based on her intense reaction to the way he trailed feather-light kisses up her neck, the probability he would thrill her for the rest of her life was exponentially greater than the odds of Navy winning.

With a low growl, he nipped at her earlobe. "Promise me you'll do that sexy football math talk when we get home tonight?"

Scarlett turned and answered him with a quick kiss as the elevator doors opened. More glorious heat spilled in. She nodded to two men in black suits who opened glass doors leading to a large suite overlooking the fifty-yard line. She stepped inside the crowded room. More men in black lined the walls.

Governor Bradley emerged from the crowd and clasped

Chris and Kane on their shoulders. "Go Navy." He fist-bumped Nic. "Go Army." He turned to Linc. "As for Air Force, better luck next year."

"Just wait, sir. We're going to take the Commander-in-Chief's trophy."

Scarlett marveled at her smiling, joking, tough-as-nails super soldiers as they huddled into a group and talked more smack about the game. Well, they were hers and Ryan's now. She'd been more than happy to relinquish the security aspect of her position to him and focus solely on enhancing the team's cybernetic capabilities. She didn't need a front-row seat to the dangers Chris and the team faced when they deployed. She only needed faith they'd come home alive.

Beth slid next to her. "This is so awesome. I got to meet the governor *and* I'm hanging out with the hot vets." She darted her gaze to Kane who piled his plate with hot dogs and fries from the buffet table.

Scarlett leaned in closer to her best friend. "Please remember that Kane and the other guys are my co-workers. You can't pick one, hook up a few times, and then ghost him."

"If I was going to sleep with one of them, which I'm not because I'm quite aware of what they are to you, Kane isn't the one I'd choose. He's not my type."

"Since when isn't a sexy cowboy your type?"

Beth shrugged. "He just isn't." She pointed to the bar in the back of the suite. "I'm going to get me a free drink and then hit the buffet. Thanks for being a geek and having the coolest job in the world."

"Being a nerd does have it perks." Scarlett glanced at the biggest perk of all.

Chris sidled up next to her. "The governor said there's someone he wants us to meet."

She entwined her fingers with his as they made their way

through the crowd toward Governor Bradley. He turned from the large window facing the field where the Navy-Marine Corps band play "Anchors Away."

"Great game so far, don't you think?"

Scarlett jerked her head up. She knew that voice.

"There you are." Governor Bradley kissed the cheek of a tall woman wearing a white sweater with the Navy logo embroidered on one side and the Army logo on the other. He motioned to Chris and Scarlett. "And here's the two you've been wanting to meet. Now if you'll excuse me, I'm going to get a drink."

"Madame President." The greeting sounded strange coming out of Scarlett's mouth. How many people got to say that?

"Dr. Kerrigan. Captain Daviani. It's an honor to meet you both." President Fisher extended her hand for each of them to shake.

Scarlett gaped at the friendly, elegant woman holding a glass of beer as if she was an ordinary citizen enjoying an afternoon at the game. She opened her mouth, but her tongue refused to work.

Chris shook the president's hand with his steel. "The honor is all mine."

"Dr. Kerrigan, I understand you've been doing some outstanding work with VIPER." She turned her soft amber eyes back to Chris. "And you deserve our nation's gratitude for your continued service."

"Thank you." He put an arm around Scarlett's shoulders and pulled her to his side. "But I'd be nothing without my genius and the rest of the VIPER team who put me back together."

Scarlett's knees shook from the joy radiating through her body.

Meeting the president.

Sweet praise from the man she loved.

Can this day get any better?

President Fisher took Scarlett's hand. "I have a proposal I hope you'll consider. I'd like you to head up a multiagency initiative to improve our military's capabilities across the board. You can do most of your work from the VIPER lab." She eyed Scarlett's fingers interlaced with Chris's and winked. "It seems like you're happy there. Sound like something you'd be interested in?"

Excitement pounded a rhythm against Chris's navy T-shirt she wore underneath her warm layers. "I'd be honored, Madame President."

"Fantastic. We'll meet after the first of the year at the White House to begin discussions. Now if you'll excuse me, I need to find something to eat before the second half begins. Go Navy." She dipped her head. "But don't tell anyone I said that. I'm supposed to be impartial." She pointed to her dual-logo jersey as she backed away with a wave.

"Wow." Chris lifted Scarlett off the floor and spun her in a circle. "This is incredible. I'm so proud of you."

"Thanks." What greater compliment could she receive for her work than a job offer from the president? She looked up at Chris. Pride shone in his eyes. Tears gathered in hers. There was nobody else she'd rather share the moment with.

Chris wiped her cheek with the pad of his thumb. "Those better be happy tears because there's no crying in football."

She laughed. "Yes, happy tears." She stared at the beautiful hero who'd brought her to this moment. "Thank you."

"For what?"

"I'd always thought the reason people couldn't see beyond my brain was because something was wrong with me. You made me realize the truth. There *was* something wrong with me."

"That's bullshit; you're perfect."

"No, I'm not. For all my intelligence, I couldn't look beyond my brain either. You pushed me to discover, to embrace everything inside. You saw all of me and made me see it too. Thank you."

He rained soft kisses on her lips. "And thank you for not running from my demons."

"Never."

"Good, because I want to talk about *forever.*" He gripped her hands with his steel and placed them over his VIPER tattoo. "If we were normal and led run-of-the-mill lives, this conversation could wait. But we're not normal. There's danger in our future. Tomorrow isn't guaranteed. Starting today—because I'm a greedy bastard and I can't wait—I want to live all our tomorrows as husband and wife."

He pulled a black velvet box from his pocket as he bent down on one knee.

Scarlett's hands flew to her mouth. "Chris."

He flipped open the lid. "This is my promise that no matter what danger we face, we will slay it together. It's my pledge to protect, love, and worship every inch of your body and mind. And when duty takes me away, knowing you're waiting for me with my ring on your finger will give me the strength to fight like the super soldier you created me to be so I can come home to you."

As she dropped to her knees in front of him, she stared at the gorgeous diamond ring surrounded by stones as red as the gown she'd worn to the governor's gala.

The night their story had begun.

With his steel fingers, he pulled the ring from the box and held it between them. "Dr. Jacqueline Scarlett Kerrigan, will you marry me?"

"Yes." As she breathed the simple life-changing word again, she threw her arms around him.

The suite erupted into applause. Her heart soared along

with congratulatory shouts as Chris slipped the ring on her finger.

Beth pulled her to her feet. "Let me see that rock."

She showed off her ring that felt as right on her finger as Chris's arms around her body as she accepted hugs and heartfelt wishes from the team.

Their family.

As the band stopped playing, Chris pulled Scarlett away from the well-wishers. "Give me my fiancée back."

She floated on air as he led her to a quiet corner and kissed her with a possessiveness that claimed her body, heart, and soul.

"Tell me, Dr. Kerrigan, are you ready for this forever mission we're about to embark on?"

She ran her fingers down his arm as she arched into him. "Absolutely Commander, but it could get intense."

His teeth teased her skin. "Well, then I'm all in. What do I need to do?"

"As soon as we get home, get naked and show me again how super you are." She pulled back and gazed into those eyes that had captivated her even before they'd met. "And then you can spend a lifetime loving me."

"That's a pretty tall order, but I'm confident I can exceed your expectations. I'm a superhero, after all."

Yes, the superhero who'd saved her from the bad guys and from herself. And who loved all of her.

Forever.

The End

Thank you for reading *Too Dangerous to Love*.
If you enjoyed the book, please consider leaving a review. I greatly appreciate it.

Would you like a sneak peek into my next romantic suspense series?

Knife to the Heart (Blood Snow Series Book One)
is coming in the Spring of 2024. To read the first chapter, sign up for my newsletter at https://www.kristiewolf.com and I'll send it to you.

Craving more Project VIPER?
Book Two, *Too Lethal to Love,* will be out in the Fall of 2024

ACKNOWLEDGMENTS

Whew! I did it! I got my book baby out into the wild.

Holy crap it wasn't easy, and I couldn't have done it without the loads of support I've received from so many people.

When I first started writing novels, I thought it was a solitary endeavor. Man, was I wrong! It takes not just a village, but a whole country of diverse talents and wisdom, and an army of cheerleaders to write and publish a book. I've been putting off finishing this part because I'm afraid I'm going to forget someone who deserves a big fat thank you. If I do, my apologies, but know that I appreciate everyone who has helped me survive this wild journey.

Drum roll please as I gush about the amazing people in my life who helped me achieve my sixteen-year-old self's dream.

My husband **Gary Clement**. Yes, honey, you are absolutely the sole inspiration for my steamy scenes. (None of the superheroes I ogle in the movies ever enter my mind when I sit down to write.) Thank you for being my tech support, listening to me talk for hours on end about my plot and characters, giving me advice about how to fix things, answering my endless technology and military questions, and believing in me so hard that I believe in myself. My name wouldn't be on the cover of a book if you hadn't pushed me to overcome my fears. Love you to pieces.

My son **Alexander,** they say the best conversations you will have with your teenage son are in the car. That must be true because that's where we talk about my plot problems. I appreciate you listening and am constantly impressed by your thoughtful, creative advice. Keep that beautiful imagination flowing, my boy. My daughter **Charlotte, y**ou have no idea what it meant to me the day you held my hand while I cried over a rejection. Remember baby girl, darkness comes and goes, but I will always be your light just like you are mine. Your bravery inspires me every day to never give up. Kids, love you both a bushel and a peck.

My mom **Kathy Wolf,** I said it all in the dedication, but I'll say it again. Thank you for your unconditional support. My dad **Al Wolf,** book format tester. Logo creator. Laptop doctor. Kid chauffeur. Knower of all things I need answers to and fixer of everything I need fixed. You're the best dad a girl could ask for. Love you so much!

My author bestie and writing sister, **Aria Wyatt,** remember how clueless we were when we sat next to each other at lunch at RWA? Look at us now! I'm so blessed to have such a wonderful friend, so lucky that I get a sneak peek at your novels before you share them with the rest of the world, and so honored you trust my opinions. Your work is incredible. (Even the words I cut out of your manuscript.) I can't wait to start that special project we've been talking about. It's going to be bestseller material for sure.

When I decided to indie publish, I was so nervous about finding good people to help me. I didn't need to worry though. My author tribe pointed me to the best, starting with two phenomenal editors who treated my book baby with so much love. Editor **Jen Graybeal,** thanks for your guidance when I had no idea where to start, and for teaching me that less words make a bigger impact. Editor **Miranda Grant,** your encouraging feedback from when you read the first few pages of this book will always stick with me. Thanks for your spot-on edits and for inviting me to my first Facebook party. That made me feel like a legit author! **Rosa Sharon of Fairy Proofmother Proofreading, LLC,** your skills are as awesome as the name of your company. Thanks for fitting me in last minute. My formatter for my ARC's **C.R. Riley**, you are my savior. Thanks for answering my desperate plea on Instagram for help. **Linda Russell and the team at Foreword PR & Marketing**, thank you for the gorgeous teasers and for making the business side of publishing less scary. **Dez Purington of Pretty Ink Creations,** thank you for my beautiful author branding. **Taylor Berry,** thanks for your patience with teaching this middle-aged author about Tik-Tok.

I have been dreaming about the cover of this book since I wrote it in 2017. Holy crap did my vision come true. **Eric at Eric Battershell Photography**, thanks for taking gorgeous photos. I can't wait to pour through your work again and find my next hero. Super special thanks for introducing me to Laura. To my cover model **BT Urruela,** thanks for your service. I hope you don't mind that I made you a bionic super soldier. **Laura Hidalgo of Spellbinding Design**, I'm so grateful that Eric introduced me to you. My cover and interior design exceeds my wildest dreams. Thank you for taking me under your wing, telling me what I should do, and sharing your knowledge about the industry. You are amazing! **Nalini Akolekar**, thanks for believing in this book and for all your advice these past few years.

Beth Prellberg. Romance is so not your genre, yet you still listen to me talk about my books as if they were Dean Koontz bestsellers. Someday I'll write your kind of story, with a whole lot of steam of course. I love you, my best friend since birth. To my other mother **Carol Prellberg**, thanks for taking the time while we were at Beth's house to proofread. Love you! **Tammy Ward, t**hanks for being my cheerleader and for reading every word I've ever written. I don't know how you catch all those typos, but I'm so grateful for your eagle eye. Love you, cuz!

To the talented authors in my super supportive critique group who inspire me every day to keep writing even when I think I suck at it. **Alexa Jacobs,** you were my first fangirl. (I have it in writing from your very first critique.) You have no idea the confidence it gave this newbie writer. **Jenn Bloch,** aka Alexa Jacobs, I'm so thankful you are also part of my work tribe. I don't know how I would juggle my life without you. **Mary K. Tilghman,** I so appreciate your cranky red pen. Keep the bloodbath coming. **Nellie Jane,** thanks for uplifting my spirits and calling to check on me when I'm down. **Kimberly Butler,** remember that doll you sent me to bang around when I get frustrated? It's an integral part of my writing process. **Nonna Henry,** I should be thanking you in the editor section because the attention you put into beta reading this book was incredible. Thanks to you all for being part of my tribe. Love each and every one of you.

Dr. Joe Ronzio, thanks for taking the time to answer my questions when I first began writing this book. If anyone I know comes close to being as smart as my genius heroine, it's you.

To my Bel Air friends. **Heather Johnson** and **Zandra Donarum,** thanks for listening to me drone on for miles as we walk and talk about my books. **Jessica Fessler,** remember the time you answered my questions about gunshot wounds? Thanks for your expert advice. I hope I got it all correct. **Samantha Rose Heil,** Beta reader extraordinaire and fellow author. I'm so happy we connected on Facebook. I look forward to writing many more words with you at Starbucks. **Laura Ames of Laura Ames Photography,** thanks for the beautiful headshots on my website. Someday I'll make enough money from my books to buy that second diving board. **Sandy Frounfelker,** thanks for always asking me how my book is coming, and thanks for introducing me to romance novelist **Mara Fitzcharles**. Mara, thanks for suggesting I go to the New Jersey Romance Writer's Conference. The experience was life-changing.

The Hosky Clan – Peg, Tom, Claudia, and John. Where does one find a job with a flexible schedule, exciting content, fulfilling work, travel to fun cities, cowboy boot shopping sprees, and a fantastic group of people who have become dear friends and treat me like family? Oh, at FedInsider. Thanks for not minding when I ask federal technology leaders what the biggest threats to their agencies are and then write books about them. I am blessed to have you guys in my life and truly appreciate your continued support for my passion. Here's to another two decades—and more—of continued domination in our corner of the market and to lots more fun.

Finally, to my **readers.** I sincerely appreciate you taking a chance on this debut author. I've got many more books in my future and look forward to sharing them with you. Thank you for reading.

Lots of love,

Kristie

ABOUT THE AUTHOR

Kristie Wolf is an award-winning author of steamy romantic suspense. When she was a teenager, she read her first romance novel and connected with it so deeply that she immediately told her mother she was going to publish one. Many years later, she did just that.

While her career as a marketing professional in the government technology space hasn't taught her to troubleshoot a computer, she's fascinated with what happens when technology spectacularly fails. The chilling stories she's heard from the nation's tech leaders are the catalyst for plots about maniacal terrorists but don't worry. Her military and law enforcement alpha heroes and badass heroines always save the day while burning up the pages and finding happily ever after.

Kristie resides in Maryland with her husband - aka her tech support - and her two teenagers who participate in nearly every sport or activity ever invented. Many of her words are written on the pool deck, on the sidelines and in the bleachers, or in her car. When she's not behind her computer, she can be found:

• Walking her Vizsla and her Pittie-mix rescue while listening to her favorite authors.

• Watching cheerleading videos on her phone because she misses being a coach.

• Learning everything she can about Elvis Presley because she's going to write a novel based on him someday.

• Making space in her closet for another pair of cowboy boots she doesn't need but has to have.

Want to be notified about Kristie's upcoming releases? Sign up for her newsletter at https://www.kristiewolf.com/

Kristie loves to connect with readers. Drop her a note on social media.

facebook.com/KristieAWolf

instagram.com/kristiewolf_author

tiktok.com/@kristiewolfromance

ALSO BY KRISTIE WOLF

Project VIPER Series

Too Dangerous to Love

Too Lethal to Love (Coming Fall of 2024)

Blood Snow Series

Knife to the Heart (Coming Spring of 2024)

Made in USA - North Chelmsford, MA
54857_9798988785026
01.12.2024 1522